a town
Like ours

ALEXANDER CADE

AIA PUBLISHING

A Town like Ours
AIA Publishing, Australia
ABN: 32736122056
www.aiapublishing.com

© Copyright 2018 Alexander Cade
www.regencymatters.com

Ebook ISBN: 978-0-6484171-3-2
Paperback: ISBN: 978-0-6484171-4-9
Cover design: Velvet Wings Media.

Please note: This book is edited to Australian conventions.

Alexander Cade is the pen name of an author who writes mystery stories set in Regency England. Other titles written under this name are *Turn Up a Stone*.

For Linda Aronson, mentor and friend, who was so encouraging.

INTRODUCTION

There is, of course, no such place as Coddington St George, though parts of it will be found scattered around the country. Similarly, all the characters are fictitious, though they have been inspired by real people, as are all worthwhile fictitious characters.

PART ONE:

THE CONCEPT

one

Jack Wilcon, President of Wilcon Interglobal Consolidated Universal Pictures Inc., sat dejectedly on a camp stool in Runyon Canyon Park, a one-hundred-and-sixty-three-acre recreational area ten miles or so out of Los Angeles. Apart from the usual amenities, the park contained within its borders bushland walks and, in the canyon itself, a cave. In the mouth of this cave, Jack sat brooding over the latest disaster of his career. Until a couple of hours before, he'd been as near to being in heaven as he was ever likely to be—not because of the natural beauties of the park, but because for the first time in his life he had actually been producing a movie.

Sadly, however, a number of incidents had occurred that had brought production to an end. He now had to break the news to Maybelle, his receptionist, former occasional lover, and only true friend. She had provided the finance for the movie, having recently received $5,000 in residual fees from her participation in a television commercial that, achieving better sales for a grease spot remover than the manufacturers had expected, had been shown ten times daily for a whole year, not just for the three weeks originally planned. Maybelle had actually achieved something of a reputation over the years for being the drab, depressed, intellectually challenged housewife who always used 'other products' with their inevitable failure. As such, she'd been cast in half a dozen or so commercials a year, most of them, though, short-lived, as competing products often seemed to do better after her commercials had been broadcast.

Jack, learning of this unexpected income, had immediately, and entirely on the spur of the moment, thought up a box office certainty into which she should invest her hard-earned cash.

'This one can't fail, Maybelle,' he'd told her. 'Cable and the internet are desperate for this kind of product.'

'What kind of product, Jack?' Maybelle had asked, trying, unsuccessfully, to look enthusiastic. She'd been down this road so many times before.

'Axe murders,' Jack had told her. And then, with his creative juices bubbling over, he'd pitched the concept to her. In Hollywood jargon, it's always a concept, never a plot, because so many low-budget productions have a plot that can be summarised in ten words.

'It's set in pre-historic times, see,' Jack had said, revealing considerable budgetary acumen. Costumes would be a few cow hides, the set a cave or two, and as the male actors would be largely covered by hair, they wouldn't have to be recognisable. Jack knew, too, that it wouldn't be difficult to cast the movie cheaply from the thousands of extras who haunted the studios hoping for a day's work. As often as not, they'd even work for deferred payment if they were offered a decent screen credit, especially if they had a word or two to speak, such as, 'Ug' or 'Ouch'. An extra who uttered earned double.

Jack had soon found a casting agent who'd agreed to find him extras of simian appearance, thus enabling him to save money on make-up. On the night of the shoot, about fifty men and women of varying ages, all with sloping heads and unusually long arms, had presented themselves.

Further savings had been possible by using crew prepared to work for deferred payment in return for a credit in mainstream entertainment, even if it was only a muddy tributary of it. Two of these, Hank Shorn and Studs Collini, had been available. The two men worked as a team—when they worked at all, which was infrequently—shooting the lowest of low-budget porno flicks and corporate videos for businesses that were in such bad shape that they couldn't afford to pay proper rates. Studs, who could operate a camera and was a skilled video editor, unfortunately had a serious recreational drug habit.

Hank, who directed whatever needed direction, was a confirmed alcoholic and had been expelled from numerous AA groups for disruptive behaviour. Unlike tall and emaciated Studs, Hank was wholly spherical. His body was one balloon, his head another, but much smaller, and his legs were so short that he seemed to have only feet. When standing together, Studs and Hank looked like a failed vaudeville comedy act. A memorable partnership many producers couldn't forget, once they'd employed them.

'This crazy Neanderthal guy,' Jack had said, continuing his pitch to Maybelle, 'returns to the cave unexpectedly and finds his woman being fucked by the chief of the tribe.'

'Has he been out hunting?' Maybelle had asked, entering into the spirit of the concept.

'Sure. He's got a hunk of meat in his hand.'

Maybelle frowned, grappling with the image that came to mind.

Jack had calculated the cost of a large piece of meat that had been declared unfit for human consumption and reckoned his budget could run to it.

'Anyway, he throws the meat to the ground and runs at the chief, brandishing his axe.'

'While the others in the cave cheer,' Maybelle had said. She was a keen fan of World Wrestling Smackdown.

'Right. Then he manages to smash his axe onto the chief's head …'

'… and blood spurts everywhere.' Maybelle had seen a hundred splatter movies like this.

'Right. The chief falls down, dead, and our murderer runs off. The rest of the movie shows our hero, the chief's son, going after him …'

'… and killing him to avenge his pop's death,' Maybelle had contributed, revealing a keen understanding of the subtleties of the psychology of the situation.

'It'll gross half a million from cable alone,' Jack had concluded.

'What's your budget, Jack?'

'Five grand.'

Maybelle had parted with her most recent earnings, and *The Axeman Cometh* had gone into production. Unfortunately, the shoot had not gone smoothly. To avoid having to pay the park a location fee, Jack had set the entire production at night when the rangers were all off duty. Unable to afford a generator, he'd used flaming torches in the cave and natural light from the moon outside. However, shooting had been frequently interrupted as the moon kept going behind a cloud. Also, although Studs Collini knew which buttons to press on his video camera, he'd never filmed in the dark before—porno is always brightly lit so that no anatomical details are ever in shadow. He'd had great difficulty getting the camera to function properly in the poor light.

Jack had also omitted to check out the cave in advance. When the cast arrived, they discovered that the cave had a long-dead horse in it. The actors, not unreasonably perhaps, had refused to perform until the carcass had been removed. Studs and Hank, whose erotic masterpiece, *Teenage Temptresses from Hell,* had won Nastiest Film at the last Adult Industry Convention, had had to drag the dead animal out of the cave and into the bush. There they'd dug a large pit, pushed the carcass into it, and covered it with branches and leaves. So far so good. It was not until the chief's son was chasing the axe murderer through the bush that Jack had remembered where they'd buried the horse. By this time, it was too late. The axe murderer fell through the branches and leaves onto the dead horse, closely followed by the chief's son.

Both actors, as soon as they'd been assisted out of the pit, told Jack what he could do with his movie, and, stinking abominably, left the location.

At first Jack had not been too worried by their departure. Both their faces had been covered in hair, so he'd thought it would be easy to replace them without having to re-shoot the opening sequences of the movie. Unfortunately, this had turned out not to be possible. When he viewed the scenes that had already been shot in the cave, he'd noticed, for the first time, that Studs' camera box was in shot. Since such equipment wasn't an everyday feature of Neanderthal living, it would be necessary to re-shoot the entire in-cave sequences. This proved to be a problem as all the cave men and women, having completed their scenes, had gone home. Jack's budget couldn't stretch to getting them back for another night.

Tragically for Jack, and more so for Maybelle, but perhaps not for the entertainment industry, *The Axeman Cometh* was never going to be finished. Jack's career as a real producer was over before it had begun.

Now, depressed and emotionally exhausted, he left Runyon Canyon Park and got Hank to drop him off at Interglobal's office. Located at the far end of the ten-mile-long Sunset Boulevard, it was a long way from the Sunset Strip where tourists oohed and aahed at the homes of the stars. The office, any office, was more than Jack could afford, but he believed that having a Sunset Boulevard, Los Angeles, address impressed potential investors in his propositions.

With his heart fluttering alarmingly as he gasped for breath—years of inhaling cheap cigar smoke had turned his lungs into an emphysemic sponge—he hauled himself up the narrow stairs to his office.

An over-weight, bald-headed, untidily dressed and permanently sweating man in his late fifties, Jack was best known among his associates in the low budget end of the movie industry for his clammy, clinging handshake, the touch of which lingered long after he'd withdrawn it from the prolonged grasp intended to convey the warmth and sincerity of his personality. In this, as in everything else, Jack failed to be convincing.

Wilcon Interglobal Consolidated Universal Pictures Inc. didn't operate at the top end of the industry and was barely visible at the bottom. But Jack persevered, convinced that in spite of years of failure the day would come when he would get his hands on a really hot property, one that would make him a multi-millionaire overnight. He spent his days mostly on the phone, attempting to solicit a few thousand dollars here and there from people who knew nothing about the movie industry and even less about his marginal involvement in it. Until his current production, he'd never actually produced a movie, though his name had appeared among the credits of a handful of box office disasters as one of the many associate producers.

Jack was in the distribution side of the business, and this occasionally entitled him to a screen credit for having committed himself to a financial contribution to the budget. In Jack's case, such a contribution was always negligible and consisted of a distribution guarantee—a sum of money that he promised to pay at a later date in return for the marketing rights in one or more territories. Since the only territories that Wilcon Interglobal Consolidated Universal Pictures Inc. were able to obtain distribution rights for were countries such as Kyrgyzstan and similar places that no one else had ever heard of, Jack's contribution, when it arrived, if it ever did, was inevitably very, very small. But he sincerely believed that it entitled him to refer to himself as a movie producer.

Jack had begun his career as a warehouse packer for a small production company that specialized in low budget sex and violence epics, usually banned in the more lucrative movie markets of the world. Inevitably, he'd told anyone who would listen that he was in the movie industry. After five years in the warehouse, his employer had allowed him to work, on a commission-only basis, as the sales representative for Southeast Asia, based in Bangkok. In this position he'd developed his taste for ostentatious luxury and acquired the trappings of the movie business: the cigars; the leased, tenth-hand Cadillac; a gargantuan appetite for sex—long since satiated—and the art of living entirely on other people's money.

Jack had no interest in film as an art form, or even as entertainment. He'd been—and still was—motivated entirely by the desire to make a great deal of money along with—in previous years—a subsidiary interest in the free sex that a surprising number of ambitious young actresses were willing to provide any man who called himself a movie producer.

Realizing before long that he would never get rich as long as he remained a sales rep in Bangkok, Jack had returned to the USA and established his own company, Wilcon Interglobal Consolidated Universal Pictures Inc. The cost of establishing the company and paying for the printing of some impressive stationery—cash in advance; printers in LA knew the ways of movie people—had exhausted his small capital.

His Sunset Boulevard 'headquarters'—as he grandly referred to the single room above Dino's Bar and Diner—was badly in need of a coat of paint and a long burst of deodorant air freshener. One of four serviced offices above a row of seedy establishments, it was perhaps best described as being 'maintenance-free'. Jack's office had a single window at the back with an uninterrupted view of Dino's overflowing garbage bins.

The suite of offices also housed Joseph Steinmark & Associates, Financial Advisers (a micro-time loan shark); Cherena, Psychic Readings: Your Future in Five Minutes $29.95; and Miss Porntip, Full Thai Body Massage, Body Slide a Specialty.

Maybelle, who loved Jack and was happy to work for nothing, serviced the offices. She saw in Jack qualities that no one else could even imagine he had. She believed that in spite of his entrepreneurial and ethical shortcomings, he was, beneath all the bluster, soft-hearted, kind, never cruel or violent and a natural optimist. No matter what went wrong—and most things did—he always bounced back, sadder but none the wiser. These qualities were very rare in Maybelle's world. An optimist herself, she also believed that one day he would make enough money to retire before the inevitable heart attack arrived and that he would take her with him to a little town in the Midwest where they would live quietly and peacefully, respectable and respected senior citizens.

Maybelle was a shameless romantic.

For the present, though, she felt content to sit at the front desk of the office suite, deal with the very occasional visitor and answer each of the four phones when it rang by stating the name of the business attached to it, the theory being that callers would get the impression that the business was successful enough to employ a receptionist.

The phones rang infrequently, however, and Maybelle dozed the days away. When a phone did ring, she usually awoke with a start and in hasty confusion often answered Jack's phone in her role as Porntip's receptionist, or as Cherena, Your Future in Five Minutes $29.95. The conversations that followed were frequently surreal.

With the failure of *The Axeman Cometh* behind him, Jack now had to turn his mind to a possible distribution deal for another producer's movies, in particular *The Power Drill Massacres* and *Dropsaw Killers of Detroit*, two slasher movies currently in production in a disused warehouse on the outskirts of LA. The problem was that to stitch the deal together he needed $5,000 to acquire the Bulgarian and Latvian distribution rights.

Nodding to Maybelle, who could tell from the set expression on his face that his world had fallen apart yet again, he panted into his office, collapsed into his frequently repossessed executive chair and picked up the phone. Unable to raise anything like $5,000, he was, nevertheless, determined to persuade the producer of the two lower-than-low budget, made-for-cable features to let him have at least some territories in which to distribute them.

'It's just that I'm putting together a package of six for Steve's company,' he told the producer. 'That's where my investors want to put their money.'

The producer understood that by 'Steve's company' Jack meant Steven Spielberg's Dreamworks. He also understood that the statement was a total fantasy. It had reality only in the alternative universe inhabited by movie people who were just hanging on at the bottom of the industry food chain. In this universe, gigantic deals were imminent, and producers and directors who hadn't produced or directed anything for ten years, and frequently forever, had access to hundreds of millions of dollars for the right property, which just happened to be on their desk, even as they spoke. Inevitably they'd also lined up the services of Brad, Nicole, Julia, Tom and Al and other luminaries of the movie industry, thus ensuring record-breaking, box office success.

'I can put your two in a package of ten that I'm calling *Nightmares*,' Jack continued, though he didn't have eight other features. Since the collapse of *The Axeman Cometh* he didn't have even one, but if he could get *The Power Drill Massacres* and *Dropsaw Killers of Detroit*, this would be the beginning of the package of ten.

The producer knew that Jack was lying, but this wasn't important—he, too, lied all the time. He calculated that cable and DVD sales in Bulgaria and Latvia were worth peanuts and, hell, we all have to make a living.

'Okay, Jack,' he said. 'But I'll need a couple of thousand up front.'

Jack knew that this was as good a deal as he'd get. 'You won't regret it,' he said, and rang off.

Now he only had to raise $2,000. Unfortunately, this wouldn't be significantly easier than raising $5,000. Perhaps, he thought, Maybelle could get another commercial. Even what she'd earn as an extra on a big shoot would help.

He pressed the intercom buzzer on his desk. Expecting the summons, Maybelle closed the current issue of *Variety*—the entertainment industry trade paper—and prepared to be consoling and sympathetic. For once she thought she might even have something useful to say. She'd just read a small classified ad in the back pages of the paper that might, just possibly might, provide Jack with a way out from the seemingly never-ending flow of failures.

Before he could begin his diatribe at the causes of his latest debacle, none for which he'd been personally to blame, he was sure, Maybelle put the paper in front of him.

'Read the ad I've circled in red, Jack.'

'What the fuck for?'

'Read it.'

Jack shrugged and opened the paper. He didn't want to quarrel with Maybelle. A possible $2,000 was at stake.

The small and unimpressive ad wasn't even boxed. Clearly the advertiser either had no faith in their offer or couldn't afford to advertise it properly.

'The Coddington St George Cultural Coordinating Committee,' Jack read, 'seeks expressions of interest from producers and/or directors with experience of community film production. Coddington St George is a small, but progressive, country town in beautiful tropical Queensland, Australia. Reply to culture@coddington.org.au.' Jack looked at Maybelle with an eyebrow raised. 'So?'

'You'd stand a good chance.' Maybelle didn't need to explain that even moderately successful producers or directors in frequent work would have no interest in what was obviously going to be an amateur production with a miniscule budget. Only the detritus of the industry, in desperation, would apply.

'What the fuck do I want to go to Australia for? I can't understand a word half of them say. And the half I can understand is all fucking lies.'

'Honey, I've been thinking,' Maybelle said, ignoring the outburst. 'I don't want to be unkind, but do you honestly still believe that you have any future in distribution? I'm finding work increasingly hard to get. I'm sure we can create an impressive CV for you. Even register a suitable business name—Jack Wilcon Community Movie Productions Inc.'

'And what if these guys check?'

'A small town council? Be realistic for a change. What will they know about Hollywood? Anyway, even if they do, you'll have lost nothing. Jack, you've lied about your credits before and got away with it. This could be your last chance, honey.'

'You're talking crap, Maybelle. What the fuck have I got to offer? The script and a few scenes of *The Axeman Cometh*, for Christ's sake? Forget it and let's have that coffee. I've got a splitting head.'

Maybelle left Jack's office and went to the little kitchen to make him a coffee. She suspected that the main reason he wouldn't even discuss the job in Australia was that he was in no mood to face rejection. And she knew the odds were long that he'd be considered suitable for the position, even if it paid little more than bed and board. At the same time, she knew that as a producer and distributor, he was at the end of the road. He had no money, no credibility and no assets of any kind apart from his ability occasionally to persuade people who should know better that he had something to offer them. His future was bleak. Maybelle's future was bleak. They both faced old age living off charity, perhaps even homelessness.

That night Maybelle slept little. She couldn't help thinking that if only Jack could get the job in Australia it could lead to something better—a new start. No one knew him there. That would be a great help.

Towards dawn she dozed, then awoke with the beginnings of an idea. When Jack panted into the office later that morning, her first words were, 'You could fake a demo, hon.'

'What the fuck are you talking about?

'Get Studs to put together a demo of excerpts from some student films. There are thousands of them. These Australians won't know they aren't your work.'

Jack stopped walking towards his office and turned. There were times when his mind worked quickly and he saw a situation with total clarity. 'Go on.'

'They'll be looking for a particular kind of producer—not some high flyer after big bucks, but one who's got a background working with beginners. Students.'

Jack knew Maybelle was right. She was also right about student films, too. If they'd been shown at all, it would've been only at short film festivals. Most of them would've never left the film school where they were made.

Sensing that Jack was now receptive to the idea, Maybelle pressed on.

'Studs will know how to find the bits he wants. He'll produce an impressive demo DVD on his MacBook. It's got an editing program. You can promise Studs work if you get the job. So, what will it cost? At most the cost of a stamp and a blank DVD. At this stage all you have to do is to express interest.'

Thus it was that Jack emailed <u>culture@coddington.org.au</u> expressing interest in producing a community movie, and referring briefly to his many years' experience as a consultant producer to community film makers in the USA and overseas. He signed it, Jack Wilcon, President International Community Movie Productions Inc, (INCOMOPRO) and gave his Sunset Boulevard address. By return he received an invitation to meet Tony Andover, the Coddington St George's Cultural Coordinating Committee's representative, at MIP TV, Cannes, the following month. He could be contacted at the Australian Rural Film Industry Development Organisation's stand.

There was no suggestion that his expenses for the trip would be met.

'That's the end of that, then,' Jack said. 'Where the fuck am I going to get the cash to get myself to Cannes? And do they know how expensive Cannes is during MIP? The whole fucking entertainment industry will be there.'

'You have to go, hon,' Maybelle said. 'Come on, Jack, you've never been a quitter. You can't give up now. I'll give Freddie a ring. He might have something for me.'

Luckily, Freddie, who operated the smallest advertising agency in LA, was able to find work for Maybelle—two days as a corpse in an ad as part of a road safety campaign. She earned $3,000 and gave it all to Jack.

'As a loan, hon,' she said.

'Sure, babe, as a loan,' he agreed, knowing that when the time came to settle with her, he could always convert the loan into an investment.

TWO

Coddington St George had at one time been a prosperous country town with its own weekly livestock market. But times had changed. This uninteresting, depressed township straddling the Bruce Highway between Rockhampton and Mackay in central Queensland was now known, when it was known at all, mainly for its geriatric hospital, by far the largest in the shire. There was a great deal of truth in the observation that people came to Coddington St George to die, and then, their short-term memories being faulty, they forgot to do so.

Until the Second World War, much of the district had been grazed by cattle, but since the war it had produced only sugar cane—tens of thousands of tons of it—for the refinery. Apart from aged care, hospital maintenance and undertaking, the sugar industry provided nearly all the employment opportunities. Only the municipal council provided work for school-leavers, though this rarely involved more than holding up 'Stop' and 'Slow' signs for the pothole-filling workmen, clusters of whom could often be seen staring meditatively at the latest incursion into the macadam.

Most of the retail activity occurred in the Paradise Palace shopping mall, built on the outskirts by Milosovic Constructions Pty Ltd. The development had inevitably destroyed the commercial life of the town centre.

Michael Milosovic was the town's mayor and also a property developer and the majority shareholder in PRP Ltd (Prestigious Rural Properties), the largest of the town's three struggling real estate agents. His political loyalties were determined by whichever party seemed likely, if in control of council, to provide the most opportunities for fast-tracked, government-subsidised, infrastructure-development approvals.

Burly and beer-gutted, with a dust-pitted red face from years spent on building sites, which he usually visited to sequestrate building materials for other constructions rather than to supervise the work in hand, Michael was in his mid fifties. Thick-set and coarse-featured, he had prominent ears and out-of-control, energetic, black eye-brows that pointed up to a bald head intricately patterned with cracks and scars where it'd been repeatedly struck over the years by low-lying scaffolding. Endowed with more self-confidence and aggression than a prize bull, Michael was nevertheless a disillusioned man, and everyone he had dealings with suffered from this. His bitterness was perhaps understandable, for there is little joy in being a developer in a dying town, even when, or perhaps especially when, one is also the chairman of the municipal planning committee.

Michael felt this keenly for he was a man with vision. He dreamed of re-building Coddington St George according to his own architectural inclinations as exemplified by his own house, which he'd designed himself in a style that can best be described as Yugoslav Modern. Lavishly supplied with Doric pillars, multi-collared tiles and bricks, with concrete casts of Greek and Roman statuary dotted about what little space surrounded it, Park Court dominated the West Coddington St George Estate. This estate comprised five hectares of project homes, mini-mansions on blocks so small that their owners never had to worry about the state of their gardens, as there were no gardens to worry about.

Most of the original nineteenth-century houses, cottages and shops in the town had long ago been demolished to make way for car and builders' yards, hardware, appliance and second-hand furniture stores, as well as the inevitable branches of national chain stores. No one now lived in the town: everyone lived outside it. As a result, not a lot happened in the town during the day, and nothing at all happened during the night— apart from alcohol-inspired disputes outside licensed premises.

Coddington St George was dying because it no longer had a reason to be. With labour-intensive agriculture in decline and nothing to replace it, the town had little to offer either residents or visitors. To make matters worse, a bypass had been built round it. This had so reduced the traffic through the town that all the service stations had had to close, as had two of the town's four hotels. The crumbling, forlorn and petroleum-polluted forecourts of the abandoned service stations were silent witnesses to the town's former prosperity.

Even the Paradise Palace shopping mall didn't attract visitors, though Michael felt proud of what he believed was his greatest achievement. He'd designed the complex himself, using coloured pencils in an exercise book on his kitchen table. Built to resemble a fairy castle, complete with turrets, towers and a drawbridge to keep the hoons out at night, the Paradise Palace shopping mall housed a supermarket and franchises of those of the nation's chain stores that had deserted the High Street. At first there'd been a few local, independent retail establishments, but unable to compete with the chain stores, which, it was rumoured, were actually branches of the Shanghai People's Export Everything Cooperative, they had soon been forced to close.

A feature of the Paradise Palace mall, of which Michael Milosovic was particularly proud, was its community park—a twenty-meter square of coloured concrete in the heart of the mall, furnished with two indestructible and undefaceable stainless-steel benches. Here young women liked to meet. Many having only recently departed from Year Ten at Coddington St George High, and finding no work available, they had opted for pregnancy and motherhood on single-parent pensions. They spent their days sitting around in the mall with their screaming infants, busily smoking and gossiping, bringing one another up to date on the antics of their favourite soap-opera characters, and when they thought it necessary, or just out of habit, clouting an erring child round the head to little useful effect.

Young men, similarly lacking anything worthwhile to do without any pothole-filling or road sign-holding employment to pass the time, and unwilling to undertake apprenticeships that paid less than the dole, hung around the mall car park doing burns with their three-hundred-dollar sets of wheels. Many of them were already fathers, though they lacked all parental inclinations, and in some cases, were unable to remember the event that had brought about their parental situation.

The remaining two of the town's original four hotels—the Grand, a depressing workingman's pub, and the Central, which had pretensions and offered food and accommodation—both had gaming rooms packed with poker machines.

As for the cultural life of the town, this was not its strongest point. In spite of—or perhaps because of—the efforts of the Coddington St George Cultural Coordinating Committee, (President, Michael Milosovic), residents had to rely for live entertainment of a serious nature on performances in the town hall by the local amateur dramatic society, the Coddington Players, and for music by the occasional concerts by the Marilyn Ferguson String Ensemble, Leader, Marilyn Ferguson, a large, wide-hipped, somewhat military-looking lady, who plucked at a double bass with a panache sadly lacking in the other players who, stern-faced to a woman, gave the impression of hating rather than loving the music they were attacking—as if they were teaching it a lesson for being so difficult to play. There was also Meat Pie, a local band, none of whose occasional members could read music or play an instrument above entry level. They knew, however, how to make a great deal of noise, which seemed to be their most developed skill, and they provided live music at the Central on Fridays and Saturdays and for the annual Bachelors and Spinsters Ball, the biggest booze-up of the year after the Coddington Show Ball at which a bigger band, imported from Rockhampton, provided even louder music due to their even-more-powerful electronic equipment.

The Coddington St George Cultural Coordinating Committee was responsible for the advertisement in *Variety*. The suggestion that the committee should sponsor the making of a community movie had, inevitably, come from Michael Milosovic. His argument for making a movie had been brief and to the point.

'Last year Mackey put on a pageant and got incredible publicity for it on television and in the national press. The number of visitors to the city has quadrupled. We have to go one better. A community movie is the answer. One that involves as many people as possible—crowd scenes and all that kind of thing. Fortunately, we have a number of talented young people in the town. All we need is an experienced producer to organise the movie. I suggest we advertise.'

And this is what they'd done.

They'd received two replies—one from Jack Wilcon in the US of A, and one from the art-house film-writer/producer/director Sven Larsson in Sweden.

The Cultural Coordinating Committee had promptly met to decide what to do about the applications.

Michael had said, 'I've had a word with Tony Andover.'

Tony had been given a small grant by Film Queensland to make a short film. Entitled *Trash: A Day in the Life of a Small Town Garbo*, it had been shot on a mobile phone in Coddington and had been highly commended at the Queensland Festival of Five-Minute Movies. Its grainy realism, in particular, had impressed the judges. This recognition had made Tony the town's expert on all matters cinematic.

'He suggested,' Michael had continued, 'that we send him to MIP TV in Cannes—some kind of film and TV festival—where he'll meet the two applicants and report back to us about them. It's a sensible suggestion. It'll be cheaper to send him to Cannes—he's young and can stay at some kind of backpacker hostel—than pay for the applicants to come here for an interview.'

Thus it was that Tony Andover, twenty-two years of age and currently employed part-time as the station manager of Coddington FM 103, had found himself at MIP TV Cannes, where the world's film and TV great and not-so-great congregated once a year to lie about themselves and their latest productions.

***

Fortunately for Jack, his hotel in Cannes was almost opposite the bus station, so he found it easily. He checked into a room the size of a broom cupboard, irritated by the knowledge that more successful producers were staying at the better hotels that cost a minimum of $750 a day plus taxes. He also knew that if anyone asked where he was staying, he'd have to say that he was staying with friends who had a villa in the hills behind the city.

As soon as he recovered from his flight and the bus ride from Nice airport, Jack walked slowly, perspiring heavily in the Mediterranean heat, to the exhibition centre where ARFIDO had a stand and where he expected to meet Tony Andover. His lips moved as he walked, rehearsing the lies he'd tell to support his application for the position of producer. Passersby thought he was a madman talking to himself and moved out of his way.

Jack banked on the likelihood that the Coddington St George representative would be ignorant of everything to do with the film industry and its participants. The man would likely turn out to be a local councillor, probably a builder or real estate agent by occupation, in Cannes on an expensive junket. If this were the case, Jack felt confident of impressing him without too great an investment in hospitality and carnal entertainment. Jack had had problems with the latter in the past. In Bangkok he'd procured a Thai woman for a visiting British DVD distributor, but the next morning, while Jack stoked up on the 'eat as much as you can' buffet breakfast in the hotel's coffee shop, the producer had approached his table and informed him—with none of the friendly warmth of the previous evening—that after the sex, which had not lived up to expectations, the woman had taken a small, ivory-handled revolver out of her handbag and demanded double the agreed fee or else.

The producer had declined Jack's invitation to join him for breakfast, and there'd been no hope of a deal then or in the future.

Jack now checked his wallet. He had enough cash to buy Tony Andover a drink in one of the hotels. With a little careful manoeuvring, he might even manage to get Tony to buy the first drink. And the first drink would also be the last, as Jack would remember another appointment before it came to his turn to buy. With the money saved he'd be able to afford a meal in one of the many comparatively cheap mom and pop side-street restaurants that had no menu, just served the dish of the day.

When Jack arrived at the ARFIDO stand, shortly before noon, he found only two people there, a soulful-looking young woman behind the desk, wearing a blouse that did everything for her figure but nothing for her modesty, and a young man with thick, black hair down to his shoulders and an intense expression on his not unattractive but fast-food-pale face. He sat at one of the small tables, leafing through *Sight and Sound*. Other representatives of the Australian film and television industry were either visiting business contacts on their stands or at lunch, after which if they were even half way up the industry career ladder, they'd rest in their hotels until the serious eating, drinking and deal-making began in the evening. Then as alert as their digestions permitted and wary of treading on a snake and sliding to the bottom of the ladder, or even off it completely, they would begin the tortuous process of deal-making.

'I'm Jack Wilcon,' Jack announced. 'INCOMOPRO. I have an appointment with Tony Andover.'

The young woman, who wasn't impressed by Tony—he wasn't her idea of an up-and-coming producer—said nothing, but pointed at him.

Jack nodded and approached Tony, hand out-stretched. 'Jack Wilcon, President, INCOMOPRO. It's a pleasure to meet you, Tony.'

The two men shook hands.

Tony didn't find it a pleasant experience. He needed to wipe Jack's perspiration off his hands, but he was too embarrassed and polite to do so. He hoped they'd soon dry in the fiercely conditioned air.

Jack sat down at a small table and looked around. A coffee machine sat on the ARFIDO stand. Jack eyed it hopefully. The coffee would be free. There might even be a biscuit or two.

Tony caught his glance. 'Would you like a coffee, Mr Wilcon?'

'Jack, please. Yes, that would be great. Milk and four sugars.'

Tony moved towards the machine, but the young woman at the desk waved him back to his seat. Although Tony didn't look as if he'd ever amount to much in the industry, she was prepared to give him a little face, especially as her boss was due back soon.

'So, Tony,' Jack said. 'Tell me all about this movie your town wants to make. And your role in it.'

It seemed to Tony that he was the one being interviewed, but as he'd never interviewed anyone before, he was unsure of the protocol, so he decided to let Jack lead the way. 'Well, the Cultural Coordinating Committee—it's a subcommittee of the Coddington St George Town Council—gives grants to local cultural organisations—you know, the amateur dramatic society, the local history people, that sort of thing. Well, there's always been rivalry between Coddington and Rockhampton, that's the next town, and last year Rockhampton—no, perhaps it was Mackay, I forget—anyway, they put on a community play, a sort of historical pageant, and it got a lot of national publicity.'

'I'm with you, Tone,' Jack said. 'So, this year, not to be out-done, Coddington St George—I love the name—has decided to make a community movie. Fantastic. And you need an experienced producer. Well, Tone, there's not much I don't know about community moviemaking. It's why I've established the International Community Movie Productions Inc. INCOMOPRO. Yes, sir. To provide production management and distribution know-how to committees just like yours.'

He took a deep breath and cut to the chase.

'Your committee gives out grants, you said. So presumably there's a budget for this movie you're planning.'

'Sort of,' Tony said.

Jack's internal organs trembled in preparation for a fall. 'Sort of?'

'For a producer. Everyone else will be expected to give their time for free.'

'Ah!' Jack recovered quickly. 'Exactly. That's what community moviemaking is all about. Involve as many locals as possible.'

Jack badly wanted to discuss the financial aspects of the project in more detail, but he was aware that too much interest in money might antagonise the young man, who was probably some kind of art-house film freak.

'But tell me about yourself, Tone. I like to know something about the people I'm going to work with. What's your interest in the film industry?'

'Well, I really want to produce a feature film.'

'Of course, you do. It's what every young film-maker wants to do. What have you produced so far?'

'Just a few short films. On video.'

'Ah ha!' Jack smiled encouragingly. 'Just the kind of film-maker I'm used to working with.'

The boy—Jack thought of Tony as a boy as he was so slim and obviously immature—was clearly little more than an enthusiastic amateur. He'd be easy to impress. 'I guess you have to have a day job,' he said. 'Make your movies in your spare time.'

'Well, yes. Actually, I manage Coddington St George 103.5 FM.'

Jack assumed wrongly that this was the local commercial radio station and was a little surprised that Tony had the necessary qualities for such a position. In fact, FM 103.5 was a community radio station that had a small audience of mainly retired citizens, most of whom lacked either the technical know-how or the manual dexterity to change to another station. Even the members of the station's managing committee rarely listened to it.

Apart from managing FM 103.5 for a wage equivalent to the dole, Tony Andover also presented the breakfast, lunch, afternoon tea, drive time, dinner and bath time shows. *The Coddington St George News Gazette* displayed advertisements referring to it as 'The voice of Coddington St George: hard-hitting local talkback radio.' However, there was never any talkback, hard-hitting or soft. This was not due to any kind of censorship, but simply because no one ever phoned the station. As a result, Tony did all the talking—hours of it. He believed that his catchphrase, 'Hey, people! You're getting it from Tony Andover!' would eventually become household words in the district and that before long he would be head-hunted by one of the Rockhampton or Mackay—or even, bigtime, a Townsville station. To encourage this, he tried to emulate successful commercial radio talk show hosts by stressing all the wrong words and syllables in his spiels. But he lacked the brash personality and excessive over-confidence to be convincing. He sounded like the kind of young man that he was: softly spoken, diffident, anxious to please, and usually drifting in a world of his own.

Between Tony's hour-long 'spots' six days a week, the station broadcast almost continuous golden oldies, interrupted only by the station's most popular program—and, some people maintained, the only possible justification for its existence—the daily readings for the locally print-handicapped by Ernie Wrench from the Central Queensland Daily News.

Ernie's readings, which included all the advertisements, were difficult to follow. He had a significant speech defect caused by the mobility of his false teeth. He also needed to move his finger slowly along the lines of print to keep from losing his place. Tony had confided to his friend Howard Grant—proprietor of the bookshop *Between the Leaves*, Artistic Director of the Coddington St George Players and a member of the Cultural Coordinating Committee—that these daily readings were by the voice-handicapped for the print-handicapped.

It was perhaps not surprising that FM 103.5 FM competed with a total lack of success with the ABC's national and local networks as well as with sundry commercial stations whose powerful transmitters frequently encroached on it. In fact, much of Tony's broadcasting was accompanied by a thudding background of heavy rock from other stations.

It was just as well, perhaps, that his ambition lay not only in radio but also in the film industry.

'Tell me about your most recent production,' Jack said. If he'd learnt anything in his fifty years, it was that it pays to listen. With the right encouragement, people often revealed information about themselves that could be put to good use.

Tony's raincoat hung over the back of his chair. He took a DVD out of one of the pockets and handed it to Jack. 'It's called *Trash*,' he said. 'It's about a day in the life of a garbo.'

'Garbo?' This was Jack's first encounter with the oddities of Australian English. He was to have many of them, some resulting in serious confusion.

'Garbage collector. He works for the Resource Recovery Centre. You know, the tip.'

'Right,' Jack said. 'Got it. How long is your movie?

'Five minutes.'

'A short day,' Jack said, hoping for a laugh, but Tony didn't seem to have a sense of humour.

'It's edited down, of course.'

'Of course.' Jack sighed. He'd no experience of idealistic young people who were not interested in fame or money but just wanted to be original and creative. Tony wasn't going to be an easy young man to get along with, he decided. And it would be very easy to offend him. A wrong word now and the trip would turn out to be a waste of time and Maybelle's money. Fortunately, though, Jack thought, it seemed that Tony Andover was as concerned to impress him, and get some free advice, as he was to impress Tony. *If I can convince him that I can help him to get to Hollywood, the job's in the bag,* he decided.

'I'll watch it in my room this evening.' This was his cue to neatly segue into his prepared spiel. 'I think you should see the kind of movies I've been involved in, too, Tone. You see, I get a lot of invitations to advise on community productions.'

He unzipped his fake leather document case and took out a DVD. 'Here are some extracts from some short films I've produced or been associated with. All very low-budget, of course, but multi-award winning. Experimental, some of it, but none the worse for that. Have you got a DVD player with you?'

'I've got my laptop.'

The soulful-looking girl brought the coffee. One biscuit, a digestive, sat in the saucer. Jack looked at it suspiciously. He thought it looked like a treat for a fashionable dog. But he was hungry, so he smiled winningly, he hoped, at the girl and said, 'I could manage two. I haven't eaten since five o'clock this morning on the plane.'

The girl returned to the coffee machine and the packet of biscuits. When Jack bit into his, crumbs flew to the back of his throat and he immediately had a coughing fit. 'Sorry,' he spluttered, spewing crumbs into the air.

Tony surreptitiously removed one from the corner of an eye.

'Got a crumb on my epiglottis.' Jack cleared his throat. More crumbs emerged, seemed to hover briefly, then landed gently on the table. Jack sipped the coffee. It was weak and barely warm. 'So, what is the selection procedure for the producer's position?'

'Well,' Tony began carefully, not wanting to give the impression that Jack impressed him, because he didn't. He'd never met anyone like him. Forceful personalities were rare in Coddington St George. Tony didn't suspect Jack of lying about himself, though he realised that this was a possibility, rather he took an instant dislike of Jack's effusive over-sincerity. Tony told himself that this was probably because Jack was not only an American but also a Hollywood producer. However, this explanation of his personality didn't make him any more attractive.

'I have to meet all the applicants who have come to Cannes,' Tony said, 'and then I'll sort of make a report to the Culture Committee.'

'A short list of the short list.'

'Sort of, yes.'

'How many applicants are there?'

'Oh, quite a few.' Tony was learning how to lie—an essential part of his development if he were to succeed as a producer.

Jack opened his document case again, took out a wholly fictitious resume and handed it to Tony. 'Your committee will need this,' he said.

All the referees Jack had listed were producers of the cheapest pornography—Jack's only remaining friends in the industry. But the names of their companies gave not even a hint of the nature of their films: Xenophon Productions, Minotaur Films, Starwise Entertainment—for all anyone knew they could be major feature film production companies. Jack was relying on the likelihood that the Coddington St George Cultural Committee wouldn't bother to take up references and that even if they did, they wouldn't go to the trouble of finding out the bona fides of the people providing the glowing—though probably misspelled—references.

He stood up. 'I have other people to see, Tony. The ABC are interested in my latest productions. Why don't we meet here the same time tomorrow? By then you'll have had time to view my demo DVD.'

Though young and naïve, Tony was sensible enough to know that he ought to keep Jack at bay. He had the other applicant to see and didn't want Jack hanging around. 'I've got a few people to see, too, Jack. Can I contact you at your hotel if we need to meet again?'

Jack didn't like this suggestion for several reasons. He especially didn't want Tony to know where he was staying—a cheap boarding house masquerading as a small hotel.

'Tone, I've got a full book, too.' He opened his document case again and took out a diary. 'We ought to fix a time now, then I can work around it.'

Tony began to feel pressured. Fortunately, he'd had enough pressure from his mother to know how to deal with it. Polite, implacable firmness was the only solution. 'Sorry, Jack. No can do. I'm only here for two days. I need to be free to move around as necessary. Have you got a mobile number?'

'Mobile? Oh, you mean cell phone.' Jack's immediate problem was to decide whether or not to accept Tony's offer. If he gave his cell phone number, then he'd be dependent on Tony's decision whether they should meet or not. If Tony decided it wasn't necessary, Jack would have no opportunity of finding out anything about the other applicants; without this knowledge it would be difficult to decide his next move. But if he declined to give Tony the number, then the young man would have every reason to be suspicious. Jack decided he had no choice in the matter. He gave Tony the number.

'I'd be grateful, Tone, if you could contact me first thing. I've got a full day ahead of me.'

'Of course, Jack. Same here.'

Unable to leave well alone, Jack had to promote himself more, just in case Tony hadn't fully understood his importance and success in the industry. 'A lot of famous people come here, you know. On my way here, I ran into Steve Spielberg.'

Name-dropping was the default mode of everyone attending the Cannes Film Festival and Television Market. A detritus of dropped names covered the floors of every hotel bar and restaurant in the city—and there were hundreds. Jack had never mastered the art, but it wasn't for want of practice. Now he launched into a long and incoherent account of all the big Hollywood names he'd helped in their careers and counted among his hundred or so closest friends. Fox, Paramount, Universal, Disney, Warner, MGM, and the other major studios were all apparently in Jack's debt and were begging him to produce multi-million-dollar features for them.

'But I've had enough of the studio system, Tone,' Jack said. 'Now I want to do something to help communities understand moviemaking. Your project's a great idea, Tone. I'd be honoured to work with you. I was telling Frank Somers—he's head of drama at MTV (there was no such person, but Jack was confident that Tony wouldn't know this), and we go back a long way; he always contacts me as soon as he arrives in Cannes—anyway, I was telling him about the Coddington St George project. "Jack," he said, "if there's anyone who can make that a movie to be remembered, it's you. They couldn't choose a better EP."

'You see, Tone, what you need is a guy who knows his way around the industry. Making movies is one thing; getting distribution and exhibition is another. With my contacts, I can guarantee to get our movie shown in major festivals throughout the world. I can also guarantee to get our movie onto cable and satellite and onto DVD. It'll be a trailblazer, Tone. Audiences worldwide will want to see what a small community can achieve.'

Jack took a last gulp from his now cold coffee, and then, after thrusting out his hand, which Tony tried not to grasp too tightly in case the gesture was misunderstood, Jack risked asking the all-important question. 'By the way, Tone. What is the budget?'

'There isn't one yet.'

This was good news to Jack. It was easier to inflate a non-existent budget than one that had already been approved. 'Have you decided on your own fee, Tone?'

He still held onto Tony's hand, as if afraid that if he let go Tony might disappear in a puff of smoke, like a genie who'd granted the traditional wish and now had other matters to attend to.

'I'm getting a small grant, as the director. No one else will be paid except the producer,' Tony said. 'The idea is that everyone, you know, gives their time.'

'Sure, sure!' Jack exclaimed, 'but there'll be some costs. Equipment hire, tapes, costumes, sets, catering, editing expenses. Reimbursements. Petty cash. That sort of thing.' He paused to give weight to the last item. 'There are always petty cash expenses. You can't make a movie without handing out cash.'

'We're hoping to keep costs to the minimum,' Tony said. 'You know, shoot it on handy cam; edit it on a computer, like I did with *Trash*.'

Jack now took Tony's hand in both of his, and then slid one hand up as far to the young man's elbow as he could. It was intended as a fatherly gesture—indicating the desire of an older man to help a young one in his career—but it succeeded only in alarming Tony. Unsure of Jack's sexual orientation, Tony didn't want to risk being propositioned.

'You can trust me, Tone. You'll never regret taking me on board. It'll be an honour to be working with someone as talented as you. I was saying only yesterday to Rupert Murdock—he owns Twentieth Century Fox, you know—it's experienced old-timers like me who can act as mentors to the new generation of film-makers.' His eyes moistened. 'It's time,' he croaked, 'that I gave something back to an industry that's been so good to me.'

THRee

Tony's only other appointment was at ten o'clock the following day. He had arranged to meet Sven Ingersson, a Swedish film-maker of some repute, at his stand. On the way, he called in at ARFIDO to check if there were any messages for him. There were not. He was relieved to find that Jack was not there waiting for him on the off-chance of a meeting. However, though Jack wasn't waiting on the ARFIDO stand, he was— unbeknown to Tony—waiting for him on a nearby stand, wasting the time of a producer of cheaply animated children's programmes. When Tony left ARFIDO, Jack followed him at a safe distance. The exhibition hall was so crowded that he had little chance of being seen.

Tony, who was early for his appointment with Ingersson, made straight for the Short Film Corner in Le Palais. The number of young film-makers who'd taken the opportunity to promote their work amazed him. The booths buzzed with enthusiasm and film talk. And everyone was friendly. Several young producers and directors thought the concept of a day in the life of a resource recovery centre operative was awesome. One suggested that he should film a day in the life of a cemetery. Tony, being the kind of young man that he was, took the suggestion seriously.

When he began his tour of the rest of the exhibition halls, especially the basement of Le Palais, he began to have doubts about where he would fit into the film industry. Most of the booths seemed to be offering 'R' or even 'X'-rated sex and violence movies. The posters for these movies depicted an abundance of naked flesh and gouts of blood. There seemed to be thousands of them. The film industry was not what he thought it was. He realized for the first time that the Hollywood box office blockbusters screened in cinemas represented a tiny fraction of the total industry. Most of it seemed to be concerned with making very low budget videos for cable, DVD and the Internet.

As one of the distributors explained to him, 'It's porno—hard core and soft—that keeps the industry going, son. Two hundred porno movies are made a week in Hollywood alone. The adult industry grosses more than all the mainstream productions put together.'

When Tony stopped at a booth or stand, either to chat to whoever was manning it or to stare at the posters and help himself to the publicity postcards and flyers, Jack had to nip quickly into the nearest place of temporary concealment. There he handed out his business cards, either as president of Wilcon Interglobal Consolidated Universal Pictures or as his new identity, president of International Community Movie

Productions. As neither entity had any current functioning capacity, it didn't matter which he represented himself as being president of. In any case, producers and distributors who had a worthwhile product on offer were far too busy with appointments made weeks in advance to spend time with casual visitors with business cards that looked—as they had been—hastily printed out by the machine at Nice airport.

Only if they were finding it difficult or impossible to get interest in their product did they welcome Jack, offering him coffee, alcohol or both. For such people, Jack was happy to provide a fictitious account of his operation until it was time to move on. Then he excused himself with a promise to return another year, adding, 'If only my list wasn't full, I'd be seriously interested in distributing your slate of productions in the territories I specialise in. Stay in touch and do keep me informed of anything new you have in the pipeline.'

Producers and distributors new to the market allowed, even encouraged, themselves to believe this nonsense. On their return to their offices they even hinted to potential investors that they had a major distribution deal almost sewn up. The old hands, on the other hand, knew Jack for what he was, a time-wasting, washed-up minor player, working his way through the last chapter of his fantasy.

For Tony it was all fascinating, surprising, exciting, but sometimes depressing. The real life-changing experience came for him, however, in Le Riviera where Sven Ingersson waited for him in a booth the size of a cardboard box that could have, and probably had, at one time contained a large refrigerator. Now it contained a card table, a deck chair and a morose Sven Ingersson, reading a Swedish newspaper.

Film posters and enlarged stills from his films—all of which seemed to depict different methods of committing suicide—lined the walls of his booth. Men, and occasionally women, hung from beams and trees, lay dead in cars from breathing in carbon monoxide, were walking into the sea, jumping from tenth floor balconies, popping handfuls of pills, and shooting themselves. One especially gruesome photograph showed a man committing hari kari. The films had titles such as *Cries and Whimpers*, *Murmurs and Screams*, *Sobs and Moans*, and most had won prizes at various festivals. One had won the Golden Twig at Nuremberg, another the Silver Branch at Woopikedia, Kansas. Three had even won The Bronze Saucer at Nuuk, Greenland.

Tony assumed correctly that the man who sprawled in the deckchair, apparently enveloped in gloom, was Ingersson in person. A long man, rather than a tall one—long because he spent most of his time lying down—he also had long and huge, heavily-lobed ears that looked as if they were made of pink plastic and had been hastily stuck on, not quite in the right places. His blonde hair had been badly cut and showed parts of his mottled and flaky scalp. Aged somewhere in his fifties, he exuded weariness.

'And you are from where?' he asked as Tony approached. His voice moved up and down like a small boat on a windy lake.

'From Coddington St George, I am,' Tony replied, unconsciously parroting the Swedish grammar. 'An appointment, we have.'

For a moment, Sven seemed not to remember this, then his memory returned and he sat up and offered Tony his hand. 'Schnapps?' Not waiting for a reply, he poured Tony and himself large glasses of colourless liquid.

'Skol,' he said and drank the lot in one gulp.

Not being used to alcohol at any time of the day, let alone at ten o'clock in the morning, Tony sipped the drink slowly, coughing only a little as the spirit seared his throat.

Sven poured himself another schnapps and began to talk, softly and gently at first but with increasing ardour as he warmed up to his favourite and—as his eighth wife had discovered—only subject. He spoke with animation of the importance of being true to one's vision as a film-maker, of never compromising for commercial reasons, and of never being concerned if all one's films lost money, especially if it was other people's. He also spoke strongly and at length of the absolute duty of governments to support independent film-makers in their never-ending struggle against the dominance of Hollywood.

When Tony told him about his award-winning film *Trash*, Sven immediately begged for permission to remake it in Sweden. He wanted to develop the concept so that the resource recovery centre attendant who, overwhelmed by being surrounded by the rubbish of other people's lives, commits suicide by shutting himself in an abandoned refrigerator.

Tony told Sven he was happy for him to do this. He then managed to interrupt the Swede and ask him why he'd applied to produce the Coddington St George community movie.

Sven, now well into his sixth schnapps, burst into tears and threw his arms around Tony. The Swedish equivalent of 'soulmate' poured from his lips.

Gradually getting drunker as Sven became increasingly incoherent, Tony eventually fell asleep. He spent the rest of the day unconscious with Sven on the floor of his booth, which had just enough room for them both if they kept their knees bent.

Concealed behind a partition in the adjacent booth, Jack heard most of this, and became deeply worried. He suspected that Tony would never forget his meeting with the Swedish director. He'd met a man totally dedicated to his art, with only side trips to marriage and alcohol. Compared to himself, he realised, Ingersson would be a saint in Tony's estimation. The man would make him feel capable of achieving great things in the art-house genre, even one day of winning the Bronze Saucer at Nuuk.

Jack was convinced, too, that Tony would suggest to the Coddington St George Cultural Coordinating Committee that Ingersson should be invited to be the producer of the community movie. He was equally sure that if he didn't do something drastic, he personally would stand no chance of getting the job. One possibility, he thought, would be to approach Tony as he left Ingersson's stand, as if by coincidence, and then insist on taking him for a coffee. There he'd casually warn him about Ingersson, inventing a history of embezzlements, fraud, sexual deviance—anything and everything he could think of that would make Tony hesitate before recommending the man to his committee.

The problem was, as Jack knew from past experience, this kind of thing could backfire. He couldn't be sure that Tony wouldn't meet someone of impeccable reputation who admired Ingersson and contradicted everything Jack had said about him, pointing out, not unreasonably, that Jack might have an ulterior motive in passing on such slanderous gossip.

On balance, Jack decided, therefore, that he needed to explore another possibility. The only one he could think of was to get himself to Coddington St George before Tony returned and somehow chat up key members of the Cultural Coordinating Committee. Once in the town, he thought, it shouldn't be difficult to find out who they were.

Man of action that he was, Jack immediately left his hiding place—and Sven and Tony snoring happily—and hurried to the communications centre. There he googled Coddington St George, worked out an itinerary, and then emailed Maybelle.

'Hi, babe. All going well here. I'm really in with a good chance. The Coddington St George guy is just a kid. He knows nothing about the industry, just made a short. He's eating out of my hand and thinks I should go immediately and talk to the committee. Not wait to be invited. I'll need some money—extra airfare to Australia, car hire, train fare, hotel, that sort of thing. I've got enough to get me there, but that's all. I've looked up somewhere to stay on the internet—the Central Hotel. Can you get money to me there by Western Union? I'm on a roll, babe. This is what you wanted, and I'm going for it. Ever. Jack.'

He then returned to his room, packed his bag and caught the next bus to Nice. There, he found a flight to Paris with a reasonable connection to Sydney within the hour. Shortly after his arrival in Sydney, he flew to Rockhampton, where he could hire a car to drive to Coddington St George. He arrived at the country town thirty-four hours later, totally exhausted and as near to cardiac arrest as he had ever been.

FOUR

A permanently homesick Englishman, the current proprietor of the Central Hotel, had decorated it in the style of a typical English country pub. He'd added a motel wing at the back and covered the walls of the hotel's public rooms with every conceivable design of horse brass, items of saddlery and hunting prints—all purchased through eBay from Genine Antiqes, Shen Zhen, China.

Alec lived upstairs in the main building with his wife, Peggy. Their children had long since left home and were 'in relationships', though not often in work. The ground floor consisted of the bar—the Snuggery, as Alec, but no one else, called it—a dining room, a kitchen, and a games room where the unemployed of the district—a large percentage of the under-forties males—played pool, placed their bets online and played the pokies. The pub also boasted an outside beer garden, rarely used because the winds that blew in from the arid west carried so much dust that in the hot summers breathing out of doors could be difficult.

Peggy looked after the bar, cooked the meals—such as they were—and complained, hardly pausing for breath, that Alec never did any work: he only occasionally served behind the bar and had never been known to polish a glass or install a fresh keg. His idea of being a publican was to engage the customers in conversation. He liked to sit with visiting diners, much to their surprise and stifled fury, often helping himself to their wine. He maintained that this behaviour was expected of him. It was part of his being 'a character'.

Unlike Jack Wilcon, however, Alec was not a lying braggart. He told the truth, nothing but the truth and the whole truth endlessly about his life's work, begun long before he emigrated to Australia—the study of weasels, stoats, ferrets and skunks, about which there was little he didn't know or insist on communicating to anyone he could corner.

Fascinating though these creatures are, they are not a significant component of Australian fauna. Nevertheless, it was his habit to sidle up to a completely innocent couple quietly masticating their lamb chops or T-bone steaks and say, 'You probably don't know it, but the collective noun for weasels is a "confusion" of weasels. What do you think of that, eh?' Then given the slightest encouragement, such as not being told to piss off, he would sit at their table, help himself to their wine, and begin one of his set-piece lectures on the family Mustelidae.

Weasels, stoats, ferrets and skunks being semi-nocturnal— they preferred to hunt at dawn and dusk—Alec had spent most of his spare time before leaving rural Sussex in England with video camera at the ready, waiting for the action to begin. Such action invariably comprised a stoat, weasel, skunk or ferret killing another small animal and eating it.

Alec's ambition was to edit the footage into a documentary and become the David Attenborough of the Mustelidae family—which also included otters and ermine. He had twice offered a television series to the BBC's Natural History Unit in Bristol, but both had been rejected. He couldn't understand why, because most of the Attenborough series seemed to dwell in a similar fashion on animals killing and eating other animals.

Until a legacy from an Australian uncle, payable on his becoming an Australian citizen, had made it possible for him to emigrate and purchase the Central Hotel in Coddington St George, Alec had worked for many years as a cinema projectionist. His main interest was, not unnaturally, photography, which he'd refined to natural history photography and further refined to the study of weasels, stoats, ferrets and skunks. In recent years he'd become obsessive in his hobby, leaving the running of the hotel almost wholly to his wife, who now insisted on separate rooms. Sometimes Peggy thought she would prefer a loose woman in his life than his obsession. She'd even encouraged several of the looser women in the town to flirt with her husband, but the competition from the family Mustelidae had proved too powerful even for them.

When Jack checked in after his dash from Cannes, he gave Alec his business card. Alec immediately attempted to engage him in filmic conversation. Having a Hollywood producer as a guest in his hotel, the president of Wilcon Interglobal Consolidated Universal Pictures Inc., no less, was an opportunity, he thought, too good to be missed. He had to interest him in his proposed TV series, *The Night Life of Weasels, Stoats, Ferrets and Skunks*. A Hollywood producer, he was sure, would have contacts in the National Geographic and Discovery Channels.

As Jack signed the guest book, Alec said, 'You probably aren't aware of the fact, Mr Wilcon, but ferrets are crepuscular, which means they spend fourteen to eighteen hours a day asleep and are most active around the hours of dawn and dusk.'

Jack was not aware of this, but he said nothing, being unsure that he'd heard correctly. Alec's Sussex accent was determinedly broad.

'Most ferrets will live happily in social groups,' he continued, unfazed by the startled expression on Jack's face. 'A group of ferrets is commonly referred to as a "business" of ferrets. Isn't that delightful? They're territorial animals, of course, and like to burrow, and prefer to sleep in an enclosed area.'

Confused by this outburst of unexpected and somewhat irrelevant information from a hotelier—Jack was used to having the accommodation's facilities briefly described—he assumed that Alec was quite mad and might even be dangerous. He backed away.

Alec followed him, room key in hand. 'Like many other carnivores,' he continued, 'ferrets have scent glands near their anus, the secretions from which are used in scent marking. It has been reported that ferrets can recognize individuals from these anal gland secretions, as well as the sex of unfamiliar individuals. Ferrets may also use urine marking for sex and individual recognition. They are absolutely fascinating creatures. As, of course, are their relations, weasels, stoats and skunks. I'm making a TV series about them, you know.'

Jack snatched the key from Alec's hand and half ran to his room, one of the twelve motel-style rooms in the courtyard at the rear of the hotel. There, he quickly locked himself in. When his heart stopped thudding against his chest and the vein in his forehead stopped throbbing, he told himself not to be stupid. The innkeeper was almost certainly harmless, just an English eccentric. English TV series were full of them. At least half the acting profession in Britain seemed to earn their living by pretending to be totally dotty.

At breakfast the next morning, served by Peggy, who seemed to be normal, though harassed, Jack felt much better. He'd slept well in the Spartan but comfortable and clean room, and wondered if perhaps he had imagined Alec—a kind of waking nightmare. However, when only half way through his fat-soaked hash browns, scrambled eggs, mushrooms and tomato, Alec arrived. He immediately sat down at Jack's table and helped himself to the now cold and brittle toast and the remains of a small dish of jam.

Jack debated with himself whether to glower at Alec or humour him. He decided on the latter. It occurred to him that it was possible that he might be able to persuade Alec to offer him a night or two free board and lodging.

'Tell me what you've you been up to?' he said.

This was exactly what Alec liked to hear, but rarely heard. 'I've got some magnificent footage of two weasels fighting. The word "weasel" of course, comes from the Anglo-Saxon root "weatsop" meaning "a vicious bloodthirsty animal". And my goodness they are.'

Then he provided Jack with a detailed synopsis of *The Night Life of Weasels, Stoats, Ferrets and Skunks*—a thirteen-part series of fifty-minute episodes.

'To be honest with you, Alec, in my opinion,' Jack said, 'Hollywood is finished as far as the independents are concerned. Production costs, distribution monopolies, union problems—the writers are a nightmare—are making it just too hard for us. No, sir, the future—the artistic future—is in natural history for television and community movies. And that's why I've established my company. I know the movie business inside and out. I've made my pile'—he didn't say what of or what size, leaving that to Alec's imagination—'and now I want to concentrate on helping people make the movies they really want to make.'

'This is all very interesting,' Alec said. 'You've come to Coddington St George at the right time. There's a plan to make a community movie of some kind here.'

This was the opening Jack needed. 'I've just come from visiting the BBC in London,' he said. 'I'm putting together a package of five community movies for them. I thought that as you people are planning one, I'd better visit and find out if I can help in any way. And if there's anything I can do to help you find a buyer for your series, I'll be happy to do what I can.' He smiled, trying to make it appear self-deprecating. 'I know a lot of the right people, you see. Studio heads. TV programme buyers. I might be able to find a channel to take your series.'

In the thirty years Jack had been in the movie business, he'd never managed to get an appointment with anyone above secretary level at the BBC, National Geographic or Discovery Channel, but Alec didn't know this. Jack had a business card, and he talked knowledgably and convincingly, so Alec had no reason to believe he was lying about his contacts.

'I shall probably be invited to be the DOP on the Coddington St George movie,' Alec said. 'I have so much experience. And all the best equipment.'

'Great!' Jack enthused. 'If I become involved in your movie, we'll be working together. I'll need somewhere to stay, of course. Do you have special terms for long stay guests?'

Jack wasn't interested in any such special terms. He knew that if the Cultural Coordinating Committee employed him to produce the movie, they'd pick up the tab. His immediate concern was to get Alec to waive the costs of this night's accommodation, and thus avoid embarrassment when he presented his credit card.

'Most definitely,' Alec said. 'And your accommodation for last night will be on me.'

Jack raised his hands to protest—though not too quickly— but Alec was insistent.

'Well, that's real generous of you,' Jack said, then he moved into the all-important pumping of Alec for information. He assumed that being a publican, he'd know everyone of importance in the town, if only by repute. 'Who's in charge of the movie project?'

'Well, I guess Fleur Robertson. She's the vice president of the Cultural Coordinating Committee. Nothing much happens here if she isn't involved in it. The president is Michael Milosovic, but he's far too busy to do any of the day-to-day work. He's just a figurehead. And a benefactor.'

Fleur Robertson—who'd not been well-named by her parents—was a short, stout woman with tightly-permed grey hair. A lonely widow, she was on almost every committee in the town and the president or chairperson of many organisations—due not to her popularity, which was far from universal, but to the simple fact that few people wanted to sit on committees and even fewer to accept office. Members of organisations in Coddington St George who accepted nomination were unanimously elected, even though the people who voted for them often personally loathed them. Another reason for Fleur's small-town success was that she got things done. Although she often felt confused and had no clear idea how to chair a meeting, she was hard-working and well meaning. If she said she'd do something, it got done, though usually by someone else—a less-assertive person she'd cajoled into doing it. Fleur was a great persuader and showed considerable qualities of leadership.

'Widow woman, is she?' Jack asked.

'Yeah. I reckon she wore out her husband. He owned the local bus service—sold now, of course. But it was a nice little business. Ten buses, he had, mostly used as school buses morning and afternoon, but he ran daily services to Rockie and Mackay. And he did quite a lot of charter work. Fleur and he didn't have much in common. He was a mechanic by trade. I've heard say she gave the impression she'd married beneath her.'

Jack made a mental note that Fleur Robertson was probably a culture snob. She'd want to talk about the art-house movies she'd seen. This could be a problem.

'So, she's the driving force,' he said.

'Yes and no. The idea for a film is Michael Milosovic's. He's our mayor. Thing is, Jack, there's a local government election in December. Michael's desperate to be elected to the shire council, but he's up against real competition—Edwin Bland. He's the manager of the Coddington St George branch of the Central Queensland Building Society. Half the people in town have their mortgages with him—or are planning to. If you ask me, the real purpose of the movie is to promote Michael Milosovic.' Alec helped himself to what was left in the pot of Jack's coffee.

'Got money, has he?' Jack asked. 'This Milosovic?'

'Rolling in it. Estate Agent. Builder. Developer. Timber merchant. Between them, Fleur Robertson and Michael Milosovic run this town. The other members of the Cultural Coordinating Committee are the Reverend Greg Small and Howard Grant. And me, of course. Howard owns Between the Leaves, a book shop of sorts, and is the artistic director of the Coddington St George Players. Pleasant enough man but not very politically savvy, if you know what I mean.'

Jack nodded to indicate total understanding, though he wasn't at all sure what political savvy meant in the context of Coddington St George. In any case, he was more interested in finding out Tony Andover's position. 'What about local talent? Apart from yourself, of course.'

'There's Tony Andover. He's very keen. Made a short film that won a prize. He'll probably want to produce. Manages the local radio station. Howard will want to direct. And, of course, half the town will want parts.'

'Any writers?'

'There's Elsie Woodmarsh. She reads her children's stories on the radio. Load of rubbish if you ask me. And Thistle O'Reilly.'

'Thistle?' The name surprised Jack. He knew that some women were called after the days of the week or the months of the year, even after fruits. He'd encountered a Peach or two in his time. Herbs, too. Rosemary was quite common, he thought. But he couldn't remember having met a weed. He wondered idly if Thistle's conception had been an uncomfortable experience for one or both participants.

'Yeah. Odd name,' Alec said. 'Mind you, she's an odd creature. Talented, they say, but she's a wild one. Works part-time in Between the Leaves, and does a bit of waiting here when we have a function.'

'All very interesting, Alec.' Jack folded his napkin, put it on the table and sighed. 'Well, I guess I ought to go for a walk around the town. Get the feel of the place.'

'Can you stay another night? On the house? You're most welcome.' Alec wondered whether to risk showing Jack some of his footage. He seemed to be the kind of man who would appreciate it. 'I've got some fantastic footage of a ferret's war dance. They do it to hypnotise their prey, you know. Then when it's in a trance, they strike. One quick bite behind the neck and it's all over.'

Jack's cooked breakfast heaved within him, but he managed to say, 'That's very good of you.'

'A pleasure.' Alec stood up. 'Perhaps I'll see you at lunch.'

As the lunch would be free, there was no possibility that he wouldn't.

Five

Jack decided it would be safer to approach Michael Milosovic before risking an encounter with Fleur Robertson. Michael, he thought, a man with political ambitions which would advance his financial interests, was less likely to want to discuss the movies of Ingmar Bergman and others of that ilk. He might even respond favourably to Jack's entrepreneurial initiative. Accordingly, Jack walked slowly down the almost-deserted High Street to the premises of Prestige Rural Properties Ltd.

A young woman with such badly bleached hair and unkempt appearance that she had to be Milosovic's daughter or mistress—for who else would employ her as a receptionist?—looked up from her magazine as Jack entered, took a fag out of her mouth and said, 'Yeah?'

'I'd like to see Mr Milosovic.' Jack handed her his Wilcon Interglobal Consolidated Universal Pictures Inc business card. He thought it would impress Michael more than the INCOMOPRO identity.

The girl looked at it, her lips moving as she struggled through the rather long words. 'You in pictures?'

'Producer,' he said.

'Dad will be pleased,' she said, confirming Jack's suspicion. 'He wants to make a film.'

'So I understand.'

'He's out somewhere, but if you don't mind waiting, I'll call him.'

'Thank you.'

Jack sat down and picked up a copy of *The Coddington St George News Gazette* from a small table on which also sat a number of building industry trade magazines. The newspaper would contain, he knew, a lot of useful information about the district and its movers and shakers.

The girl spoke quietly into a phone, then said, 'He won't be long. He's on a building site. D'you want a coffee?'

Jack declined and leafed through the newspaper. On the first inside page, he found a photo of Michael above a column headed, 'From the Mayor's Parlour'. Michael had a weekly column in the paper that had been running since he'd been elected mayor. Jack wondered if he wrote it himself. He somehow doubted that his daughter wrote it for him.

Ostensibly intended to inform the citizenry of all the splendid things the town council was doing for them, its main purpose was to promote Michael as an energetic and trustworthy community leader. Although Jack wasn't to know it, the column generated a lot of correspondence, all of a critical nature, but as Prestige Rural Properties and other Milosovic enterprises bought many pages of advertising in every issue of the publication, none of these letters ever appeared in print.

Michael Milosovic had settled in Coddington St George soon after the collapse of the Balkans. Possessing little more than a few clothes, he'd worked as an odd-job man, offering whatever anyone needed in the way of house maintenance. For five years he'd saved every penny he could until he had sufficient capital to invest in a block of land. He then borrowed enough money to build a house on it. This he quickly sold at a profit. From then on, it hadn't been difficult to raise the finance for further speculative homes, and only three years later, he'd obtained the finance to build his dream project, the Paradise Palace shopping precinct.

Now the majority shareholder in PRP Ltd (Prestigious Rural Properties) and for two years the town's mayor, his ambition was to get elected as a shire councillor and then, in the course of time, be appointed chairman of the planning committee, a position he was confident he could use to his own advantage, if not to that of the shire's residents.

At first there had been strong opposition to his proposal to the Cultural Co-ordinating Committee that the town should make a community movie. Edwin Bland had been particularly opposed to the idea. Edwin detested Michael. Whereas Edwin was a strong supporter of the National Trust and a convenor of the local Save Our Heritage Society and believed in preserving everything of possible historical interest, and much that was not, Michael was determined to destroy it and re-build the town according to his own architectural whims.

The fact that Michael owed the building society a great deal of money further aggravated the relationship between the two men. Edwin's predecessor, a man of ambition whose final years with the society had been dedicated to lending as much money to as many people as possible, had, as an eve of retirement gesture, agreed to finance a substantial part of the Paradise Palace shopping precinct. When Edwin arrived in the town, as the new manager, he'd found himself responsible for what his cautious instincts told him might become a massive bad debt, one for which he'd be held responsible, no matter what he said in explanation to his superiors. To make matters worse, Edwin had before him an application from Michael for finance to build another aged-care facility, a project which was certain—at least as certain as anything is certain—to make a great deal of money, not only for Michael but for whoever financed the project.

Edwin knew that if Michael took this business elsewhere, he, Edwin, was likely to lose his job. He also knew that if he expressed his concerns about Michael's existing debt, his superiors would suspect he had a political motive. One way and another, Edwin spent a great deal of his time brooding about Michael Milosovic. It wasn't surprising, therefore, that he loathed Michael or that he'd decided to offer himself as a candidate for the shire council. If he achieved nothing else, he told his supporters, he'd do his damnedest to prevent Michael from destroying the shire's few remaining buildings of aesthetic or historical interest.

For his part, Michael had mentally listed all the things he could do to destroy Edwin's credibility. There weren't many. Half the town depended on the building society for their mortgages, and Edwin had a reputation for being not only fair but also occasionally compassionate, a rare quality in a banker. He was also a family man and a churchwarden at St Jude's, a fine specimen of late Victorian colonial ecclesiastical architecture. The congregation was small, but the vicar, the Reverend Greg Small, was popular and frequently delivered what could be considered a 'Green' sermon. The town's mortgagees, the St Jude's congregation and all their friends and relatives were a formidable voting block. Only people whose applications for loans had been declined or who had strong religious convictions of a different kind, had any real grievance against Edwin. His only problem was that he had a colourless personality and completely lacked a sense of humour.

Michael's support came mainly from his employees, their relatives and friends, from small business people who depended on him for much of their custom, and a surprisingly large number of people he'd helped one way and another. His generosity always had an ulterior motive, but this didn't negate its value to the people who received it.

Another major difference between the two men—though it wasn't something that Edwin ever thought about—was that Michael wanted more than anything, more even than architectural dominance of the town, to be accepted by the 'squattocracy', the 'old money' and the poor but equally old families in the district. As a caste, they had little contact with the town's *hoi polloi*, inviting only a select few to their social events. Fleur Robertson, by dint of her dominance of the community's cultural and social welfare organisations, was accepted, though grudgingly, as was Howard Grant who held the social position of local intellectual. They automatically accepted Edwin: he was nearly everyone's bank manager.

The largest land owner was Harold Frobisher. He farmed 2,000 hectares of sugar cane and kept a small herd of Herefords. His family dated back to the First Fleet, and his son, Trent, aspired to be an actor.

Knowing that no matter how rich he became, and no matter how much property he owned, 'the squattocracy' would never accept him for his wealth alone, Michael had decided that entry to their society would be possible only by dint of largesse to St Jude's or sponsorship of every cultural event at which he could point his cheque book. The film would need some money, and he was prepared to provide it. This would ensure that he'd be centre stage at the premiere. His generosity would be there for everyone to see, and it would do his election campaign no harm at all. And if he could make sure that Trent Frobisher was given a major role in the film, this would also advance him socially. To achieve his objectives, Michael believed, he needed to get onside whoever was appointed producer.

'I'm Milosovic,' he said, extending a hand.

'Jack Wilcon.'

'My girl says you're a film producer. You've heard what we're planning to do.'

'Yes, I met Tony Andover at MIP TV,' Jack said. 'Brilliant young man. He'll go far.'

'He told you we're looking for an experienced producer to work with him?'

'Yes. I've already expressed interest. I had to have a meeting with the ABC so I thought I'd visit the town on my way back to the States.'

'Very sensible. The film is my project, you know. I had to fight hard for it. There was a lot of opposition. Have you made community films before?'

'Most of my work has been with amateurs,' Jack said, for once speaking the truth. Although cast and crew in Jack's productions had hoped to be paid, few of them had ever received professional rates. They usually received nothing.

'Can I get you a cup of coffee or something?'

Interpreting this, as she did all of her father's utterances, as an implied criticism of her behaviour—as it usually was—the girl said, 'He said he didn't want one.'

'Perhaps he's changed his bloody mind,' Michael snapped.

'I had a late breakfast,' Jack explained.

'Let's go into my office.' Michael looked at his watch. 'It's a bit early for lunch. We'll go to the Central later. You've met Alec?'

'Yes. Interesting man.'

Michael led the way into the glass-partitioned room that served as his office, and Jack followed him.

So far so good, he thought. As he sat down, he said, 'I expect you've had a lot of interest in the project.'

'What we're looking for, Jack,' Michael said, deliberately ignoring the question, 'is someone with the right kind of experience who's willing to supervise young Tony—a sort of project manager in building terms. We need someone who really enjoys working with the community and knows how to handle volunteers. They can be the very devil, as I'm sure you know.'

'People skills,' Jack said. 'I've sure got those.'

'Good. It could be disastrous if we get a few people offside.' He didn't explain why. He didn't need to. Jack was happily riding along the same wavelength.

'We can't offer a lot of money,' Michael continued, coming to the point quickly. He didn't believe in wasting time. If Jack was the kind of man he thought he probably was, establishing the financial situation had to be a first step. 'The contract will be for six weeks. The fee twenty thousand dollars—Australian— plus reasonable expenses: fares, motel, food, etc.'

Jack did a quick calculation. Twenty thousand at the current rate of exchange was about fifteen US. It was little short of insulting to a genuine producer who was often in work. To Jack it was more than acceptable, especially as he'd have nothing to spend it on. It would be enough to acquire more territories for *The Power Drill Massacres* and *Dropsaw Killers of Detroit*. Perhaps even Estonia, Latvia and Lithuania. There might even be enough to re-shoot *The Axeman Cometh*.

He smiled. 'It's a lot less than I usually charge,' he said, implying that he was usually paid what he asked for, not what he was offered. 'What will happen to the profits? I usually receive a percentage of the gross.'

This wasn't true. On the few occasions when he'd been offered a percentage of the profits of a movie, it'd always been of the net because there never was a net. Hollywood-style accountancy saw to that.

'Do you think there'll be any profit?' It hadn't occurred to Michael that a community film could make a profit. He'd assumed it would have to depend on a council subsidy and local sponsorship.

'If I'm involved with it, there will be,' Jack said, smiling broadly. 'I'll have world-wide distribution all sewn up before the first day of the shoot.'

Michael considered this. If the film actually made money that went into the Cultural Coordinating Committee's grants account, recouping the expenditure and then some, this would enormously benefit his election campaign and save him money. 'You're sure of this?'

'Read my lips,' Jack said. He opened his document case and took out another copy of his demo DVD. 'This will show your committee the kind of thing I do,' he said. 'I get a real kick out of mentoring young people. Tony Andover and I really clicked. It'll be an honour to work with him.'

Michael put both hands to his mouth, as if covering it to prevent himself from saying the wrong thing, while he thought about Jack. There'd been a number of applicants, none of them of any interest except for a Swede, Sven Ingersson, and about him Michael already had reservations. He thought there could be a language problem, and the man's list of films hadn't been encouraging. His most recent production was called *Rapor och Fistes*. Using the translation programme on the internet, Michael had discovered that this, loosely translated, became *Belches and Farts*.

'I suppose,' he said, 'it wouldn't do any harm for you to meet some of the other members of the committee. But just informally.'

Having decided that Jack was his man, Michael wanted to avoid any kind of formal interview with the committee. He knew it would produce only argument and ill-feeling and delay a decision. Long experience had taught him that the only way to get anything done was to do it and then inform the committee what he'd done. They could object as much as they liked, even pass no-confidence motions or attempt to rescind his decisions, but they rarely did anything of the kind. They realised that if his decisions led to disaster, they'd be in the clear. They would simply blame him, denying that they had anything to do with the situation. And this was all that really mattered. The minutes of the meeting at which they'd agreed to his decision would subtly imply that there'd been opposition to it.

The committee's main problem was that without Michael's financial contribution there would be no culture in the town. The annual budget of the Cultural Coordinating Committee was just enough to provide minimal support for the Coddington St George Players, the String Quartet, the Annual Poetry Prize (recently awarded to Elsie Woodmarsh, the part-time, voluntary, local librarian, for her Sonnet to a Goldfish) and an occasional scholarship or grant to a promising young local artist, writer, composer or—in Tony's case—film-maker. Cut-backs on all these grants would have to be made if money was to be found for a community film.

Largely motivated by the psychological need to have his own way on all occasions, Michael was determined to significantly damage Sven Ingersson. Then there would be no need for any discussion of the matter at the next committee meeting.

Hoping that Jack would have some useful dirt on Ingersson, to be used as ammunition if necessary, he asked, 'Have you seen any of this Swedish fellow Sven Ingersson's films?'

'Brilliant,' Jack said. 'One of the most respected art-house directors internationally. *Cries and Murmurs* is a masterpiece. I think it even won the Bronze Saucer at Nuuk.'

This wasn't what Michael expected to hear. Underestimating him, he thought Jack would've blackguarded the man. He raised an eyebrow. 'Oh?'

'He'd make a fine movie for you.' Jack chuckled warmly, managing to convey in the single laugh admiration, compassion and affectionate regret. 'Huh! If only he didn't always go over budget, he wouldn't find it so difficult to raise the finance for his films. Tragic, really. The man's a genius.'

Over budget. Genius. These were words of which Michael had a profound understanding and fear. He'd had to deal with architects who'd won prizes and been called geniuses.

Seeing Michael pale slightly, Jack said, 'You're a developer, Mike. You know how easy it is for costs to blow out.' He paused. 'You'd understand Sven's problems.'

Michael knew all about cost over-runs. He also knew that in order to raise the finance for a project he always deliberately under-budgeted it. By the time the project needed more cash, the bank or finance company was so locked in that the money needed to finish it was always forthcoming. Michael had discovered early in his career as a developer that if he ever budgeted properly, he'd never raise the finance for anything.

What he had yet to discover was that the film and construction industries had many things in common. Not only did most projects go over budget, they were weather-dependent, union-dominated, and usually had astute criminals—both white and blue collar—involved somewhere.

'Cost over-runs, you said.'

'Oh, not excessive.' Jack was quick to maintain his apparent admiration for the Swede. 'Twenty or thirty percent at the most.'

Michael was now totally confident that there'd be no one on the committee who would dare to speak for Ingersson once the truth about him was known. Whether or not the film would be an artistic success was irrelevant. He could prevent it from being shown before the shire council elections. What mattered was that it must not cost more than he and the council were prepared to spend on it.

'Are you staying another night?' he asked.

Assuming that Alec would provide further free hospitality—if he didn't, then Jack would ask for an invoice to be sent to his accounts department—Jack said, 'I could if necessary.'

'Good. I'm sure you're the man for the job, but for form's sake, you'd better front up to the committee. Most of them are in the Coddington St George Players, on tour at the moment, round the villages, with *Pride and Prejudice*. Go to tonight's performance—it's in Stanfield, a village about five miles away. I'll lend you a car. I'm sure there'll be drinks afterwards. Introduce yourself—just tell everyone how wonderful they are in the play, then hurry away. They won't bother to insist you come for a formal interview later—at the committee's expense.

They'll have met you, I'll be recommending you, and that'll be that.'

'Well, Mike, thanks,' Jack said. 'I'll do just that.'

'Excellent. Now let's go and have a beer and some lunch.'

six

After a heavy lunch of T-bone steak and chips, Jack rested in his motel room until the time came to drive to Stanfield and the evening performance of *Pride and Prejudice*. Fortunately, there was almost no traffic on the narrow, winding dirt road, and during Jack's short journey on the wrong side of it—a stranger to Australia, he forgot, if he'd ever known, that like the Brits, the Australians drive on the left—he experienced only a minor incident. The driver of a gigantic tractor, wending his way home after a day's brooding in the cane fields, shouted an obscenity at him as Jack forced him to move out of the way. Assuming that the scream of rage was a jovial greeting in a wholly unintelligible local dialect, Jack waved and drove on.

Sixteen people made up the audience at the Stanfield Village Hall—little more than a brick shed with a stage at one end. Jack, who grudgingly paid his ten dollars for a ticket and single sheet programme, considered telling the woman on the door that he was a talent scout for a theatrical agent and that a free ticket would be to the benefit of all concerned, but he sensibly decided that if this little lie got back to those members of the cast on the Cultural Coordinating Committee, it wouldn't do his application for the producer's job much good. It was just as well that he made this decision, since the majority of the members of the Cultural Coordinating Committee were involved in the production, which was sponsored by the Coddington St George Town Council (Mayor, Michael Milosovic) and Prestige Rural Properties Ltd (Proprietor, Michael Milosovic). Jack had enough sense to realise that Michael had all his bases covered and that as long as he kept him onside, the producer's job was his.

Accordingly, having paid his entry fee, he sat at the back of the hall and studied his programme. Fleur Robertson was listed as Mrs Bennett, Trent Frobisher as Mr D'Arcy, and Howard Grant as the director. Thistle O'Reilly was down to play Elizabeth Bennett.

The evening began badly. The stage manager had great difficulty accommodating the set and furniture on the narrow stage. The essential couch, on which the Bennett girls and their mother engaged in conversation, occupied so much of the stage that no one could move behind it or in front of it without either clambering over it or risking a nasty fall into the auditorium. The stage manager solved this problem a few minutes before the curtains were due to part by pushing the couch off the stage into the body of the hall. He replaced it with four plastic, stackable chairs.

Soon after 'curtain up' another problem quickly presented itself. There was no backstage. If a character exited stage left or stage right, as the case may be, he or she had to return the same way. However, the script soon demanded that Mrs. Bennett exit stage left as if to one part of the Bennett house, then re-enter stage right, as if from another. Fleur soon realized that there was no way she could do this without walking across the stage, in full view of the audience. Seeing a door at the side of the stage that opened to the outside of the hall, she assumed there was a similar door on the other side of the stage. She decided that if she went out of this door, she could nip round the back of the hall and come back in through the other one.

Unfortunately, her assumption was incorrect. No door existed on the other side of the stage. Fleur found herself, therefore, outside the hall with her next entrance imminent. Her attempt to return to the stage the way she'd left it failed because the door had closed and locked itself, as some Yale locks tend to do. Desperate, she ran around to the main entrance, intending to enter it and approach the stage through the body of the hall.

She turned the handle of the main entrance. It moved but the door didn't open. To prevent it from rattling in the evening breeze, the lady responsible for the front of the house had bolted it from the inside.

Fleur banged on the door and called out, 'It's me. Let me in.'

The lady responsible for the front of the house had already seen the play several times and was dozing. For some time, she heard nothing. Fleur's cue to enter passed, and the cast didn't know what to do. Fortunately, the audience became far more interested in the noise coming from the entrance to the hall than in what was—or rather was not—happening on the stage. Eventually the lady responsible for the front of the house woke up and unlocked the door. A tense exchange between her and Fleur followed, then Fleur ran through the hall to the stage to resume her performance.

Unfortunately, she'd forgotten that there were no steps up from the hall onto the stage. The members of the cast on the stage had to band together and haul Fleur—who was short, stout and no longer young—up onto it. Shaking a little, she stood for several minutes breathing heavily until she was able to resume her performance.

For a moment it seemed as if all was now well, but it was not. A young woman in the audience had her baby with her, and stimulated, perhaps, by the events it had just witnessed, the baby began to howl. The young mother attempted to pacify it, but without success. It seemed likely that the baby would cry for the remainder of the performance.

Certainly, Fleur believed it. She walked to the front of the stage and said to the young mother, 'I'm sorry, but I really cannot continue if your baby is going to cry.'

'Well!' the young mother exclaimed, standing up, her baby over her shoulder, 'if that's the way you feel, I shall leave. And I shall take my lamp with me.'

Realizing the significance of this, Fleur attempted to withdraw her complaint, but it was too late. The young mother, fitter and more agile than Fleur, put the baby down on the stage, levered herself up onto it and then swung up her legs. Once on the stage, she picked up her baby and marched with it to stage left. There she collected her lamp and departed through the side door.

The side of the stage where the cast put on their costumes and make-up was now in total darkness. The borrowed lamp had been its only source of light.

This wouldn't have mattered too much, perhaps, if it had not also been the side of the stage where the prompter sat, and if the actor performing the role of Mr Bennett had been able to remember some, or even any, of his lines. The Coddington St George Players, like so many amateur dramatic societies, had plenty of women members, but almost no men. Howard had considered casting one of the more masculine women as Mr Bennett but decided it might be misconstrued. He feared that certain members of the community would leap to the conclusion that this was a new interpretation of the play in which the Bennetts were portrayed as a lesbian household.

To avoid any unpleasant controversy, he'd decided that it might be safer to cast Mr Arthur Grimble as Mr Bennett. Arthur was over seventy and, although a keen thespian, he could never remember his lines. He relied heavily on a prompter. So heavily in fact, that in some performances the audiences—such as they were—assumed there was an echo in the hall. They heard every line of Mr Bennett's twice. Occasionally they heard it several times.

Not too long after the exit of the lady with the lamp, the play resumed and the scene between Elizabeth and Mr Bennett got underway. Fairly early in Act One, Mr Collins declared his intentions. Elizabeth made it clear she was not interested in his marriage proposal. Arthur Grimble for once managed to remember his response without a prompt.

'An unhappy alternative is before you, Elizabeth,' he said. 'From this day you must be a stranger to one of your parents. Your mother will never see you again if you do not marry Mr Collins, and I will never see you again if you do.'

Thistle O'Reilly, playing Elizabeth Bennett, smiled as she was supposed to do.

Fleur, her mother, then said, as she was supposed to say, 'What do you mean, Mr Bennett, by talking in this way? You promised me to insist upon her marrying him.'

This time Arthur Grimble awaited his prompt. It didn't come. He waited longer. It still didn't come. Sitting in almost complete darkness, the prompter couldn't see the page of the script, let alone the line.

Arthur searched his memory. To his relief and not a little surprise, lines came to him. 'I have received a letter this morning that has astonished me exceedingly,' he said. 'As it principally concerns yourself, Elizabeth, you ought to know its contents. I did not know before that I had two daughters on the brink of matrimony. Let me congratulate you on a very important conquest.'

Arthur spoke the lines clearly, enunciating every word. Unfortunately, they were the wrong lines. In one utterance, Arthur had taken the play from half way through Act One to almost the end of Act Three.

Thistle's knee-jerk response was to exclaim loudly, 'What the fuck!'

Then, collecting herself, she responded to what Arthur had said, not to what he ought to have said. Within a few minutes, the play came to an end. It had lasted for less than half an hour.

Jack, who'd heard of but knew nothing about *Pride and Prejudice*, assumed that what he'd seen was a modern, somewhat meaningless one act play. On his way out of the hall, he said to the woman at the door, 'A bit short for ten dollars,' then drove back—again on the wrong side of the road—to the Central Hotel. There, in the Snuggery, hoping to be stood as many drinks as he could down without falling over, he made himself agreeable to the locals by relating anecdotes, all fictitious, and many very old, about Hollywood's rich and famous. Only his favourite story, the one about Steve Spielberg, failed to produce hoots and guffaws of laughter, and to anyone who knew any Hollywood hopefuls, it would've rung totally true. In Coddington St George, it produced only bewilderment.

'Steve told me this himself,' Jack said through his own laughter. 'He was having dinner with Robert de Niro in Twenty-one—that's where all the top people eat—when this young fellow comes up to him and says, "I'm sorry to trouble you, Mr Spielberg, but I wonder if you can help me. I'm spending my last dollars entertaining that guy over there."—he points to the worst table in the room—"He's loaded and I want him to invest in my movie, but he's not convinced I can get all the people it needs. You must remember how hard it was when you started out." Steve nods. He remembers all right. He's a good guy. "Go on," he says. "Well," this young feller says, "Would it be possible when you leave the restaurant to approach my table and say, 'Hi, Tom. How are things?'" Steve knows the score. "Sure," he says. "Pleased to help." That's Steve all over. Anyway, he and Bob finish their meal, and as they walk out,

Steve goes up to this guy's table and says, "Hi, Tom. How are things?"'

At this point, Jack paused and looked at the group of admiring drinkers. 'Can you guess what he said?' They all shook their heads. 'He said … the guy said, "Oh fuck off, Steve; can't you see I'm busy?" Man, that is so Hollywood.'

Jack was sufficiently sober not to attempt to explain the joke to the drinkers, or to add that if he'd been the young guy, and had thought of it, this was what he would've said in his desperation to impress. Instead, realizing that if he stayed in the bar any longer he might have to buy a round, he muttered, 'Yeah, well, that's it for me, guys.' He pushed himself to his feet. 'You all take care now.'

He lurched out of the bar to his motel room and fell onto the bed. A few moments later, a knock sounded on the door. Cursing, he sat up, waited for the dizziness to fade, then shouted, 'I'm coming.' He stumbled to the door, only just staying on his feet, and opened it.

Alec stood there, a photo album in his hands. 'I thought you might like to browse through these, Jack. Examples of my work.'

Controlling the impulse to tell Alec what he could do with the photos, Jack murmured, 'Yeah, right. Er, thanks.'

He took the album, shut the door and returned to the bed. Curiosity overcoming his alcoholic daze, he opened the album and leafed through it. The book contained photographs of weasels, stoats, ferrets and skunks engaged in assorted vicious activities.

Jack dropped the book onto the floor, sighed, lay back on the bed and closed his eyes. He instantly fell asleep with his mouth wide open. A martyr to apnoea, he stopped breathing every few seconds, and then gasped for breath with a gigantic snort. A little later he shouted and screamed in his sleep. At night his unconscious took over and reminded him in the strangeness of his dreams that all was not well in his world.

seven

The next morning, Jack didn't feel like eating breakfast—repeated cups of strong black coffee were all he needed—but he went to the dining room just before the breakfast session closed. He didn't want to miss a free meal, especially as it would be the last one he'd eat before the airline meal much later in the day.

He was on his third cup of coffee when Michael Milosovic arrived and sat at his table. 'Good morning, Jack. Mind if I join you?'

'Please.'

Alec came up. 'Morning, Michael. I'll get Peggy to make some fresh.'

He, too, sat at the table, and Jack realized he was in for a few searching questions. He wondered if the two men had got together and exchanged impressions, but Alec had only one thing on his mind and wasted no time bringing it up.

'Did you have time to look at my portfolio, Jack?'

'I made time. Stayed up half the night going through it. Brilliant. Your use of lighting is truly professional. Have you done much video?'

'Oh, yes,' Alec said. 'A lot.'

Jack managed to look impressed. He realised that Alec was going to need a lot of flattery. 'I thought you probably had. I look forward to seeing it.'

'What did you think of the show last night? The Coddington St George Players?' Michael asked.

'Fantastic,' Jack enthused. 'There's real talent there.'

Michael looked startled. 'You think so? Talent? I mean, you know, acting talent?' He'd only seen one of the Players' productions, and it'd been more than enough to convince him that he'd rather watch Coddington United lose eight nil to Rockhampton Reserves than endure another one.

This was his first moment of doubt about Jack's suitability as producer of the proposed movie. He later greatly regretted not paying attention it.

Realizing his mistake and that honesty rather than flattery would've been more convincing, Jack went into damage control mode. 'Talent for the movies, I mean,' he said. 'Movie acting is totally different from the stage. On stage, the actors have only one go at it; for the movies we have take after take, often of a line or a move at a time. Movies are made in the editing suite. As long as the actors look right, they don't have to be able to act. Think Tom Cruise,' he concluded.

Alec and Michael nodded. They didn't need further convincing.

'They don't even have to be sober,' Jack went on, incapable, as always, of letting well alone. 'In one of my movies I cast'—he mentioned a famous actor—'in a cameo role, but we were shooting in a bar, and the guy was pissed from day one to the end. He couldn't remember his lines, so all round the set I had crew holding up cards with his words on them. One day he was so pissed he couldn't stand up. The director re-blocked the scene so that he stood with his back to a wall. We had a guy behind the wall with his hand through a hole, propping the actor up. D'you know what?'

Alec and Michael shook their heads.

'When the movie was released, the critics said this guy had given the performance of his life. What a fine actor he was. Huh! What they should have said was what a great job the editor did. He worked for a month working on the various takes, creating a performance a word at a time. Cost a fucking fortune.'

For once Jack's story was a true one. The only lie was that it hadn't happened on one of his movies.

'Believe me,' he went on, 'with the help of the director and editor, I'll get fantastic performances from your local talent. I've done a lot of work with amateurs.' He smiled. 'Trust me.'

This all made sense to Michael, but he wanted one more issue clarified. He'd lain awake for several hours during the night, as was his habit, going over and over in his mind the problems he had to solve. He wanted to be sure that his first impressions of Jack weren't going to let him down.

'You said, Jack, that you could arrange distribution. Can you give me a few details?'

Jack was prepared for this. He bent down and picked up his document case from where he'd left it on the floor, zipped it open and took out a sheaf of papers. 'Distribution guarantees,' he said, handing copies of contracts to Michael and Alec.

'For our movie?' Michael queried. 'It hasn't been shot. There isn't even a script.'

'Let me explain how my end of the movie business works,' Jack said patiently. 'I package movies for different distributors in different countries: six romantic comedies; three R-rated thrillers; five family movies, and so on. All for cable, DVD and the Internet. The distributors I deal with know that what I produce will be okay and the price is right. Cable and the internet markets are hungry, guys. They eat up product. If it's in focus and the right length, they'll buy it. Not for big bucks, but they'll buy it. I'm putting together a package of three community movies for film societies. Those people,' he pointed at the contracts, 'specialize in that market.'

For different reasons this all sounded very believable to Michael and Alec. Michael knew how deals were done. He'd even got finance for the Paradise Palace shopping precinct before the plans were more than a rough sketch. And Alec knew that ninety percent, if not more, of the movies produced in Hollywood were just so much junk. Very few, if any, had weasels, stoats, ferrets and skunks in them.

Jack held out his hand for the contracts, which they handed back to him unread. It wouldn't have mattered if they'd scrutinized them. The distributors didn't exist. Maybelle had invented them and produced the contracts on her second-hand laptop. Jack worked on the assumption that no one would bother to check, and when, at a later date, no distribution guarantees manifested, he had excuses. In any case, he'd be a long way from Coddington St George. It wouldn't be worth the town council taking legal action against him. The costs would be too high. In the worst-case scenario, they might send two large men with baseball bats to his office—this had happened once before—but he thought it unlikely.

'These distribution guarantees, they'll cover the budget?' Michael asked.

'The ones I've got already will. There are still some territories to sew up. You should make a profit. Not a large one, but enough to put a smile on your councillors' faces.'

'How much do you think the movie will cost?' Alec asked, adding, 'I've got all the equipment we'd need.'

'Is that so? Well, we're in luck. Apart from my fee as Executive Producer, there'll be a producer …'

'I think Tony Andover will expect to produce," Michael said. "He's rather set his heart on it.'

'Let me explain,' Jack said. 'The Executive Producer looks after the financial side of things. The producer actually organises the production. Tony can do that.'

'Howard Grant will want to direct,' Alec said. 'He directs all the plays.'

'Howard is brilliant," Jack said. "His work is so …'—he hunted for a suitable word and chose one that couldn't be contradicted—'so different. But he's a theatre director. He gets great performances, but they're rather large for film.'

'Less is more,' Alec said. He'd recently watched a DVD of Michael Caine's MasterClass on film acting. He'd found it disappointing as it hadn't been very relevant to his own needs.

'Exactly, Alec. We'll need a very experienced editor, of course. If you're going to shoot the movie, Alec, then I'd like to bring an editor from the States.'

Alec smiled, happy to have his role confirmed. 'All the local talent will be free, and all the crew.'

'I can provide materials and tradesmen if we have to build sets,' Michael offered. 'The council will look after road closures and public locations. I'm sure local people will be only too happy to lend their homes and so on.'

'We'll need a writer,' Alec said.

'I guess we'll have to have one,' Jack agreed. 'But believe me, they can be a real pain in the ass.'

'Thistle O'Reilly,' Michael said. 'I'll speak to her.' Michael had been waiting for an opportunity to endear himself to Thistle. His relationship with his Croatian-peasant wife had long since lost whatever small erotic element it'd once had. Thistle was by far the most attractive single young woman in the town.

'I could bring one from the States,' Jack said, thinking of Maybelle. It would be a way of paying her back what he owed.

'I think Thistle should have her chance,' Michael said in such a firm tone that Jack realized this was non-negotiable.

'Good. Local talent. That's what community movies are all about.' Jack smiled. He could shift his position at a speed that dazzled. 'So, I guess we're thinking, what? Two hundred thou?' He raised an eyebrow to underscore the query.

Michael frowned. He and the other committee members hadn't been thinking anywhere near two hundred thousand. 'We thought half that.'

'Fair enough,' Jack said. 'Make sure the writer knows that. It'll cost her nothing to write World War Three. It'll cost a billion bucks to produce it. You'll get some local sponsorship, I guess. Small businesses.'

'The town's not rich, Jack,' Alec said. 'Most local businesses are struggling. Even the hotel's not doing too well,' he added quickly. Peggy had given him a hard time for offering Jack free hospitality.

'Yeah well, I'll leave all that side of things to you. You can rely on me to make the most of whatever money you can raise.' Jack looked at his watch. 'Guys, I've got a plane to catch.'

He had to be in Rockhampton by midday. From there he would fly to Brisbane to connect with a QANTAS flight to LA. He stood up.

'I'll run you into Rockie, Jack,' Alec said. 'No trouble. I'll also arrange to return your hire car.'

Jack quickly accepted the offer. He reasoned that as Alec and Michael Milosovic seemed to be friends, or at least allies, he'd improve his chances by working further on Alec. The man was determined to shoot the movie, and as the producer, he'd have the final say who would shoot it. The job would be the gift of whoever produced it. Alec would know this. If he made Alec feel secure, he'd support him with Milosovic.

'Great!' he said. 'We can talk about your portfolio on the way. I know an agent who'll be crazy about your work.' He turned to Michael. 'I guess I'll be hearing from you very soon.'

'I don't think there's any doubt of that, Jack.'

Confident that there wasn't, Jack felt tempted for a moment to suggest that perhaps a small advance payment would be in order as he'd have to turn down other offers, but for once wisdom prevailed. Hands were shaken all round. Jack went to his room to get his bag.

'What do you think, Alec?' Michael asked.

'I reckon he knows what he's doing.'

'Yeah. And one thing's for sure: for what we're paying we won't find it easy to get anyone better.'

Alec drove a red MGB, which he referred to as his 'pride and joy', and Jack had to squeeze himself onto the passenger seat. He guessed that Alec drove a sports car in the hope that it would make him seem and feel younger than he was. Jack always hired a Cadillac at home. It made him feel richer and more important than he was.

They'd hardly left the town when Alec said, 'So you like my work.'

'Like it! I love it. You've got real talent, Alec. I'll get you an agent to market your work in the States. Make you famous. Trust me. I'm a man of my word.'

PART TWO:

THE
DEVELOPMENT

eiGHT

Shortly after Alec and Jack left, Thistle O'Reilly flounced into Between the Leaves. Tall, with a model's figure, Thistle O'Reilly had a lion's mane of dyed, beetroot-red hair half-way down her back, drug-dilated pupils in her dark, sleep-denied eyes, and the conversational vocabulary of a cook on a prawn trawler. A fiery, tempestuous young woman, she exuded a confusing combination of hard-core feminism and raw heterosexuality. She kept herself afloat financially with a few hours work a week for Howard Grant at Between the Leaves, and with very small payments for the erotic short stories that she wrote for Screw, an online adult dating magazine.

She sat down in front of Howard's desk and, being a chain smoker—not only of tobacco—lit a cigarette, coughed for a few moments and then said, 'What the fuck went wrong, Howard?'

Three days had passed since the Cultural Coordinating Committee had considered applications for financial assistance from local writers and artists. Thistle had applied but hadn't even been invited for an interview. She was furious, especially as she'd just heard that Elsie Woodmarsh had been awarded two thousand dollars to write a series of *Little Stories for Little Folk* to read on community radio, even though it was a matter of public record that no one under sixty ever listened to the station. Thistle wanted an explanation for her rejection and enough cups of coffee, assorted muffins and raisin toast to keep her going for a few hours.

Howard turned his head away from the exhaled cigarette smoke floating over his desk and said, 'I did what I could, Thistle, but I'm afraid I was out-voted.'

'Fucking philistines.'

Howard was lying. He hadn't said or done anything to support Thistle's application. It hadn't even been considered. In fact, as secretary of the committee, he'd deliberately lost her application, knowing it would alienate her even further from Fleur Robertson. She'd applied for a thousand dollars to 'buy time' to work on her new narrative poem entitled 'Fucks I Wish I'd Had,' a sequel to 'Fucks I Wish I'd Never Had', which she'd recently performed with enough venom to stop an outraged bull at the Cairns Festival of Performance Poetry.

'I did warn you, Thistle,' Howard said, 'that the committee would object to the title and subject matter of your poem. If you had called it something else …'

'Fucking censorship.' Thistle got up and walked to the little kitchenette where Howard prepared the light refreshments designed to tempt potential customers to browse his book stock.

Thistle's real first name was Emma, but she thought bearing the name of a plant made her more memorable. At first, she'd considered calling herself Daffodil, but she was sufficient of a realist to know that she neither looked nor behaved like a daffodil. She'd also considered fruits. One of her favourite writers was the Japanese woman, Banana. After a great deal of thought and trying out mango, lychee and pineapple over several months, she'd settled on Thistle. It seemed, she thought, very apt. She knew she was beautiful in a wild kind of way. She also knew that she had to be very carefully handled.

Her surname was plain Riley, but she thought O'Reilly gave it a greater Irish emphasis, which was appropriate for her profession of performance poet.

Over the years, she'd had several middle-aged, male patrons, but her relationships with them had always been short-lived. Even the most tolerant of men found it impossible to cope with her total unreliability. She rarely kept any kind of appointment made in advance, and when she did keep one, she invariably arrived an hour or more late. She couldn't be taken anywhere as she insisted on smoking where and whenever she felt like it, and she argued ferociously with any waiter or proprietor who attempted to explain that smoking was not permitted. She'd leave, cigarette in mouth, just seconds before the police arrived.

She was, however, not at all materialistic. She had little interest in money, and none in clothes or jewellery. She didn't drive a car and didn't want to learn. Content to live in a bed-sitting room with a hot-plate and a kettle and a miniature en suite, she didn't want the responsibility of owning or managing a home or an apartment. She never cleaned or tided her room, and clothes and books covered the floor. The remains of take-away pizzas and Chinese meals provided nightly feasts for the resident rodents and lesser creatures. When the inevitable conflict with her landlord occurred—usually precipitated by non-payment of rent—she simply threw her few possessions into a couple of battered cardboard suitcases and moved on. There was always another filthy room to go to.

Thistle needed money only for the necessities of life: rent—occasionally—fast food, cigarettes and a small, but frequently renewed, stash of pot. She lived on the fringe of society and was content to do so. Her writing and performing were the only things that mattered. Everything and everyone else existed to make it possible—even to serve it.

Michael Milosovic seriously fancied Thistle and was often seen having a coffee with her at the In Place, Coddington St George's attempt at a trendy café. However, in some ways a female version of Michael, Thistle knew that within days of her sleeping with him, he'd drop her. Only by holding out could she benefit from his patronage. She thought of him not as a friend, but as someone to be used.

She did, however, think of Howard as a friend. Whereas Michael was interested only in her body, Howard was interested only in her art. He was one of those men who are entirely asexual, though in his case, he was probably in love with himself. He enjoyed Thistle's company and let her unburden herself endlessly over free cups of coffee in his bookshop. He believed that if she could only control her temperament, which, he feared, exceeded her talent, and if she would only make the occasional small compromise and take even a modicum of advice, she might eventually achieve something as a writer. He'd even encouraged her to write something for the Players, but she'd declined, arguing that there was no way she was going to risk any of 'that fucking lot ruining my lines'. She had, however, offered to write and perform a monologue for the Players to include in their program of productions as a curtain raiser. Howard had said he'd suggest this to his committee, but he hadn't done so. He knew that whatever script his committee might approve, it would bear little resemblance to what Thistle delivered on the night.

Apart from Howard, Thistle's only friend in the town was Herbie Spratt, a homeless vagrant who spent his summer days sprawled on a bench under a tree at the oval or sitting on the bench outside the Grand. At night, during the warmer months, he lay curled up under copies of the *News Gazette* in the town's bus shelter. He was rarely disturbed. There was only one bus a day.

In the winter, Herbie usually found a straw bed in one of the abandoned cow sheds within walking distance of the town. He ate as well as the wealthiest inhabitants of the town because he lived out of their garbage bins. Whatever they ate, Herbie ate a day or two later.

A comparatively peaceful man, his face hid completely behind a bushy beard, thickened with the fermenting remnants of past meals. His skin, what little of it was exposed, was almost black with dirt. He never washed, and his smell isolated him in a world of his own.

He'd been adopted as a kind of pet by the regular drinkers at the Grand. They gave him at least a couple of schooners of beer a day, provided he never entered the hotel. A recurrent joke among the drinkers was that Herbie ought to stand for parliament as an Independent. He would be the kind of MP that the town deserved.

Thistle believed she had a lot in common with Herbie. She'd rejected society; society had rejected him. She had no compunction about using people who were better off than she was, however, especially if she thought they were undeserving, but she could be compassionate to people who had little or nothing, especially if they provided 'copy' for her monologues. She planned what she knew would appeal to the ABC in Rockie—perhaps even to one of the programmes on Radio National—a narrative poem on what it was like to be homeless. Herbie was her source of inspiration and information.

'If you'd applied for a grant to write your poem about Herbie,' Howard said, 'You'd probably have got it. The committee is heavily into social commentary. Writing about a homeless old man would be PC.'

'Fuck political correctness,' Thistle said, expertly operating the Espresso machine. 'I'll write about him when I'm fucking ready.'

Howard sighed. He knew he shouldn't have risked making a suggestion, even if she agreed with it.

'Was Michael Milosovic at the meeting?' Thistle demanded.

'Yes.' Howard would've liked to have told her that Milosovic had voted against her application, but he knew this lie could backfire. 'But he left before your application came up,' he added to be on the safe side. 'It wouldn't have made any difference anyway. We'd have been in the minority.'

There was only one thing left now for Howard to do. He took his wallet out of his pocket. 'Don't worry about it, Thistle,' he said, and gave her two fifty-dollar notes. 'You don't need petty grants when you've got me.'

'You're a darling,' she said, and pecked him on the cheek as she returned, smiling now, to her chair, coffee in hand.

Once again, a brief outburst of indignation had achieved its purpose. And once again Howard asked himself why he allowed this impossible woman to manipulate him. He wasn't sure, but he thought it was something to do with the responsibility of one artist to support another. And perhaps, one day, she'd be famous, and he'd be remembered as the man who'd made her success possible. He'd be at least a footnote in her biography.

At this moment, a potential customer entered the shop, wanting a copy of the latest bestseller, which had been reviewed on an ABC book programme. Inevitably, Howard didn't have it in stock, and not wanting to go to the trouble of ordering it, he told her it was already out of print.

Between the Leaves was so badly managed that it couldn't possibly provide Howard with even a modest wage. As he often said, 'It's a mystery to me how I survive in business. I'm just not cut out for it.'

This wasn't true. Although running a book business was beyond him, Howard secretly operated a highly successful phone sex business from The Golden Fronds Aged Care Facility in the town. It had occurred to him while studying the advertisements in certain kinds of magazines that although the ads for phone sex featured nubile young women displaying plenty of choice flesh, customers had no way of knowing whether the female one spoke to on the phone looked anything like the female in the ad. A little research had given him no indication of the age of the women at the other end of the line, though he suspected that many of them were Indians working in call centres in Madras or, if nearer home, residents of the Philippines.

His research into the phone sex industry had inspired him to approach two of The Golden Fronds more liberated and financially short pensioners, Muriel Cross and Ethel Smart. Both long-widowed and finding it difficult to obtain the quantities of alcohol they needed for a life worth living, they thought it a jolly good idea. Howard provided mobile phones, and Thistle wrote their scripts. He required only that they should put as much sultriness as possible into their voices and do their best to limit quavering. Too much quavering, he thought, might raise suspicions.

Both ladies entered into the spirit of their new vocation and devoted at least eight hours a day to providing men who needed women to 'talk dirty' to them with all the dirt they needed. Muriel, who was tiny and frail and needed a Zimmer frame for walking, had assumed the identity of Gloria. Her script began, 'Hello. I'm Gloria. I've been waiting for your call. Do you have a big one for me? You do? That's what I like to hear. You want me to describe myself. Well, darling, I'm tall with long, long legs and huge breasts you'll love to fondle.' It continued on these lines, while she crocheted tea cosies for the annual Coddington St George Red Cross Fair.

Ethel, who was sprightlier and needed only a stick to assist her, made the tea when she wasn't 'on call'. Her script aimed at the one-minute caller.

'Hello, I'm Miranda. I'm just about to take a shower. I'm going to slowly undress, letting my sexy underwear fall to the floor. And then I'm going to stand under the shower and give myself a really good time. Would you like to be with me? Of course you would. You'd like to help me have a good time, wouldn't you? I'm completely naked now. If you could see my magnificent body, you wouldn't be able to control yourself. There are so many things I'd want you to do to me. I'm under the shower now, and I'm going to turn on the water. Now, I'm stroking myself, and it feels oh, it's so good. Oh, yes. Oh, oh.'

The only really tricky moment in the venture so far had been when the contract gardener, Larry's Lawn Service, had heard their simulated noises of ecstasy and, assuming that one of them was having a heart attack or a fit, had phoned for an ambulance.

It was this business venture that enabled Howard to survive financially. It no longer mattered, therefore, that the bookshop lost money and would continue to do so as long as he managed it. And in the unlikely event of anyone wondering where his income came from, he'd created an imaginary investment portfolio. The bookshop existed to provide him with a suitable 'cover' and somewhere to meet his friends.

nine

The day after Jack's departure, Michael formed a subcommittee to manage the movie. It consisted of the existing members of the Coddington St George Cultural Coordinating Committee plus co-opted extras. He suggested to Fleur Robertson that, as chairperson of the Cultural Coordinating Committee, she should chair the subcommittee. She accepted willingly, as she accepted all such offers of official positions on committees. She collected chairpersonships the way other women collect items of craft pottery, commemorative mugs, teaspoons and various hand-made knickknacks. She wasn't elected to these positions because of her chairpersonship skills, however, but because of her lack of them. The committee members who proposed and seconded her nomination knew that her inability to control even the friendliest of meetings could be used to their advantage.

Although a large woman, Fleur had a small voice, one which could never rise above the din of heated and vicious controversy. Her pleas for order were always ignored. She also had a very limited understanding of the basic rules of procedure, and members who did have such an understanding or, more to the point, were able to give the impression that they did, could easily manipulate her. Points of order, ambiguous amendments to motions, and the devastatingly effective ploy of proposing that the motion be put confused her totally. After half an hour, sometimes even an hour, of erratic discussion on some minor matter having preceded this motion, most members of the committee, having long forgotten the exact content of the original motion, and being both exhausted and irritated by the rambling and often incoherent arguments, were in no mood for further intellectual effort. They voted for or against the motion that the motion be put, assuming that they were voting on the motion that had been so interminably discussed. This was not, of course, the case. They were voting only on a motion that they should vote on this motion. When they discovered what they'd done, one or more of them would demand that the motion on which they'd voted be rescinded as it wasn't the motion they thought it was. This required a motion to rescind the motion and a vote on that. And so the morning, afternoon and evening dragged on.

Fleur, who by this time would have very little idea what was going on, simply abdicated her authority to the most assertive members of the committee—always the members who'd nominated her for the chair. They now assumed total control of the meeting, the other members of the committee having by this time lost all understanding of or interest in the proceedings, and often having nodded off or become deeply engrossed in the most complex of doodles. Several would've gone home, this not infrequently bringing the meeting to a halt as there'd no longer be a quorum of members. If a quorum remained, they left the decision-making to the most assertive personalities. Of these, Michael, who as mayor attended policy meetings of all the committees spun off the town council, was by far the most vocal.

One way or another, he ensured that all committees voted the way he wanted them to.

Now he suggested to Fleur, 'Why don't you ask Alec Grimshaw, Tony Andover and Thistle O'Reilly to be members of this subcommittee?'

'I'm willing to work with young Tony, and I agree Alec Grimshaw should be on the subcommittee,' Fleur replied over the phone, 'but I have a real problem with that girl. She's simply not a committee kind of person.'

Michael had to accept that this was an understatement and decided not to press the matter. 'But you'll accept Alec?'

'Yes. Whatever one may think of him, he's well-known in the community. And he'll work hard."

'Exactly. We ought to have more young people on the committee. If you won't have Thistle, what about Trent Frobisher? He wants to be in the movies, I understand.'

Having got her own way over Thistle, Fleur knew she'd have to accept Trent. She didn't really object to him. He was a pleasant enough young man and his father owned half the district. He'd be good for a donation to the project if his son was heavily involved.

'Yes, Trent is a very good suggestion.'

'Excellent. That's that decided, then. You as chair, Edwin, Howard, Alec, the Reverend, Trent and myself as the subcommittee. Howard can be secretary. Edwin, treasurer.'

Michael felt content. He had the numbers he needed. If there were disagreements—and he knew that Edwin Bland and the Reverend Greg Small would see to that there were—he'd have his own vote and Alec's. He was reasonably confident that he could also rely on Trent, who he'd heard was desperate to be in a movie, and on Tony, who'd be grateful to him for supporting his trip to Cannes. Howard was another matter. He'd be all over the place, supporting Edwin and the Reverend one moment and him the next. As often as not he'd abstain. But Michael believed his vote wouldn't be important. Fleur would have the casting vote, and if there was a tie she would vote to preserve the status quo. For the chairperson to do this was one of the few rules of procedure she understood. Whichever way the voting went on any major issue, Michael felt sure he'd have the majority, if only of one.

Fleur realized, of course, that she was being used. She suffered this situation for the sake of her social position, feeling it important that she be seen as heavily involved in the community. Her ambition, though never voiced, was to be awarded an OAM 'for services to the community'. Being right, having her own way, were not important to her. Being there and noticed was what mattered.

Her only allies on the committee, she knew, would be Edwin and Greg, both of whom would vote on principle against anything Michael wanted to do. Howard was a loose cannon. Trent and Tony, she thought, would be influenced by Michael's financial contribution to the project. She wished she believed in it, but thought the whole idea far too ambitious. So many things could go wrong. No one really knew anything about film-making. Tony's five-minute short was hardly a film at all.

If she had had her way, the money they'd spent sending him to Cannes to meet the applicants for the producer's job would've been better spent on refurbishing the bridge clubroom in the town hall or on new curtains for the stage. The movie would be just a one-off project. At the end of it, there'd be nothing left for the town except a DVD that no one wanted to buy. Although Fleur was a keen thespian, she didn't deceive herself into thinking there was enough talent in the Players to cast a movie. The recent performance of The Players in Stanfield proved that. The most embarrassing evening of her amateur theatrical career, it'd been a relief to have had such a small audience.

***

The Coddington St George Community Movie Subcommittee convened in an ante-room to the council chamber the day after Tony's return from Cannes. A great promoter of democracy in meetings, Michael had had the rectangular table in the committee room removed and a round table installed in its place. This, he liked to tell people, made everyone on the committee equal. It did nothing of the kind. Regardless of the shape of a table and his location at it, Michael dominated every meeting he attended.

Fleur opened the meeting by welcoming Alec and Trent. 'I'm sure,' she said, 'you'll both make a significant contribution to our deliberations.'

Both men smiled but said nothing. Alec's only concern was to be confirmed as Director of Photography—the DOP as he liked to refer to the role—and he knew that his only function on the committee was to say, 'Hear! Hear!' to everything Michael suggested.

Trent Frobisher assumed that he'd been invited onto the committee partly because of his acting aspirations, but mainly because of his father's money. His acting experience was limited to the occasional role in a Players production, though he'd once attended a three-day workshop in Brisbane given by the Susan Watkins Academy of Acting for Television. This had been intended mainly for physically attractive, but not very intelligent, young men and women who hoped to appear on the nation's television screens. The more successful of the women occasionally obtained employment enthusing over such products as Orgon—the Ultra-Sensitive, Forest-Perfumed

Laundry Detergent—or smiling adoringly at a cherubic child as they held up a bar of Crunch, a sugar-laden confection, and spoke in the sincerest of tones the slogan, 'Mothers Who Love Their Children Give Them Crunch Every Day.'

The men, wearing brightly coloured shirts and silly hats, walked around warehouses stacked from floor to ceiling with recent imports from China, screaming, 'Everything Must Go,' or, 'Don't Delay, Buy Today,' and similar exhortations. Many of them had developed the art of speaking so quickly that not a word they shouted could be understood.

The Susan Watkins Academy also offered workshops in how to appear amazed, concerned, confused, ecstatic, grateful, and in vibrant good health, and also a very popular weekend course on 'How to Appear Sincere'.

Now Trent sat silently, gently fingering his jaw. In an attempt to achieve the chiselled look, he'd shaved too close to the bone and scraped off a layer of epidermis. His jaw was red and raw, the inflammation aggravated by too liberal an application of Musketeer aftershave.

After 'Welcome to New Members', the second item on the agenda, hurriedly prepared by Howard, was 'Report by Tony Andover'.

'I had a really great time,' Tony began. 'You can have no idea how many movies there are. It was awesome.'

'Were there any community movies?' Michael interrupted.

'I didn't see any, and no one seemed to know anything about them.'

'Good. We shall be breaking new ground,' Michael said.

The Reverend Greg Small smiled the smile of a man hoping to soften the blow of bad news. 'There's probably a reason why there aren't any community movies,' he said. 'They're so bad nobody wants to watch them.'

A pale man, the Reverend Greg Small enhanced his paleness by always wearing a black, clerical suit and dog collar. Unlike many parsons who avoid indicating their calling by their clothing, hoping to be thought of as tolerant men of the world rather than judgmental clergy, Greg wore his uniform defiantly, almost as if he were trying to convince himself of his vocation, which in fact he was. He'd long ago lost his faith. It had slid away, a little at a time, over the years. First of all, he'd had his doubts about the credibility of most religions, but more recently about Christianity.

His problem was that he couldn't reconcile the size of the universe, the billions of stars in billions of galaxies, with the theological concept that God had made man in His own image. Greg's intelligence couldn't permit him to accept that God—whatever His form and function—would go to so much trouble to create such a vast, probably infinite and expanding entity, just to have, on one of the most insignificant planets in a remote minor solar system, homo sapiens. Concern about the efficacy of prayer quickly added to this doubt. Why, he asked himself, would this God—who was supposed to look like a member of the human species and who resided somewhere in the vastness of this universe, or universes, he'd created—pay the slightest attention to the petty requirements of men, women and children on Earth? And if He did pay attention and do something about them, how could He—or even She—do anything about them without subverting the basic laws of science? To these doubts he added suspicions about the Virgin Birth, Christ's Ascension into Heaven, the authenticity of miracles and various appalling events in church history.

His reading of such works as The God Delusion by Ronald Dawkins and similar atheistic outpourings, which he'd studied in the hope of being able to refute their arguments, had done nothing to alleviate his concerns. Ripostes such as 'God moves in a mysterious way' and 'It's in the Bible' did not, he thought, really take the discussion very far.

Greg's real problem, though, wasn't so much that he'd lost his faith but that having lost it and having no skills other than those required by a vicar in a declining parish, he knew he'd not find it easy to obtain elsewhere better paid employment with all the perks attendant on his current living. The vicarage, a large Queenslander high set in spacious grounds, was an ideal place for his four young children to grow up, in spite of its increasing disrepair. And although he never had any money to spare, his wife Cynthia was a good manager and assisted by gifts from sympathetic parishioners, most of whom were over sixty, and by the sale of her own jams, chutneys, pickles and cakes, kept them all alive with her home baking and stewing, which, with other housekeeping tasks, kept her on her feet sixteen hours a day. Her complexion was even paler than her husband's.

Greg did his best to be positive, but as time passed, he found it increasingly difficult to be enthusiastic about anything. Although only forty-four, he was a sad, disillusioned and worried man. The only thing that didn't worry him was whether when he died he'd go to heaven or hell. He didn't believe in either of them.

Michael said, 'Has it occurred to you, Reverend, that the reason there are no community movies—assuming there are not—is that it's only in recent years that digital technology has made them possible? Filming and editing it were far too costly before. What do you think, Tony?'

'I think you could be right. Even short student films cost a lot of money.'

'So, we could be at the beginning of something new. Trailblazers,' Alec said, confident that Michael would approve of the contribution.

'Exactly, Alec. So, Tony, did you meet the two applicants? Jack Wilcon and …' Michael consulted the minutes of the last Cultural Coordinating Committee meeting. 'Sven Ingersson?'

'Oh, yes,' Tony said. 'I spent a lot of time with each of them.' He then proceeded with a paean of praise of Sven, maintaining that a film-maker of his experience and integrity, to say nothing of his reputation among serious cinema-goers, was ideally qualified to produce their movie, especially as he was famous for making great art on very small budgets.

'He sounds wonderful,' Fleur said. 'Just the kind of man we need.'

'It would be fantastic,' Howard added, 'if our community movie could aspire to being a work of art.'

'Especially if costs can be kept down,' Edwin concurred.

'I'm glad you mentioned that, Edwin,' Michael said. 'The only trouble with Ingersson, I understand, is that his films always go over budget—which is why he makes so few. He has the devil of a job raising the money to make them. Is that true, Tony?'

Having no experience of committees, Tony gave a straightforward, truthful answer. Over the umpteenth schnapps, Sven had confessed that the five-year gap between each of his films was due to financing difficulties. 'I'm afraid it is. He's, like, a perfectionist, you see.'

'Exactly. A fine film-maker, but a perfectionist. And unfortunately, one who repeatedly goes over budget. That could be a problem for us, couldn't it, Edwin?' Michael turned towards the banker, knowing there was no way he wouldn't agree with him.

'Well, yes,' Edwin said. 'We'll have a very tight budget indeed. Really only just enough to pay for a professional producer.'

Fleur said, 'I suppose we do need a professional. I mean, it's not as if we're aiming at a professional standard.'

'Mackay employed a professional director for their pageant,' Michael declared, wagging a thick, dirty-nailed finger at Fleur. 'That's why it was so good. Do we want to be compared unfavourably with that lot?'

This was the decider. The rivalry between the two towns was deep and dated back to before Federation.

'What about this Mr Wilcon, Tony?' Fleur asked. 'What did you think of him?'

'He talked a lot about all the famous Hollywood people he knew and how successful he was,' Tony said. 'I looked him up on the internet. His name appears in the credits of a lot of films—all rubbish. He's never actually produced a movie. He's always listed as one of the associate producers.'

'When you say "rubbish", Tony, what exactly do you mean?' Greg asked quietly.

'Well, you know—'

'Low-budget productions,' Michael cut in. 'Made for cable and the internet.'

'Well, yes. I mean, I doubt if anything he's been involved with has ever had a theatrical release,' Tony said.

'In the cinemas, you mean,' Howard interjected. He was the only member of the committee apart from Tony who knew what a theatrical release was.

'Well, yes, but—'

'We don't need our movie to be screened in cinemas,' Michael said. 'DVD and cable will do us very well.'

'It's not just that ...' Tony wanted to provide the committee with a short list of Jack's productions, but Michael cut him short.

Michael didn't know what these productions were, neither did he care. Knowing nothing about the movie industry, it didn't occur to him that they were, in fact, the kind of films that they were. He knew only that Jack had convinced him that his involvement in the project would be what it needed. He played his trump card.

'Jack Wilcon's been here, actually. Stopped over on his way back from Cannes to LA. I found him very impressive.'

'Hear! Hear!' said Alec.

Michael then explained to the committee about Jack's distribution guarantees and how they would take care of the budget. With Jack Wilcon in charge of production, he argued, there'd be no risk, and the finished film would be screened internationally on one or more of the cable networks.

Edwin and Greg had serious reservations, but as these were mainly related to their antagonism to Michael, rather than to Jack Wilcon, whom they didn't know, they were at a loss how to deal with the situation. At the end of his recommendation, Michael proposed a formal motion that Jack should be offered the position, and Alec seconded it. He insisted that Fleur put it to the vote immediately as he had to leave for another meeting. Michael, Alec and Trent voted for. Edwin and Greg, wanting more information before committing themselves either way, voted against as did Tony. Howard abstained. Fleur cast her chairperson's vote. The motion was carried.

Despondent, Tony said he had to get back to the radio station and left the room.

The committee moved on to the next item on the agenda. The date of the next meeting.

Ten

Twenty-four hours later, Jack Wilcon walked slowly into his LA office, head down, shoulders hunched, wearing his disaster look—an expression with which Maybelle was familiar. Jack would need to be carefully helped back into a positive, 'the break-through is just around the corner' mood. This was her main function in his life: Jack was easily depressed, though quick to recover at the slightest glimmer of a light at the end of whatever tunnel he happened to be in at the time.

'Welcome home, hon,' she said. 'Coffee?'

He looked up.

She thought she saw tears starting in the corners of his eyes. *Ah, well,* she thought, *there goes my five grand.*

Then suddenly his face changed. A broad grin appeared on his mouth. He straightened up, held out his arms to her and exclaimed, 'We did it, babe. We did it!'

Mouth and eyes wide open, Maybelle leapt up from her chair and hurried round to the front of the receptionist's desk. She took Jack's hands in hers. 'You don't mean …?'

'Meet the producer of the Coddington St George Community Movie.'

'Oh, Jack! Jack, I knew you'd do it. This is it, isn't it? The chance of a lifetime.' The usual element of doubt approached rapidly over the horizon. 'You do have it in writing?'

If Maybelle had been religious she would've immediately fallen on her knees and prayed, *Dear God, don't let him fuck this up*. But she wasn't, so she added, 'It really is confirmed, isn't it?'

'As good as.'

She took her hands away and walked to the coffee machine, wishing she had as many dollars as she'd heard Jack say, 'As good as' about a deal he'd been negotiating. Controlling her disappointment, she said, 'When will you hear definitely?'

'Perhaps today. Tomorrow at the latest. Trust me, Maybelle. It's in the bag.'

Maybelle wished, oh she wished, that Jack had not said, 'Trust me.' In her way she loved him, but she certainly didn't trust him. She knew that whenever he told someone to trust him, he'd already be rehearsing in his mind what he'd say when he didn't deliver what he'd promised. It was not, she repeatedly told herself, that he wanted or even intended to lie and cheat— a little exaggeration or wishful thinking was not necessarily dishonest—it was just that when things went wrong, or when they needed a bit of a push, he had to do what he had to do in order to survive in a very dog-eat-dog industry. Everybody in it lied, fiddled the books, broke promises, dishonoured cheques, breached contracts, welched on guarantees, plagiarized and stole concepts, ideas, and even large chunks of scripts. It was that kind of industry. Maybelle had convinced herself that Jack was no worse than the others. It was just unfortunate that the ethics of the industry he worked in overflowed into his personal life.

A 'ping' from her computer interrupted her thoughts. An email had arrived. Jack waddled quickly round her desk and opened the email. It was from Michael Milosovic and informed him that The Coddington St George Community Movie Subcommittee had confirmed his appointment as producer of the proposed movie. A draft contract for his consideration was being drawn up and would follow shortly.

Jack let out a huff of air, like a balloon suddenly going down. He collapsed into Maybelle's chair, the relief overwhelming. 'Read this, babe,' he said. 'Can you trust me or can you trust me?'

Had Jack been up to it, he and Maybelle would've celebrated by having sex on her receptionist's desk, but his libido wasn't adequate for it. The most he could manage without a tremendous and prolonged effort that would probably bring on stroke or cardiac arrest was a grateful embrace.

'It's all thanks to you, babe,' Jack said, doing his best to put his short arms right round her plump body. 'It was your idea that I apply. You invested the cash to get me to Cannes. I love you, babe.'

Maybelle noted the word 'invested'. She'd thought she'd made Jack a loan to be repaid if he got the job. Clearly she'd yet again been mistaken. She'd invested 'loans' in a score or more of Wilcon Interglobal Consolidated Universal Pictures' projects. None had ever been repaid or declared a dividend. None had ever made it possible for him to earn more than just enough to keep himself alive and the business going.

Releasing her, he said, 'We must get Hank and Studs into this. I need their expertise. Get them over. We'll have a pizza in Dino's downstairs. Can we put it on the tab?'

'I'll tell Dino you've landed a big job in Australia,' Maybelle said. 'That should keep him quiet for a while.'

Maybelle and Jack both lived on their credit with Dino. The food he served them was always a day or two old, but it was edible.

Jack walked away to his office, turned at the door and blew Maybelle a kiss. 'You're a great broad, babe. I dunno what I'd do without you.'

Maybelle smiled, but said nothing. She knew exactly what Jack would do without her. He'd find some other worn-out woman and pay her just enough to rent a dingy room in a semi-derelict boarding house and buy sufficient junk food to stay alive while her arteries hardened and her kidneys and liver complained as the diabetes gradually took hold.

She'd stood by Jack for over ten years, helping him out with loans that, without any discussion, he'd turned in his own mind into investments. And in spite of all the failures, his fantasies of success, his pointless boasting and his less than adequate grasp of reality, she'd lived, and still lived, in the hope that one day he would get a piece of a movie that took off and make millions. There was always the possibility that even at his end of the market, a movie could make a fortune, reach the 'blue sky'. Horror made big money if it was well done. Vampire movies were currently making fortunes for their makers. And *Friday the Thirteenth* had grossed seventy million and cost ten. It was still possible, Maybelle thought, that Jack would strike lucky, and she assumed that when he did, he'd repay her investments and then some. In any case, she didn't think she had any option but to stay with him. She had a very limited future in television commercials, and not just because she was approaching sixty. The supply of talent far exceeded demand.

Maybelle sighed, picked up the phone and keyed in Studs' number.

***

Jack knew that he had to be careful what he told Hank Shorn and Studs Collini. Though his oldest and, he sometimes thought, his only friends, there was a limit to how far he could risk taking them into his confidence. He needed to enthuse them about the community movie, but avoid giving them the impression that there'd be much money up-front. He wanted to be straight with them, but if he were too straight, they mightn't show any interest in the project. He needed to dangle before them the likelihood of some kind of future work without actually lying about it. His main problem, however, was that he was sufficient of a realist to know that if his idea for a Coddington St George College of Community Movie Production—a fantasy dreamed up during the long flight home—ever became more than an idea, Hank and Studs were the last people he should involve in it. Hank's alcoholism and Studs' drug dealing and dependency wouldn't be hidden for long.

Over one of Dino's yesterday's pizzas, the three of them met in his office to discuss the project.

'What's the budget?' was Hank's first question. He hadn't worked since the debacle with *The Axeman Cometh*, and for what little direction he'd done on that, he still hadn't been paid.

'That's what's so interesting,' Jack said. 'There isn't one yet. There's no script. Not even a concept. I'll need you to prepare a budget as soon as we get a script.'

'But there'll be money, won't there?' Studs demanded. 'I can't leave my business too long,'

'Oh, yes, there'll be money. It's just that at this point in time, I don't know how much.'

Jack had never budgeted a movie. He knew almost nothing about the nuts and bolts of film production. Having always been on the distribution side of the business, he'd rarely visited a set or a location. He had no idea how to schedule a shoot—organize the shots in such a way that, if possible, the cast and crew only went to each location once and that the most efficient use was made of time, extras and equipment.

The work of all the other departments of a movie production also remained a mystery to him. He'd never shown any interest in it. He knew roughly what an art director did—designing and dressing the sets, choosing and organizing the props, supervising any construction needed—but he didn't know enough to do any of this work himself. His single venture as a location manager had been a disaster. Not only had he not obtained permission to use the park and the cave, thereby creating a legal nightmare for the movie had it been completed, because the park administration would have taken out an injunction to prevent it from ever being shown, but he'd failed to check that the cave was in a usable condition and didn't have a dead horse in it.

In the matter of legal technicalities, Jack was also ignorant. He'd never been responsible for negotiating the contracts with cast and crew or obtaining waivers from members of the public whose premises were used or who appeared in shot. He knew something about insurance—the necessity of taking out a complete package that covered all possible eventualities, such as sickness or injury to key cast and crew, damage to locations, camera and other equipment failure and general public liability—but he'd never been responsible for obtaining such insurance. He knew about completion guarantees—a kind of insurance by which the insurer guarantees to provide enough cash to finish a movie if it runs out of money during production—but he'd never taken out such guarantees and neither had the producers of most of the movies with which he'd been involved. Their budgets had been so ridiculously low that no completion guarantor would have considered them.

What Jack did know about was deferrals and producers and director's points—the percentages they were entitled to from the profits of the movie.

'What I'm proposing to do,' he said now, 'is negotiate for you a percentage of the profits.'

'Of the gross,' Studs said.

'I can try for that, but you know how difficult it can be.'

'We can't defer our fees,' Hank said. 'We need money to live on. And what about airfares and accommodation?'

Jack had worked all this out. Maybelle had looked up airfares on the internet. A business class return LA to Sydney on United Airlines was ten times the cost of an economy fare on a low-cost airline. Jack was confident that he could persuade the movie subcommittee to fly him business class. He'd make it clear to them that Hollywood producers usually flew first class and that he was doing the committee a favour by agreeing to fly business. In fact, he'd fly economy with Hank and Studs on one of the budget airlines, such as Trans Pacific Air, and have cash to spare.

'You'll be accommodated at the Central Hotel,' he told them. 'A room each, with an en-suite, and full board. The food there is great. Believe me.'

Jack hadn't had an opportunity to discuss this with Alec, but he felt sure that giving him the title of director of photography on the movie would be adequate compensation for the cost of accommodating and feeding the three of them for six weeks or so. Hank's bar bills would be a problem, but he'd be able to 'have a slate', as Jack thought the expression was, and he'd be out of the country before the day of reckoning.

'And there'll be per diems,' he said. 'The idea is that Michael Milosovic, he's the mayor and loaded, will invest in the movie. So will local businesses. And probably some of the actors.

Everybody, of course, will give of their time. That's what community movies are all about.'

Studs asked, 'Will there be a lot of people involved?'

'I'll see to it that the script calls for hundreds of extras and a big crew—runners, standby props, make-up, hair, catering, drivers—the usual mob of hangers-on.'

'Good,' Studs said. 'I like a big production.' And he genuinely did. If the number of people involved in a production was large enough, his pharmaceutical side-line brought in far more cash than his always-small fees.

'What will you do, Jack?' Hank asked.

'The finance. And community liaison. And I'll need to work with the writer. I expect she'll be new to scripting.'

Like all producers since the beginning of time—which for people like Jack was since the beginning of the movie industry—he believed that he knew more about writing a movie than even the most successful and grossly overpaid of writers. He wasn't alone in this attitude; directors thought the same. Although most movies began with a script that the producer and director enthused about, by the time they'd finished with it—to say nothing of the contribution of stars determined to enlarge their roles or re-write their lines in a way they were able to say them—the writer often found it difficult to find in it anything that he or she had written. Novelists who allowed their work to be adapted for a movie were usually appalled by the result. Gerald Kersh, a minor but briefly popular British author of the 1940s and 50s, had boasted that he was the world's highest paid writer. For his novel *Night and the City* Hollywood had paid $40,000— several million in current terms. Kersh had maintained that as the movie contained nothing of the novel except the title, he'd received $10,000 a word.

'The point is, guys,' Jack said, 'this community movie deal could be the beginning of a new part of the industry. I mean, just think about it, there's more porn being made now than all the other kinds of movies put together. That wasn't so twenty, thirty years ago. If we can create something that pleases the community, there's no reason why we can't specialize in producing movies of this kind. There could be hundreds of them being made, and we'd be leading the crowd. A new genre.'

Maybelle spoke for the first time. 'Every community has some kind of amateur dramatic society,' she said. 'With the technology being as cheap as it is, it won't be long before every community has its own movie production society.'

'Jesus!' Hank said. 'There could be hundreds of them in California alone.'

'Multiply that by every state,' Jack said, smiling warmly at Maybelle. There was no doubt, he thought, she was one in a million. He'd try to show his appreciation somehow. Perhaps she'd like a box of chocolates. 'We get this right,' he said, 'and we'll be made for life.'

The three men—and occasionally Maybelle—talked and talked, wandering around the subject of the movie until way into the night. Neither Hank nor Studs had any employment pending, and so as long as they didn't have to find any money for the project and wouldn't be out of pocket, they were prepared to defer any fees. They couldn't imagine that an almost wholly amateur movie could possibly make even enough money to cover the airfares, but that wasn't their problem. As far as they were concerned, they were being offered an all-expenses-paid holiday in an Australian country town. The fact that—apart from themselves and possibly the young film-maker Tony Andover and the video guy, Alec Whatshisname—no one in Coddington St George had any relevant skills wasn't important.

They'd have a good time, probably lay some local dames—there'd be plenty of those wanting to impress the men from Hollywood—and possibly a new career at the end of it. They'd be fools to turn the offer down.

'It's agreed, then,' Jack said, summing up the evening's discussion. 'You'll production manage, Hank, helping out young Tony with his direction when necessary, and you'll edit, Studs, and operate the camera for Alec Grimshaw. Light it the way you want to light it. Alec won't interfere. It's the position he wants, not the work.'

'Yeah, well, that's not unusual,' Studs said.

Nothing had been said about Maybelle joining the team. Jack now faced up to this. 'I'd love you to come with us, babe, but I need you here to look after the office.' He patted her hand. 'But if everything goes according to plan, there'll be a big job for you in the future.' He winked.

She smiled ruefully. She would've loved a trip to Australia and a holiday with the others. 'Sure, hon,' she said. 'Sure.'

PART THREE:

PRE-PRODUCTION

eLeven

Alec met Jack's flight, and during the drive to Coddington St George, he told him what he thought he ought to know about the committee. He particularly wanted Jack to know that he was on his side and that Jack would need his support.

'You ought to know,' he said, almost before Jack had managed to click on his seat belt, 'that the decision to offer you the job was not unanimous. There were three votes against and one abstention.'

Jack shrugged, hoping to give the impression that such opposition to his appointment didn't worry him. 'You can't win them all. What was their problem?'

'Well,' Alec explained, 'Edwin Bland—he's the manager of the local building society—and Greg Small—the vicar—usually vote against anything Michael Milosovic wants to do. It's political. Nothing to do with whether or not what he wants to do is good for the town. You see, Edwin is standing against Michael in the shire council elections this year, and as he's a churchwarden and chairman of the parish council, he and the Rev are in cahoots.'

'That's understandable,' Jack said. 'I guess local politics were bound to be a factor. Who was the third 'no' vote?'

'Young Tony Andover.'

'Oh?' This was a shock and a disappointment. Jack had assumed that he'd impressed Tony. 'Did he say why?'

Alec prevaricated. 'Oh, you know what these young people are like. Arty farty. No business sense. He wanted to work with the Swede. Preferred his kind of film.'

Jack felt disappointed by Tony's decision, but he put it down to youthful idealism. 'He'll have to grow up,' he said, 'if he wants a career in the industry.'

Alec nodded. 'I guess so.'

'Will he still produce?'

'Probably, Jack. Nothing's been said against him.'

'Have any of the committee ever seen any of Sven Ingersson's movies?' Jack asked.

'Howard probably has—he was the abstention. Don't worry about him. He procrastinates about everything. Michael never goes to the cinema or watches TV—too busy planning to rebuild the shire. Fleur's knowledge of film probably begins and ends with *The Sound of Music*. And I doubt if Edwin or Greg are into art house. Too much sex and violence in them for their liking.'

'Yeah, well, thanks for putting me in the picture,' Jack said. 'And now, Alec, if you don't mind, I'll have a bit of a doze. I can never sleep on planes.'

He closed his eyes and soon pretended to snore quietly, but he was far from asleep. The lack of unanimity on the committee about his appointment was a worry. Jack suspected it could be a problem. There'd been a clause in his contract permitting the committee to cancel it if they weren't satisfied with his work. He'd accepted it because he had no option. He was also used to such clauses in distribution guarantee contracts—they always contained an out if the product didn't meet the guarantor's requirements. As a distributor, Jack had only had to enforce the clause once. The producers of a movie in which he'd had a very small stake had guaranteed to deliver an R-rated production, but the end result had been classified MA. He'd had to tell the producer that his customers demanded an R—this was the part of the market he served—and unless they re-edited the movie to get an R, he wouldn't be able to pay up. He'd suggested to the producers a few little bits of explicit three-cornered sex and blood-spurting violence that had nothing to do with the plot and could be easily excised for that part of the market requiring nothing stronger than an MA. These brief scenes, using the bodies of porno actors hired for the purpose, had been inserted and had resulted in the necessary R for Jack's customers. Such is the artistic commitment at Jack's end of the movie industry.

As far as his contract with Coddington St George was concerned, he suspected that his enemies on the committee— and as Edwin and Greg had opposed his appointment he had to consider them enemies—would be watching his every move. And Tony's opposition was a major setback. Jack sighed. Nothing ever went smoothly. Unwittingly, he'd become a pawn in the Coddington St George political scene. Bland and Small would be on the lookout for ways to make use of him in their campaign against Michael Milosovic. He'd have to be careful not to provide them with any ammunition. And as for Michael, the movie was just part of his election campaign, nothing more, Jack thought. He desperately needed a trouble-free production if he was to gain, not lose, votes. It didn't matter to him what the finished movie was like—the election would be over before it was released, if it ever was. It would be the daily involvement of the community in the production that mattered. Any kind of scandal or major disaster would play into Edwin and Greg's hands.

Jack considered everything that could go wrong—an intellectual exercise with which he was very familiar. He wondered whether he should email Maybelle and ask her to tell Studs and Hank that he was sorry but he wouldn't be needing them. In their different ways, they were both seriously unreliable and a health hazard if nothing worse. The problem was, he did need them.

Jack now realized that getting the job had been the easy part. Keeping it was going to be much more difficult. This meant that as soon as possible he ought to get his hands on all the money that would be due to him. Unfortunately, Michael, exercising his developer's skills, had structured his remuneration as a series of progress payments, as if he were a builder. Ten percent on arrival, twenty percent at the end of pre-production—script development, casting, location survey and so on—fifty percent at the end of the shoot and the balance on delivery of the finished movie. Jack decided that to be on the safe side, he'd need to cream off part of the budget as early as possible—and do his damnedest to inflate it so that there was some cream to be had.

***

As Alec drove into the courtyard of the Central Hotel, Jack pretended to wake up. 'Sorry about that,' he said, yawning. 'I was tired.'

'The committee would like to welcome you as soon as you've had time to freshen up,' Alec said. 'Then we'll all have lunch. Peggy's done a roast specially, complete with Yorkshire Pud.'

'Great.' Jack hoped his stomach would be able to cope with the food. Pizzas and Big Macs were his usual diet.

He let himself into his hotel room and sat on the bed. He'd arrived. What could turn out to be the most important few weeks of his life were now underway. He felt as if he were sailing into unknown waters, and he'd have to be careful that he didn't founder on submerged rocks that suddenly appeared as if from nowhere. He shivered with sudden foreboding, then told himself not to be stupid. Nothing could go seriously wrong. The usual problems—insufficient money, temperamental actors, bad weather, illness and injury, equipment failures—wouldn't be his fault; and because the whole venture was non-commercial, the worst that could happen would be that the production took longer than scheduled. If anything had to be reshot with a different actor, then it would simply be reshot. Apart from himself—Studs and Hank had tacitly accepted that they were just having an all-expenses-paid working holiday—no one else would be paid. *So what,* he thought, *could go wrong?* He tried to tell himself that he was being unnecessarily anxious.

***

Alec took Jack to the committee meeting, held, as usual, in the ante-room to the council chamber. Everyone except Tony was there. Michael introduced Jack to the others, and there were smiles and handshakes all round. Trent Frobisher, anxious to be cast in whatever happened to be the major role, attempted to put on Expression Twenty-four from his Manual of Facial Expressions. Expression Twenty-four indicated intelligence, alertness and a willingness to participate in whatever was being proposed. Unfortunately, the message from Trent's brain to his facial muscles failed to connect properly and he produced Expression Twenty-five—a ferocious scowl, indicating serious suspicion and more than a suggestion of violence to come. The look puzzled Jack, but he said nothing.

Fleur, as chairperson, welcomed him to Coddington St George. 'We're delighted you were able to accept our invitation to produce our little film, Mr Wilcon.'

'Jack, please. I'm not heavily into formality,' Jack said, smiling.

Michael and Fleur laughed. Howard wondered whether to laugh or not, and by the time he'd made a decision, the moment had passed. Trent guffawed, then realizing he might have overdone the response, turned this into a cough. Edwin and Greg twitched slightly at the corners of their mouths. Alec grinned, as was his way when he thought someone had made a joke but wasn't too sure.

'Jack,' Fleur said. 'Of course. Yes. Well, Jack, I'm sure it will be a very challenging, fulfilling and enjoyable experience for all concerned. We are, of course, all amateurs, and so I do hope you won't expect too much from us. We know we have a lot to learn from you. '

'And I from you,' Jack said, hoping to endear himself to the committee.

'Well, you know, Jack,' Fleur said, 'this is going to be a first as far as we know. Blazing a path into the … well, you know.'

Not sure to where the path would lead, she let the statement hang unfinished and changed the subject. 'Now,' she said, 'Alec has very generously offered to accommodate you at the Central. I know he and Peggy will make sure you're well looked after.'

Fleur shuffled some papers. She had an agenda somewhere. Though she couldn't find it, she knew from her experience of a thousand committee meetings what the first item would be. 'Yes, well, I suppose we'd better start with apologies. I'm afraid

Tony Andover, who was to produce the film, has had to withdraw. I'll read you his letter.'

It took her only a few minutes to find the letter. It had managed to get itself pinned to the minutes of the previous meeting.

'Dear Mrs Robertson,' she read, 'I'm very sorry to have to resign from the committee and take no part in the production of the community movie. Unfortunately, my work as manager of FM 103.5 takes up most of my time. Sorry about this. Yours sincerely, Tony Andover.'

'Huh!' Michael exclaimed. 'A pity he didn't think about that before. We wouldn't have sent him to Cannes if we'd known he was going to do this. Huh! That's what comes of giving young people grants. No gratitude. They expect it as a right and then let you down. So, we don't have a producer.'

Everyone on the committee knew the real reason for Tony's resignation. He obviously had no wish to work with Jack. Fleur couldn't help wondering, not for the first time, if they'd made a bad mistake. The trouble was, Michael had been so determined to have the American.

Jack said, 'No problem. I'll produce. My EP work won't occupy me full-time.' Knowing nothing about the workings of small-town cultural committees, he thought he was putting himself in a strong position for a fee increase.

'Thank you, Jack, that's very generous of you,' Fleur said.

Jack realized he'd made his first big mistake. He'd not been offered extra payment to take on all the work of an actual line producer, and he'd given the impression that he didn't want to be paid.

'Howard has agreed to direct.' Fleur turned to Jack. 'Howard has a lot of experience directing the Coddington St George Players. I'm sure he'll more than fill Tony's shoes.'

Jack remembered Howard's direction of Pride and Prejudice. Alec had also said the man procrastinated about everything. There was, Jack was sure, nothing more likely to create chaos on set than a procrastinating director with only amateur theatre experience. He forced a smile. 'It'll be a real pleasure working with you, Howard,' he said.

'Each of us on the committee has agreed to accept certain responsibilities on the production,' Fleur went on, completely ignoring the agenda, which she still hadn't found. She thought she might have left it on her desk at home. 'Edwin, being a banker, has kindly agreed to be treasurer.'

'Production accountant,' Jack said. 'Excellent. We'll need to work out a budget together, Edwin.'

'If we have any money,' Edwin said, his smile tight-lipped.

'Michael,' Fleur pressed on, 'who as you know is our mayor and an important developer in the town, has offered to provide a production office. He'll also be responsible for obtaining sponsorship and raising whatever money we need.'

'There's a vacant shop at my Paradise Palace shopping plaza,' Michael said. 'We can use that. I'll have whatever you need installed. No doubt you'll want to shoot quite a lot of the movie in the plaza. It'll be a great location.'

'I'm sure it is, Mike,' Jack said, though he felt far from confident about that. He remembered attending the shoot of the pilot of a puppet series for children. He'd had a miniscule investment in the show, believing with some justification that as a lot of children's television had a long shelf life—think *Thomas the Tank Engine*—he couldn't go far wrong. The life-size puppet had been manipulated by one puppeteer lying on his back on a trolley with his arms working the puppet's arms and head, while another puppeteer some distance away behind the camera operated the radio-controlled eyes and mouth. The scene had taken place in a supermarket, of which the manager had been less than co-operative. He'd not only refused to close the place for an hour while they shot the scene, but he'd refused even to shut off the aisle in which the action took place. Consequently, every time the director shouted, 'Action,' and the trolley—pulled on a rope by one of the crew—moved down the aisle, an insistent and persistent shopper, usually a female old-age pensioner with powerful elbows, forced her way into shot to get her can of beans or packet of tea or whatever she could not wait five minutes to obtain. The scene, which on screen lasted ten seconds, had taken six hours to shoot, and by the end of it, no one on the crew was speaking to anyone else. Traumatized, the producer had cancelled the project as puppetry and redesigned it as cell animation, a much safer but more expensive format. Jack's already small investment had suddenly become micro-miniscule, and all he'd been left with had been distribution rights in Luxemburg and Liechtenstein, two territories in which the demand for children's television programming was non-existent. This had been Jack's first and last involvement in productions for children. He'd also sworn never to invest again in any project that had to be shot in a supermarket that wasn't closed to the public. If Michael wanted to shoot in the Paradise Palace shopping plaza, there would have to be security on all the entrances, and it would have to be peopled with extras who would do what they were told.

'And Trent,' Fleur continued, 'will be what I understand is location manager. He'll organize wherever you want to film. And there you are.' She smiled broadly, pleased with the way the meeting was going.

Jack looked at Greg. 'And the Reverend?' he asked. 'Is he just going to pray?'

Michael—but only Michael—roared with laughter. Trent thought Jack was being serious. Howard didn't know what to think. Edwin thought the remark was in bad taste. Fleur knew Jack was joking and tried to show that she was amused and not easily offended.

Greg said, 'If you think it will be necessary, Jack, I'll be happy to, though I'm not sure that there's anything suitable in *The Book of Common Prayer*. A hymn perhaps 'for those in peril on the set'.

It wasn't a bad joke, as Anglican jokes go, and it helped to restore the co-operative mood of the meeting.

'I'll issue a press release for the *Gazette*,' Michael said. 'It's important we get plenty of publicity.'

'Of the right kind,' Edwin muttered cryptically.

'I suppose, Jack,' Fleur said, 'the first thing we need is a script. Michael, that is, the committee, feels that Thistle O'Reilly should be given an opportunity to write it. We've asked her to contact you at the hotel.'

Fleur was far from happy about this, but she knew she mustn't cross Michael if she was ever to get the OAM she so badly wanted. The recommendation would have to come from the mayor's office. She wasn't confident that anyone else of any importance in the town would think of recommending her for the honour. She ground her teeth slightly. The problem with Thistle, she believed, was that she would be incapable of writing a happy family movie that everyone in the community would enjoy. She was convinced that Elsie Woodmarsh would be a far more suitable choice of writer. Whatever she wrote might be bland and boring, but it would never be controversial and cause offence. And, of course, Elsie would be desperately hurt by not being asked. Fleur knew she'd never hear the last of it. It was so difficult to know what to do.

'We'll need to screen test everyone who wants to be in the movie,' Alec interjected, determined not to be overlooked. 'I'll organize that. Perhaps, Michael, you could state a day and time for it in your press release. And we'll need a hall to do the tests in, of course. Greg?'

Greg wasn't happy about the St Jude's Church Hall being used, but he could think of no good reason for refusing. He thought it important that the church should be involved in community activities, especially as the movie was likely to attract young people. He was only too aware that if he made difficulties, Michael would immediately approach the pastor of the Hill Song Evangelical Congregation, whose brand-new building on the outskirts of the town—designed and built by Michael— accommodated five thousand worshippers, most of whom were under thirty, every Sunday for what, in Greg's opinion, was little more than a rock-and-roll sing-song that mentioned Jesus in every other line.

'Of course,' he said. 'I'm sure the hall will be ideal.'

'Excellent.' Fleur smiled broadly. In spite of a few problems, the meeting seemed to be going much better than most of the meetings over which she presided. The last meeting of the Coddington St George branch of the United Nations Association, of which she was, inevitably, president, had ended in the secretary and treasurer coming to blows. It had been almost as bad as the violence at the last annual general meeting of the Central Queensland Cat Protection Society, the secretary of which was still awaiting trial for causing grievous bodily harm to the president.

'Excuse me,' Howard said, 'I may be wrong, and of course, I'll defer to your greater experience, Jack, but isn't it usual to have a script before one does screen tests? I mean, won't people want to audition for specific roles? I'm not sure how they can do that if there are no roles to audition for, if you see what I mean.'

'That's a good point, Howard,' Jack said, 'but in a movie of this kind, I think what we need to do is get a few minutes of video of everyone who wants to be in it, and then you and I will invite people who look right for a part to audition for it. What Alec will do is create a mini spotlight—that's a directory of actors. Most productions,' he went on, 'have a casting director who knows who to cast in the different roles. We don't have that luxury.' He smiled at Alec. 'Thanks for bringing that matter up, Alec.'

Alec bowed his head slightly to acknowledge the thanks and the implied compliment.

'Well,' Fleur said, 'now that we all know what we have to do, I suppose we had better get on with it. I'll leave you, Jack, to arrange meetings and so on with your, er, heads of department.' With considerable relief, she closed the formal part of the meeting.

Jack had said nothing about bringing Hank and Studs over from LA. He decided to wait until something happened, as it surely would, that would give him an excuse for sending for them.

TWELVE

As soon as the meeting ended, Michael phoned Thistle on her mobile. For once he got more than the aggressive, 'I'm busy but if it's important leave a message.'

'Yeah?'

'Thistle, it's Michael. How are you?'

'Okay.'

'I've got news for you. Can we meet for a coffee? The In Place?'

'Give me half an hour.'

'Right.'

Michael went straight to the café, but not because he thought Thistle would be early. He knew she'd be late, at least half an hour. She was late for everything. It was a mystery to him—who was never late—how anyone could always be late for an appointment unless they did it deliberately to show that they didn't care what people thought of them or needed to test their power in some way. He thought it possible that Thistle was late because she was incapable of getting herself organised, but he didn't think this was very likely.

In Howard Grant's case, it was a genuine excuse. He suffered so badly from procrastination that as often as not he didn't turn up at all for a meeting or an appointment. He pottered about his shop, trying to make up his mind which coat to put on, which tie to wear—or whether to wear one at all—whether or not he should take his mobile phone with him, whether to walk, ride his bike or drive his car, and so on. So many minor decisions had to be made that, as often as not, by the time he'd made the final one, there was no point in going anywhere, so he didn't go.

Michael was content to sit in the cafe and pretend to read *The News Gazette* while he worked out in his mind exactly what he intended to say to Thistle. The opportunity had at last arrived that he'd been hoping would eventually present itself—to set Thistle up in a studio apartment he was keeping vacant for the purpose in a small block of flats he owned. The idea had been in his mind for some time, but he knew he'd need an excuse. Thistle was very touchy, easily enraged. If he was to have any chance of making her his mistress, he had to create a situation in which one thing led inevitably to another, and before she fully realised what was happening, they'd be in bed together. The only way he'd be able to create such a situation, he'd decided, would be for him to own the place where she lived so he could innocently call on her to see if everything was okay. She'd feel she had to invite him in for a coffee, and once he was in, events could take their natural course. He didn't think for one moment that she fancied him, but he suspected that a strong sexual attraction wasn't necessarily her only reason for sleeping with a man—or with a woman for that matter. Her reasons would depend, he was sure, on varying circumstances. In his case, once she got used to living in a decent flat, he felt sure she'd want to stay there—at least for a few months, perhaps even a year. Occasional sex with him would be a small price to pay.

The arrangement would be short-lived, he felt sure of that. She wasn't the kind of woman who'd accept the role of kept woman for long. Soon there'd be a fierce quarrel, she'd storm out of the flat, return to her former way of life and that would be the end of it. Michael accepted this. In fact, he wanted it. He had no interest in keeping Thistle indefinitely. He'd soon tire of her, as she would of him. He quickly tired of most things. His relationships—sexual, social and business—were like his buildings: not made to last. He needed to be constantly moving on to greater things. He only stayed with his wife because she was his excuse for not committing himself to another woman. The time to get a divorce would be when he met a glamorous society woman who could become a trophy wife to enhance his position and perform as an elegant hostess.

Once clear in his mind what he'd say to Thistle when she arrived, he opened *The News Gazette* to read his column, 'From the Mayor's Parlour'. The self-promotion was blatant, but if he didn't blow his own trumpet, no one else would.

The headline read: 'Coddington St George to Have Community Movie'. The article, written by Michael but sub-edited by the paper's senior reporter, an elderly man who could spell and knew the difference between a verb and a noun, was as follows:

'Well friends, the community movie I suggested to the Cultural Coordinating Committee is on its way to becoming a reality. The producer I found in Hollywood for our project, Jack Wilcon, has accepted the position. He'll be staying at the Central. Jack is the president of International Community Movie Productions Inc. and a highly regarded and experienced producer. A scriptwriter, director and other key crew members will be appointed this week. I will be keeping a firm eye on the project to make sure that everything is as it should be. As I always say, making a movie is like building a house—it needs careful planning if things aren't to go wrong.

'Our movie will cost the ratepayers just a few thousand dollars, no more. I shall be contributing to the budget, and I know most local businesses will also. What we need more than money, though, is your active participation, as cast or crew. There will be something for everyone to do.

'There will be a screen test for everyone interested in auditioning for a role, large or small, on Saturday in the St Jude's Church Hall at 10 am. Come as you are. We'll give you something to read before the camera.

'See you there.'

If that didn't get him elected to the shire council, he thought, nothing would.

Only an hour and five minutes later, Thistle left her rented room, which looked as if it had been ransacked by a posse of secret-service agents looking for a microchip with the nation's nuclear missile launch code on it, and strolled to the In Place.

Michael looked up and smiled as she entered the cafe.

She pecked him on the cheek, sat down at the gingham-clothed table and lit a cigarette, as usual ignoring the no-smoking signs.

'It's a lovely day,' Michael said. 'Let's have our coffee in the courtyard.' He wanted to avoid the inevitable confrontation with the proprietor if they stayed inside.

'Suit yourself.'

They stood up, and in a gesture of defiance—Thistle knew that the proprietor of the cafe was standing at the Espresso machine watching her—she dropped the cigarette onto the floor and ground it out with the heel of her shoe.

When they'd settled in the courtyard and the proprietor had taken their order—after heavily banging a large glass ash tray on the table, Michael said, 'The committee has agreed you can write the script of the movie. I've told the producer. Jack Wilcon. He's at the hotel. Expecting you.'

'Bless you, Michael.' Thistle smiled and patted his hand, giving it a gentle stroke as she did so.

'There's just one thing. Well, two really.'

Thistle narrowed her eyes, immediately suspicious. She didn't respond well to suggestions of a creative nature. 'They are?'

'If possible—but only if it's not a problem—can you have a major role in it for Trent Frobisher?'

'That wanker! Have you seen him act? He's wood, Michael. One hundred percent timber. Jesus! Did you see him as D'Arcy in *Pride and Prejudice*?'

'I was fortunately able to avoid exposure to that production.'

'What's the other thing?'

'We need to get sponsors for the movie. People who'll contribute a few dollars. I thought I'd put the hard word on the tenants of the shopping plaza. I need to be able to tell them that their shops will appear in the film. So, could you write a few scenes set in the plaza? Nothing big. Just so the camera can sort of pan around. I think that's the expression.'

'I'll think about it, Michael,' she said. 'If the story requires it.'

'Quite.'

Thistle liked to begin by being cooperative. Only when her creativity took hold did she insist that there could be no outside influences or interference in what she wrote. Then she became stubborn and, as the poetry producer of ABC Radio Rockhampton had discovered, somewhat abusive.

'It's a major project, love,' Michael said, coming gently but firmly to the point. 'You'll need peace and quiet—a decent environment in which to write. And hold meetings with the director.'

'Tony Andover? He's nice.'

Michael decided to say nothing yet about Tony's decision. 'You know that block of flats at the end of River Lane?'

Thistle nodded.

'I own it. A studio apartment—one large room with an en suite and a small kitchenette—has suddenly become vacant. The fellow lost his job and moved away. It would be ideal for you.'

Thistle's eyes opened wide, revealing black dots of pupils.

Michael guessed she'd had a joint or two already. 'Just for the duration of the movie.' It was essential, Michael knew, that Thistle shouldn't think he was suggesting any kind of permanent arrangement. He had to proceed very carefully.

'How long will that be?'

'Six weeks, two months at the most. We'll need you during the shoot in case we need to make changes for any reason. A movie scriptwriter,' he added quickly, 'is rather like an architect of a building project.'

'What kind of reasons?'

'Bad weather. An actor falling ill. Problems with a particular location.'

Thistle nodded. 'I guess so.' She could accept this since no suggestion had been made that something she'd written might not be good enough. 'What am I going to do for money?' she demanded.

Michael sighed inwardly. All was well. She'd accepted the accommodation offer. 'There's a budget for a writer.'

'How much?'

'Oh, several thousand.' There was no such budget for a writer—or for anyone except Jack. Michael intended to provide Thistle's fee himself. At this stage, however, he didn't want her to know this.

'Sounds good. When do I start?'

'As soon as you've had a chat with the producer. Jack Wilcon.'

'What's he like?'

'American. If the weather was warmer he'd be wearing a Hawaiian shirt, Bahama shorts below the knee and a baseball cap backwards.'

'Shit!' Thistle laughed. 'I can't fucking wait.'

'You'll get on with him all right. He's very experienced.'

'I hope I'm not expected to sleep with him.'

'Over my dead body,' Michael said.

For one long moment, Michael and Thistle looked into one another's eyes. Nothing was said, but everything was communicated.

'I'll be off then.' She stood up, kissed Michael—this time briefly on the mouth—and left the cafe.

So far so good, Michael thought. Thistle would move into River Lane Lodge within a couple of days.

***

Jack was just coming out of the shower when Thistle knocked on his door. As soon as he'd arrived in Coddington St George, Alec had taken him to the committee meeting. He'd had no time to wash or unpack.

'Coming!' he called, thinking it was probably room service bringing the iced water he'd optimistically ordered. He opened the door.

'Hi, I'm Thistle O'Reilly,' she said.

139

Jack saw before him a tall, too-slim, red-haired young women dressed in a thin, almost transparent, black dress that finished its journey ten centimetres above the knee. She wore black-net stockings with only a few ladders and holes in them, and scuffed, black, flat-heeled shoes. Dark purple lipstick glistened on her lips, and eye-liner accentuated her eyes. She had large, black, pear-drop earrings hanging from her ears almost to her shoulders.

Thistle saw a large, fat, bald man, naked except for a too-small towel around his waist. She thought she also saw a great deal of body hair and wobbly breasts but couldn't be sure as she'd omitted to put in her contact lenses. Jack was mercifully little more than a blur.

'Come in! Come in!' he exclaimed, trying to sound pleased. 'I've heard so much about you.'

Suffering from jet lag and with most of the bones in his body aching from having been forced into strange positions by the cramped conditions on board Trans Pacific Air's no-frills or leg-room elderly 747, Jack had no idea who Thistle was or what she wanted. He assumed, though, she was something to do with the movie and that he ought to make some effort.

Thistle followed him into the room. Suspicious of all men and especially of men like Jack Wilcon, she was quite sure he'd never heard anything about her except her name. Her ego was vast but not of intercontinental extent.

'Forgive the mess,' Jack said. 'I'm still unpacking. You won't mind if I carry on. Find a chair and sit down.' He resumed his unpacking.

'I'm the writer for your movie,' she said.

'Well, that's just great!' Jack said. 'I guess we might need a writer.'

He didn't ask her if she'd written for the movies before. That wasn't important. In any case, as he liked to say, 'The past is just history'. Most of the writers on the movies he'd been involved with had been cut-price, non-union, first-time writers. And they'd never written for the movies again. The experience had been too traumatic.

'I've already got an idea,' Thistle said. 'It's called *The Countryman*'. She'd dreamed this up during the short walk to the hotel. When her mind worked, it worked fast.

'I love it already,' Jack enthused. 'It's new. It's vibrant. It's catchy.' Swaying slightly from tiredness, he opened another case, took out two pairs of loud socks and an even higher-volume tie and put them into a drawer.

'It's the story of a young dairy farmer ...' Thistle continued, taking into account Michael's request, but Jack interrupted.

'Milkmaids,' he said. 'I can see them now. Gorgeous broads in low-cut peasant blouses, their blonde heads against the flanks of steaming cows as they squirt milk from the full udders. Fantastic symbolism.'

Thistle ignored the interruption. 'He can't make a living on his farm,' she said, 'so he goes to the city. But he can't get a job. He's got no skills.'

'Except milking, 'Jack said, his mind full of udders and other mammaries.

Thistle took a deep breath. 'He has to live rough,' she said. 'Sleeping on the streets. Eating what he can find in the bins behind supermarkets.'

'And then he meets this fashion model,' Jack said, sitting down suddenly on the edge of the bed. All he wanted to do was lie down and close his eyes, but he felt he ought to maintain his producer's persona a little longer, just in case this appalling young woman had important contacts in the town. 'She falls for

141

him and they become lovers,' he said, so tired that his speech was now barely intelligible. 'She introduces him to her agent, who gets him work. He becomes a famous male model. *Brokeback Mountain* meets *Pretty Woman*. It's got everything, Briar.'

'Thistle.'

'Right, Thistle. This is the best pitch I've ever heard. I'm going to make you famous. Trust me.'

Thistle decided not to bother trying to tell Jack how she intended ending her film. The man was obviously a fuckwit, she thought. He wasn't worth wasting time on.

'Thank you for your time, Jack,' she said. 'I know how busy you must be.'

'Great to meet you.' He grinned. 'I'm really looking forward to working with you.' He tried to stand up to walk her to the door but gave up when half bent. The movement was beyond him. 'You take care now. Writers are precious.' As she closed the door behind her, he said under his breath, 'Fucking writers. Nothing but fucking trouble.'

But at the back of his mind, a thought slowly formed. There could be something in Thistle's concept. What he needed to do was think of a way of making it his own. Perhaps after a sleep, something would occur to him. He lay back on the bed, and within twenty seconds, his snores reverberated through the thin walls of the hotel.

THiRTeen

Thistle phoned Michael while she walked out of the hotel courtyard. 'Jack Wilcon,' she said, 'is a fucking idiot. If you think I'm going to work with him, forget it.'

For Michael, this was a completely unexpected development. It'd never occurred to him that Thistle would react to Jack in this way. Then he remembered that Tony Andover had also withdrawn from the project. It was as if there was something about Jack that young people couldn't stand.

'What did he say that's upset you?'

'I'm not fucking upset. I just don't want to waste my time with idiots. Sorry, Michael. I'm surprised Tony's agreed to work with him.'

'He hasn't. He's resigned from the project.' There was no point, he thought, in keeping this information back. She'd find out soon enough and then be furious with him for not telling her before.

'Well, I'm not fucking surprised. See you.' She rang off.

Michael's plans for Thistle were ruined. He decided to advertise immediately for a tenant for the apartment in River Lane Lodge. He was just losing money leaving it vacant. He cursed Jack Wilcon and wondered whether he might have made a terrible mistake. He could understand Thistle taking against the man—she was hypercritical of nearly everyone—but Tony Andover was mildness itself, self-effacing and always anxious to please. *Ah well*, he thought, *there's nothing I can do about the situation except watch out for future problems.*

Thistle phoned Tony at the radio station. She had to wait while he finished reading aloud the credits from the CD he'd just played. He listed everyone named—vocalist, every member of the band, recording engineer, publicist, business manager—the list seemed endless. At last he answered the phone.

'Coddington St George Community Radio. Tony Andover here. Sorry to keep you waiting. I hope you're enjoying the program.'

'Hi, Tony. It's Thistle. Can we meet?'

'Sure. I'm off air in half an hour. Ern will be reading *The News Gazette* for a couple of hours.'

'Let's meet at Howard's place.' She suggested this because the coffee and muffins would be free, she'd be able to smoke without argument, and Howard ought to know what was going on.

'Have you met this fuckwit, Jack Wilcon?' she said later as she walked into Between the Leaves.

'Good morning, Howard,' Howard said. 'And how are you today? I'm very well, thank you, Thistle. And how are you?'

'There's no need to be sarcastic. I'm pissed off.'

'Really? I'd never have known. Flat white, is it?'

'Oh, Howard, you're really a dear.' She sat down at his desk and lit a cigarette, dropping the still burning match into his waste paper basket. Fortunately, he'd recently emptied it. Now he busied himself at the coffee machine.

'To answer your question, Thistle, yes, I have met him.'

'And?'

'Hard to say. He's not my type of man, but then I'm not sure if any Hollywood producer would be. All that hype and false bonhomie.'

'I'm not going to write the movie. And Tony's off it, too. Have they asked you to direct?'

'Mm,' Howard said.

'Are you going to?'

'I honestly don't know. I don't really want to. I'm a theatre person, as you know. But I don't want to let the Committee down. If I don't direct, who will?'

Thistle laughed. 'Fucking Jack Wilcon himself, no doubt. Jesus, it'll be a disaster.'

'There's always Alec Grimshaw.'

'You're joking. You are, aren't you?'

'At least he knows something about film.'

'A movie is more than pictures of weasels, stoats, ferrets and skunks, Howard, and you know it.'

'Trent?'

'Well, he'll be less awful behind the camera than in front of it. What does it matter anyway? The movie's going to be a complete fucking disaster.'

'Why have you taken against Wilcon?'

'If you'd been there you'd be feeling the same. I was trying to outline a perfectly reasonable storyline for the film, and he just kept on interrupting with the most absurd suggestions. I'm telling you, Howard, the man's a complete fucking idiot. I can't believe he's a successful producer.'

'A lot of rubbish comes out of Hollywood, Thistle. I often think the movies must attract a certain kind of man.'

Howard handed Thistle her coffee and two muffins on a plate. She ate hungrily. It was her first meal of the day. Michael hadn't ordered food for her. He'd had other things on his mind.

'If Tony's pulled out of the project,' she said, chewing slowly, 'why don't we make a movie ourselves? Show the town that we don't need some Hollywood hotshot. I've got an idea for something worthwhile—not what I told Jack Wilcon. All we'll need will be Tony's talent as a director, and a camera. I reckon I can learn how to use one. You could do the producer's job, whatever that is.'

'I've got a business to run, Thistle.'

'So what. This can be the production office. You wouldn't have to come on the shoot.'

Howard went into dithering mode, and his mind walked around all the possible reasons for and against his becoming involved as a producer. Thistle left him to his thoughts while she searched the shelves for something to read. She settled on Anais Nin's *Delta of Venus*. She'd read it before and been very influenced by it. Like Nin, she lived off her earnings from erotica. She wanted to read the book again.

When Tony came into the shop half an hour later, she brought him up to date with her thinking. They'd known one another for years and been mildly friendly, but never close. Thistle thought he was sweet and gentle and clever. He thought she was clever and frightening. There'd never been anything romantic or sexual between them and there never would be. Tony was one of those seemingly asexual men who go through life quite happily making lots of friends but never entering into any kind of serious relationships. He was what used to be called 'a confirmed bachelor'. People who thought he was gay were mistaken.

'Why did you resign from the movie, Tony?' Howard said, as he made yet another flat white. For Tony, as for Thistle, Between the Leaves was the coffee and muffins equivalent of a soup kitchen.

'I don't like him,' Tony said. 'I think he's a fraud. He's nothing more than a small-time distributor of R-rated rubbish for cable. He's never been involved in a decent movie in his entire career.'

'Then why did the committee appoint him?' Thistle demanded.

'Michael Milosovic gets what Michael Milosovic wants, Thistle,' Howard said. 'You know that. He owns half this town. He's got Fleur Robertson eating out of his hand. God knows why. She must want something from him. Or be in his debt.'

'Yes, but why did Michael want him?'

'Birds of a feather, perhaps. They'd talk money, not art,' Tony suggested.

Howard said, 'Only you Tony, Edwin Bland and Greg Small voted against him. Michael, Alec Grimshaw and Trent Frobisher voted for him. This gave Michael the numbers because Fleur had the casting vote.'

'You abstained,' Tony said accusingly.

'Yes, and I'm sorry about that. I didn't actually mean to, but the vote was taken so quickly, it was all over before I could get my hand up.'

'One of these days, darling,' Thistle said, 'you're going to really miss the bus.'

'Anyway,' Tony said, 'what's done is done. 'I'm just sorry to have lost a chance of working with Sven Ingersson.'

'You met him!' Thistle exclaimed.

'I spent most of my time with him. He was interested in coming here and making the community movie.'

147

'But he's a genius,' Thistle said. 'I adore his films.'

'Me too.'

Howard said, 'I feel really bad about letting you down, you know, not getting my vote in. As you say, Tony, why don't we make our own movie? We don't need a professional. You can direct, Tony.'

'I'd prefer to work with Sven. I'm sure he'll come just for his fare and keep.'

'Tony, if Sven Ingersson's films are anything to go by,' Howard said, 'he's a disturbed man. Probably bipolar. Certainly a depressive. I've been in amateur theatre long enough to know that to direct amateurs one needs to be patient, calm, unstressed and always friendly and supportive to them. Demand too much and they walk. Most of them won't put up with what professional actors have to cope with from directors. You've got the perfect temperament and local knowledge to direct a community movie.'

'Maybe, but I'd be better used shooting and editing the film.'

'How good is your equipment?' Howard asked.

'I made the short on my mobile. To make something decent, I ought to have at least a cheap Handycam, some filters, a reflector, lights. Oh, and Final Cut Pro—a proper editing programme, not the basic one that comes with Windows.'

'I'll be happy to put in some money.'

'That's fantastic of you, Howard, but, I mean, are you sure you can afford it?' Tony asked.

The shop hadn't had a single customer that morning. Only Thistle knew about Howard's side-line.

'I couldn't pick up the whole tab,' Howard said, 'but I reckon Edwin Bland would contribute something. If only to spite Milosovic.' He was thoughtful for a few moments, then he said,

'Go and talk to Edwin at the building society. I assume he knows you. You go to St Jude's, don't you?'

'Yeah. I'm in the choir. He's a churchwarden. Chairman of the parish council.'

'There you are, then. If I put in a thousand, I'm sure Edwin will put in at least the same. Would that be enough?'

'Almost. I'll have to price everything.'

'Are you feeling all right, Howard?' Thistle asked. 'This rush of blood to the head isn't like you. All these decisions.'

Howard smiled weakly. He was quite surprised himself by his decisiveness. Probably his guilt at letting his young friends down had spurred him into action.

'I've been working for months on an idea for a radio feature,' Thistle said. 'It'll be even better as a film. It's a winner as a community project, Tony. I promise you. And Edwin will love it. And,' she added, planting an essential seed, 'it won't cost much, and with Sven Ingersson directing we'd get international distribution.'

***

Late that afternoon, Jack awoke after a restless sleep. Because of his apnoea he stopped breathing at least ten times a minute while he slept. As soon as his brain registered this fact, it sent frantic messages to his lungs. En route, these conjured up assorted nightmares, causing Jack to cry out in horror and panic as he gasped for breath before subsiding into comparative calm for another half minute or so. When staying in motels, neighbouring guests banging on his door or walls further interrupted his sleep. Fortunately, at this time of the day the other rooms at the Central were vacant.

He lay for a few moments, trying to remember where he was. Looking around the room, he slowly realized that he was in a motel, then where it was and then why he was in it. The images of his repeating nightmare faded: him, lost in a strange city—a weird, science-fiction kind of place like Dubai—and desperate to find a toilet. When he eventually found one it was either occupied or so filthy as to be unusable. He then had to hurry on through deserted streets, down dark, narrow lanes that seemed to lead nowhere, thinking of nothing except that he was totally lost and always would be, and he was desperate to relieve himself. There was never anyone he could ask for help. He was always completely alone.

Now, as soon as he was wide awake, it occurred to him, with surprise, that he seemed to have the beginnings of an erection, such a rare event that he thought he ought to make use of it. Not wanting to risk the inevitable erotic failure in a face-to-face encounter, he reached for one of the magazines conveniently provided by Alec and turned to the classifieds. He was not disappointed. Several pages listed advertisements for phone sex. The one that caught his eye contained heavily photo-shopped images of a blonde and a brunette, both in their thirties with substantial, upwardly forced breasts, adequately revealed. The expressions on their mouths and in their eyes implied that there was nothing he could possibly want to hear that they wouldn't provide and then some. Jack dialled the mobile number and was immediately connected to Gloria, aka Ethel Smart. With considerable skill, she kept Jack on the line for twenty-four minutes and forty-three seconds and could have kept him enthralled even longer if he hadn't realized that the beginning of the erection had, as usual, amounted to nothing worth having and had been a false alarm.

Within minutes of Jack putting down the phone, Howard Grant arrived at Golden Frond Aged Care Facility. Thistle, inspired by her re-reading of *The Delta of Venus*, had invented two more characters for Muriel and Ethel to add to their repertoire: Olivia and Jessica would be twin sisters who offered stimulation to clients requiring a double act. Howard had arrived to deliver the script in person.

Muriel and Ethel welcomed him warmly, plied him with tea and cake, and then, barely controlling their giggles, told them about their latest client.

'I thought, Howard,' Muriel said, hiding her mouth with her hand, rather like a Japanese housewife, 'that we'd heard everything, but this gentleman, well, really, such an imagination. The things he said!'

'Bizarre, Howard, isn't the word,' Ethel added. 'We could hardly keep ourselves from laughing.'

'I know we were being a bit naughty,' Muriel went on, 'but we couldn't resist trying to find out something about him. Our mobiles keep a record of all received calls, of course.'

'And,' Ethel said, unable to control her excitement, 'the number is a local one. What do you say to that?'

'Would you like to hear him?' Muriel asked. 'He really is a hoot. As you know, we tape everything—just to be on the safe side in case, well … you know.'

Howard wasn't at all sure that he wanted to listen to the fantasies of a frustrated Coddington St George citizen, but he didn't want to disappoint the two ladies—they were both excellent earners—so he accepted the tape and left them to practice being Olivia and her sister, Jessica, offering double delights.

Back in his car he put the tape into his cassette player and turned it on. To his surprise—and then to his intense pleasure—the voice was American. More than that; it was Jack Wilcon's. Howard listened. He smiled. Then he burst out laughing. He assumed that Jack must have seen Gloria and Miranda's advertisement in a magazine, offering uninhibited, no-topic-too-torrid, erotic talk. Jack had then not only chosen them to stimulate him but he'd also required them to follow his own imagination and explore his fetishes—at two-dollars-twenty per minute plus GST, plus network charge, plus three dollars a minute for requiring deviation from their scripts. Howard thought Jack the most profitable and entertaining client the ladies had had for a long time.

FOURTEEN

Jack had only just recovered from his far-from-satisfactory phone call to Gloria aka Ethel, when a brisk rat-a-tat sounded at his door.

'Just a minute,' he called, hoping that Thistle hadn't changed her mind and returned with further script suggestions.

Sitting up too suddenly, he waited for the room to stop circling, then got to his feet and padded slowly to the door. It was secured on the chain, so he opened it just enough to peer out and see a tiny, very old woman, with small round spectacles, a tight bun of hair and a dress, with frills around the neck and sleeves, that reached down to her ankles. She looked, he thought, like a fairy tale granny who would turn into a wolf at any minute.

'Yes?' he said, looking her up and down.

'Mr Wilcon, I'm Elsie Woodmarsh, president of the Coddington St George Writers' Circle and Ladies' Literary Society.'`

'Of course you are,' Jack said, thinking that the safest thing to say.

'I've come on behalf of the members to offer our services as scriptwriters.'

'All of you? I mean, how many members are there?"

'Seven. We intend to produce a collaborative work.'

'Sounds promising,' Jack said. Seven writers would be so occupied quarrelling with one another that nothing usable would be produced and he'd be spared much contact with them.

'Why don't you go over to the hotel?' he said. 'I'll join you for a drink in the bar in ten minutes.'

Elsie thought it definitely preferable to have a meeting in the hotel than in this repulsive-looking man's room. 'Very well,' she said, 'and please don't be late. I have another appointment.' She turned on her heel and marched away.

Jack thought she was, in spite of—or perhaps because of—her small size, a most formidable woman.

When, fifteen minutes later, he joined her in the Snuggery she was on her second sweet sherry. He ordered a double bourbon on ice for himself, then joined her at the table in the bay window which overlooked the town's main street.

'Now, Mr Wilcon,' she said as he lowered himself into a chair.

'Jack, please.' False charm oozed out of him almost like drops of perspiration.

'We have decided, Mr Wilcon,' she continued firmly, 'that the concept of a community movie is a good one, but it has to be developed in the proper way.'

'Of course,' Jack said. 'My experience—'

'I know nothing about your experience, Mr Wilcon,' she interrupted, 'and I don't want to know anything. I know everything, as do the members of the Writers' Circle, about this community.'

'Making a movie involves—'

'I know perfectly well what making a movie involves. What you don't know is what making a movie in this community will involve.'

Jack decided to shut up and let the old bag talk. He knew he wouldn't get anywhere with someone who showed such blatant hostility.

She signalled to Peggy Grimshaw, who tended the bar, to bring her another sherry. Rumour had it that she drank a bottle a day of the cheapest Australian that the supermarket carried, and that her doctor had suggested she donate her kidneys to medical science. They'd already be preserved in alcohol.

Elsie had been a widow for most of her adult life. Her husband had died a hero's death in the Vietnam War. She'd never remarried, never even considered any kind of romantic relationship. Her husband's memory was sacred to her. With only a captain's widow's pension, she'd continued to live in the family home in Coddington St George after her parents' death, writing wholesome verse for the cheaper kind of greeting card and religious magazines aimed at an elderly, working-class readership. From her writing she earned barely enough to feed her cats. She wrote poems in praise of Christmas and Easter for *The News Gazette*—for which she received ten dollars each. She made jams, marmalades, relishes, pickles and chutneys that she sold from a stall at the gate of her house every Saturday morning. Financially, she just about got by. She'd been president of the Writers' Circle since its inception in 1976. As the only published member of the group—all female and even older than she was— the members accepted her opinions as literary law. Her eulogies for departing friends were always in verse and a feature of many local funerals.

The gentleness of her literary efforts was not, however, mirrored by her public behaviour. Elsie was known, not very affectionately, by the checkout girls in the supermarket as 'Elbows' Woodmarsh, the allusion being to her skill in getting to the red light when the special of the day was announced over the store's loudspeaker. In short, Elsie had realized early on in her widowhood that if she didn't stand up for herself, if she didn't push herself forward, no one else would, and she'd be taken advantage of by shopkeepers, tradesmen, public servants—everyone, in fact, she encountered. Jack Wilcon, whom she detested on sight, didn't stand a chance. Neither did Fleur Robertson, whom Elsie had long ago relegated to the ranks of spineless social climbers. Elsie didn't attempt to climb any kind of ladder in the town. She didn't need to. Her family had lived in Coddington St George for over two hundred years. Although she had no money to spare—her house frequently shed part of its fabric, and all the land surrounding it had long been sold off to the Frobishers—Elsie Woodmarsh was 'squattocracy'. This was what mattered.

'A community movie,' she said, '—I prefer the term "film" but I'll accept "movie" for the time being—must involve as many members of the community as possible.'

'Oh, I do so ag—'

'Furthermore, it must be about the community. We have an opportunity as never before to depict the life of this town in all its variety. A great deal happens here, Mr Wilcon. There are all kinds of community activities. And there are organisations that make great contributions to our lives: the police; the fire service; the St John's Ambulance; the CWA; the Lions; Rotarians; the schools' P & Cs; the churches; the many different clubs and societies, and of course, the local businesses.'

'I'm sure these are all very worthy,' Jack began, 'but—'

'We also have left a few fine buildings dating back to Colonial times. They need to feature in the film before, like everything else, they are torn down by the mayor in his pursuit of immortality.'

'It will be difficult to include—'

'Nonsense. It will just be a question of listing the most important features and activities in the town: the annual picnic races; the Coddington St George Show; the Country Music Festival, to name but three, and of course, the annual football and cricket matches between Coddington St George and neighbouring towns, school sports days and concerts. Major events, Mr Wilcon, involving hundreds, thousands of people.'

'A movie needs plenty of action, Miss Woodmarsh.'

'I can assure you, Mr Wilcon, that there is plenty of action at these events. Now ...' She took a folder out of her shopping bag. 'Here is a synopsis of the film. We've called it *A Town Like Ours,* and it will consist of a series of short films, linked together by a narration in verse.'

'I don't think—'

'You're probably not aware of one of the greatest poems in the English language, Mr Wilcon. Dylan Thomas's *Under Milk Wood,* a poem about a Welsh village.'

'No, unfortunately, I—'

'And I suppose you don't even know *Our Town,* the fine play by your compatriot, the playwright, Thornton Wilder.'

'I've heard of that, of course.'

He hadn't, and Elsie knew he hadn't.

'Our movie,' she said, '*A Town Like Ours* must become part of our artistic heritage. We shall talk again.' She delicately licked the dregs of her sherry, stood up and walked steadily and with great dignity out of the bar.

Jack sat silently for a few moments. He'd never met anyone like Elsie Woodmarsh, and he hoped he'd never meet anyone like her again. At the same time, he suspected that she knew what she was talking about. The concept was a good one, and it would certainly be appropriate for his own future as the guru of community movie making. Everything would depend on the content of each sequence. The movie would need plenty of action to maintain viewers' interest. This meant that there would have to be a car chase, he thought. Every movie he'd ever been involved with had at least one car chase. Most of them had several.

The problem was that *A Town Like Ours* could turn out to be bigger than *Ben Hur* and *The Ten Commandments* combined. No way could he produce such a monstrosity without help. He'd have to risk sending for Hank and Studs.

Jack was due to have a working dinner with Michael and Alec in a couple of hours' time. He decided to bite the bullet with Michael then. In an odd sort of way, he thought, Elsie Woodmarsh had provided the ammunition he needed.

***

While Elsie brow-beat Jack, Tony and Thistle sat in Edwin's office at the building society trying to convince him that he personally, or the building society, should sponsor a rival community movie.

'The point is, Edwin,' Tony said, 'it will be really sad if all the town can produce is the kind of thing that Jack Wilcon has been involved in. Frankly, I don't know why Mr Milosovic supported his application.'

'It probably didn't occur to him to google Wilcon on the internet,' Edwin said. 'It's not the sort of thing that Michael would do. And the demo DVD Wilcon provided was very impressive.'

'I don't believe Wilcon had anything to do with those films,' Tony said. 'The DVD could be a montage of bits and pieces from shorts and student films. The credits at the end could all be fake. How would anyone here know?'

'He provided references,' Edwin said.

'Were they contacted?'

Edwin knew they hadn't been. Desperate to get the movie into production before the shire council election, Michael had forced the committee to make a quick decision. Edwin was sufficiently experienced in business to know that references often meant nothing. Sometimes they meant even worse than nothing. They could mean that the applicant's employer so badly wants to get rid of an employee that they praise him or her to the skies. Unless provable dishonesty is involved, there can be no comeback.

'What are you suggesting, Tony?'

Tony looked at Thistle. The alternative movie was her idea, and he felt that she should pitch it.

'I think a community movie should be about something important,' she said.

'Such as?'

'Homelessness for a start. It's not just a national problem. It's local as well.'

'You're thinking of Herbie,' Edwin said.

'Yes. Everybody in the town knows him, but how many people know anything about him? About what it's really like to be him? He sleeps rough every night, winter and summer. He eats other people's garbage. If he's not well, he can't go to a doctor or buy anything from a chemist. I'm probably the only friend he has, and I'm not much of one. I want to help Tony make *A Day in the Life of a Homeless Man*. We can do a theme like justice.'

Tony said, 'I think it's an awesome idea, Edwin. I'd really love to make it. Thistle will write any narration and get Herbie to talk to the camera. We just need a little money to buy some decent equipment.'

'How much?'

'Howard's offered a thousand. Another thousand should do it,' Tony said.

'Don't you two need to be paid?' Edwin asked.

They both shook their heads.

'We get by, don't we, Tone?' Thistle smiled, and the warmth and radiance of her smile explained why so many people put up with her coarseness and temperament. 'Anyway, we're both a fucking sight better off than Herbie.'

Edwin winced at the seven-letter version of the hated four-letter word. A deeply religious man, he never swore, not even an occasional 'bloody' as he knew it meant 'by our lady'. Even the common 'struth' was short for 'by God's truth, and 'Jiminy Cricket' and similar JC expressions were American euphemisms for Jesus Christ and unacceptable to him. But Thistle's heart, he believed, was in the right place. She might be a foul-mouthed Magdalene on drugs, but she had her own moral code, odd though it was to people like him. He suspected that like many serious artists, she did what she believed she had to do in order to survive. If that meant living off other people's generosity and bending a few rules from time to time, it was not for him to be judgmental. No banker, he knew, could afford to be.

'I need to think about it,' he said. He wanted to talk to the Reverend Greg Small. 'There are a few issues involved that I need to think through. Come and see me tomorrow. I appreciate your coming to me.' He stood and escorted Tony and Thistle to the door of his office. They shook hands.

Once outside and walking along the High Street to report to Howard at Between the Leaves, Tony said, 'I reckon he'll do it, just to get even with Milosovic.'

'That's not very fucking Christian,' Thistle said.

Tony grinned. 'The Rev will help him square his conscience. I often think Greg should be the banker and Edwin the priest.'

'Why do you go to church, Tony? You don't believe in all that garbage, do you?'

'It's not a question of belief. In his autobiography, Graham Greene wrote about his conversion to the Catholic Church. He said that he converted not because he believed in all the doctrine and so on, but because the priest who instructed him was a totally good man. It made him think that it's not what we believe that's important, it's the way we behave.'

'There are times, Tone,' Thistle said, 'not often but very occasionally, when I think I could fall in love with you.' She squeezed his arm. 'Can you lend me a few dollars for a packet of fags?'

FiFTeen

Three separate meetings took place simultaneously early that evening: Jack had a drink with Michael and Alec in Michael's office; Edwin and Greg had a coffee with Howard at Between the Leaves; and Fleur had a long discussion in her kitchen with her cat, Tibbs, an elderly, grey, fur-shedding Persian of unpredictable temper, with whiskers that looked as if they were nicotine-stained but surely couldn't possibly be. The meetings were of equal importance. The outcome of each would have a significant effect on Jack's future hopes and dreams; on Michael and Edwin's electoral chances; and, depending on which of them was elected to the shire council, on the future make-up of the planning committee. This, in turn, could result in the re-zoning of agricultural land for high-density housing development, the further destruction of small-town high streets by the provision of large suburban shopping centres modelled on the Paradise Plaza basic design; and the total destruction of the character of a town's central business district by the erection of high-rise office buildings, already planned in one of Michael's many exercise books and known in his fantasy world as the Milosovic Buildings.

Michael knew that if he could get himself elected, he would have enough support from other councillors to be appointed chairman of the planning committee. Two of these councillors were estate agents; one was the proprietor of the shire's largest hardware store and timber yard; one was the county manager of the Acme Mortgage and Finance Corporation, and one was his wife's sister's husband, who operated a demolition and earth-moving business that had shares in a company that supplied ready-to-pour concrete.

There was very little that Michael was not prepared to do to ensure he was elected. He knew, as did Edwin Bland, that as few as a hundred votes would determine the outcome of the election and that the number of citizens who voted would be very small, probably less than twenty percent of the Coddington St George ward, even though voting was technically compulsory. Apathy among the electorate would, as always, put the future of local government in the hands of a minority of the population.

Michael could do very little to wholly ensure his election. The blatant buying of votes was out of the question. His powers as mayor were very limited, and street lighting, sewage, parking meters, potholes and similar matters, though important, were not vote-getters. Michael needed something that would get a great deal of free publicity, involve a large number of satisfied members of the community, provide a distraction from the everyday cares of living under cost-cutting state and federal governments and of coping with failing health and education services. A community movie, for which he could claim most of the credit, was, he thought, a godsend. It would cost him little or nothing financially; he could beat it up in his newspaper column, and he could ensure that the premiere didn't take place until after the election, by which time it would be no more than a very small footnote in the town's cultural history.

Jack, having been advised by Alec of Michael's political ambitions, knew when he proposed Elsie's concept that he was backing a winner.

'What I want to do,' Jack said, 'and why I've developed this concept, is to create a movie that will show this wonderful little town in the best possible way.'

Jack's short-term memory performed miracles when he was plagiarizing someone else's ideas.

'It must be about the community,' he went on. 'We have an opportunity to depict the life of this town in all its variety. A great deal happens here. There are all kinds of community activities. And there are organisations that make great contributions to your lives: the police, the fire service, the St John's Ambulance, the schools, the churches, the many different clubs and societies, and of course, the local businesses.

'I've talked to a number of people since I arrived,' he continued, 'and they've suggested the most important features and activities in the town: the picnic races, the annual football and cricket matches between Coddington St George and ... er ... other places, school sports days and concerts. Major events, Michael, involving hundreds, thousands of people.'

Michael sat open-mouthed as Jack continued with his pitch. A movie like this would get him the votes of many people who would otherwise vote for Edwin Bland. He had no doubt now that appointing Jack to produce the movie had been a brilliant decision. Accordingly, he needed to make it absolutely clear to the electorate that appointing Jack had been his idea. In his mind, he began planning his next column for *The News Gazette*.

'I've called my movie *A Town Like Ours*,' Jack continued, 'and it'll consist of a series of short films linked together by a narration in verse. A kind of visual version of that great er ... Australian poem, *Under Milk Wood*.'

Goodness! Alec thought. *The man's an intellectual. Who'd have thought it?*

'Our movie,' Jack said, 'will become part of Coddington St George's artistic heritage.' He sat back, exhausted by the mental effort of remembering Elsie's words.

'This is a fantastic idea, Jack,' Michael said. 'Break open a bottle of bubbly, Alec. Your best. Not just fizzy fake Chardonnay.'

'Right!' Alec said, and went off to get a bottle of French champagne and three glasses.

'Who will you get to write the script? I suppose we could offer it to Thistle O'Reilly,' Michael said.

'Sure, but I was thinking of the Ladies' Literary Society—a collaborative effort.'

Seven votes were worth more than one, even though the one would be Thistle's—not that Michael felt confident that he could rely on such an unpredictable girl. 'Brilliant,' he said. 'I'm sure they'll leap at the chance.'

'Good,' Jack said. 'I'll contact the president. What's her name? Elsie something.'

'Elsie Woodmarsh. Funny old bird. Be careful with her, Jack. Her bite's worse than her bark—and that's saying something.' He laughed hugely at his witticism. He hadn't felt so optimistic about anything for months.

Alec returned with an already opened bottle and glasses, and as he poured the slightly flat champagne—Peggy had been celebrating the birth of a baby with a friend—Jack said, 'There is just one problem. I have the solution, but it needs your approval.'

'And that is?' Michael asked.

'It'll be a much bigger movie in every way than what I first thought we'd make. I'm going to need more professional help.'

For a moment, Alec saw his role as DOP disappearing, but Jack was not that stupid. 'Not in the cinematography department, Alec,' he said quickly. 'No, no. I'm going to need an experienced director. I'll be stuck in the production office all the time, making sure that hundreds of people are where they ought to be when they ought to be. I'm also going to need an experienced first AD.'

'That is?' Michael asked.

'Assistant director. He's a sort of floor manager,' Jack said. 'He runs the shoot, freeing up the director to concentrate on the creative side of things.'

'I suppose,' Michael said, 'we could advertise for such people. There must be plenty of them looking for work.'

'Oh, yes,' Jack said. 'The trouble is, such people are very expensive. You'd be looking at a thousand a day.'

'Each?

'Oh, yes.'

'Bloody hell,' Michael said. 'And how long would you need them for?'

'Five or six weeks.'

Michael did a quick calculation. 'That's about eighty thousand bucks.'

'I'm afraid so.' Jack smiled. 'Fortunately, I can help you avoid such an expense. Two close associates of mine, both very experienced men, have often said they'd be willing to work for nothing on a not-for-profit community movie. They'd need just their airfares, food and accommodation.'

Jack had thought very carefully about how much to ask for. On the one hand, he wanted to get as much cash for himself as he could—insurance against something going wrong and the movie never being finished—but on the other, he knew that the more he asked for the less likely he was to get it.

'An extra ten grand should cover it,' he said, thinking mainly of the airfares—which were already paid for anyway—and assuming that Alec would pick up the tab for the food and accommodation.

Michael thought the same. 'I'll put it to the committee this evening,' he said. 'Tell me about your associates.'

Jack provided a totally fictitious account of Hank and Studs' achievements, even giving Studs a safety certificate from the State of California entitling him to work with explosives and pyrotechnic effects. He thought that a burning building with a dramatic fire service rescue would make a good scene.

'I don't think I'll have much problem persuading the committee to approve their employment, Jack,' Michael said. 'What you've suggested for our movie is superb. It couldn't be better, could it, Alec?'

'Absolutely,' Alec said. 'I'm really excited about being part of it, Jack.'

In fact, Michael was far from confident that he'd get more expenditure through the committee. Edwin and Greg would definitely oppose it, and if Howard didn't abstain again, so would he. The votes for would be his, Alec's and Trent's. There'd be a tie. Although he didn't hear what Fleur was, even then, saying to Tibbs, he suspected that she was far from happy about Jack's appointment. Tony's resignation had clearly worried her. Had he been within earshot of Fleur's kitchen he would've had his fears confirmed.

'I should never have voted to employ Jack Wilcon, Tibbsy,' Fleur was saying as she chopped a piece of stewing steak for a meat pie. 'He's a horrible man; I'm sure of it. I can tell from his eyes. And his greasy skin. There's something not right about him. Tony disliked him intensely, and Tony is a very sensible young man. It's awful that he's resigned. Oh, Tibbsy, what am

I to do? The committee will be equally divided as it was last time. Alec and Trent will vote whichever way Michael wants them to. If Howard abstains again, the silly man, he's such a ditherer, then Michael's motions will be carried whatever they are. If Howard doesn't abstain, and if he votes with Edwin and Greg, then I'll have to vote for the motion if I'm not to make an enemy of Michael. Oh, Tibbsy, do you think I should resign from the committee before things start to go wrong? Well?'

'Meow!'

Fleur assumed from this response that she should not resign. It wouldn't do her position as a community leader any good not to be actively involved in what promised to be the biggest cultural event in the town's history.

'I must just hope that Michael doesn't want to do anything that might turn out to be controversial,' she said and dropped a piece of steak onto the floor for Tibbs.

Not three kilometres away, Michael also counted the numbers. He suspected that Howard would not abstain again. Edwin would've got at him. This meant that Fleur's vote would be crucial. He'd looked up the rule book for council subcommittees to make sure that the same rules applied to subcommittees as applied to full council meetings. It was there in black and white: the chairperson of each committee was entitled to a vote as a member of the committee. This was his or her deliberative vote. If the voting tied, the chair could exercise a casting vote as well. By convention, this should be to vote against any motion that involved any kind of change. It was possible, he thought, that one day Fleur would risk his wrath by opposing him. Her conscience might overcome her lust for the OAM that he'd intimated was in his gift. She might even decide that Edwin was equally likely to put her name forward to the honours committee. Michael thought that in spite of Edwin

168

being a pathetic, God-bothering dullard, he had to face the fact that the man was not only well-known in the community but also respected. His recommendation would count, and Fleur would know this.

Michael felt convinced that he needed to do something—he wasn't yet sure what—to ensure that the committee, due to meet in an hour's time, would provide the airfares for Jack's associates. As for their board and lodging, he'd talk to Alec about it. There wouldn't be a problem with Alec. He'd realize that *A Town Like Ours* depended on his and Peggy's co-operation.

***

At Between the Leaves, Edwin had just finished outlining Tony and Thistle's project to the vicar.

'I know we should support it, Greg,' he concluded, 'but I'm not at all sure how to go about it. I mean, for us, me in particular in view of the election, to sponsor a rival production to the Cultural Coordinating Committee's wouldn't look good at all. I'd be accused of being petty and treacherous, supporting the project for political reasons.'

Howard nodded. 'An added complication is that I think sooner or later we should resign from the committee. As long as Fleur casts her chair's votes for whatever Michael proposes, our votes will be worthless. He'll have the numbers for whatever he wants to do whether we approve or not. And if the project fails, then we'll go down with him. We'll just be wasting our time and our reputations by staying on the committee. If we resign and promptly sponsor another production, that could really muddy the waters.'

'I'm sure you're right, Howard,' Edwin said. 'It's not a simple situation at all. And in fact, there's another complication. You see the society'—by which he meant his employer—'has a budget to sponsor local community and cultural events. If I

169

don't approve an application from Tony, my boss is going to want to know why. And I have no good reason for making such a decision. In fact, even if Tony doesn't apply to us, I ought to get the society attached to the project somehow. I mean, think of it; a documentary by two talented, local young people about a homeless man! It's the perfect project for a building society to support. What excuse can I possibly give for not getting the PR and advertising benefits for the society from being a major sponsor? I can hardly say that I was worried about losing a few votes in the shire council election.'

'In my opinion,' Greg said, speaking very slowly—he needed to choose his words with care—'we need to make it clear to the community that Edwin's support has nothing to do with the election. He needs to be in a position that makes it almost impossible for him not to be a sponsor. I'm wondering, therefore, whether it might be a good idea for the film to be a St Jude's fundraiser for the Church Roof Repair Fund. The subject matter is perfect. The Anglican Church is very concerned nationally with the problem of homelessness and operates a number of hostels. As chairman of the parish council, Edwin would be duty bound to ask his boss to agree to the society being a sponsor. And having the church involved should remove any political bias. Although my congregation is small, the church is still important for weddings and funerals, so there's hardly anyone in the town who is opposed to keeping it in decent repair.'

Edwin brightened, and he beamed at Greg. 'I think that's a splendid suggestion. Don't you, Howard?'

Howard smiled. 'I'm not sure how Thistle will respond to being involved in a fundraiser for a church,' he said, then added, ruefully, 'and there's always the possibility that you may want to exercise some control over the finished product. I can assure you that she'll not take kindly to the slightest suggestion of censorship. In fact, I wouldn't want to be in the room, even in the town if you dared to suggest—for example—that Herbie watch his language or that any remarks of a sexual nature should be edited out.'

'Oh dear,' Greg said. 'I hadn't thought of that. I would have to have some say in what was in the film.'

'He's right,' Edwin agreed. 'And so would I if the society were a sponsor.'

'Perhaps I can persuade her to be reasonable,' Howard said. 'I'm not optimistic, but I can at least try.' An idea occurred to him. 'It might help if we could pay them both a small honorarium. They are both as poor as church mice.'

'And St Jude's mice are very poor,' Greg said, laughing, 'but I have a better idea. I'm often asked if I know anyone locally who makes wedding videos. As far as I know, there isn't anyone. The nearest is in Rockhampton. Perhaps Tony and Thistle could have a little business. I'll be happy to recommend them.'

And so they agreed that the film would be a St Jude's fundraiser, sponsored by Between the Leaves and the building society, but it wouldn't be announced or go into production until after the election. In the meantime, Tony and Thistle would be told that sponsorship would be forthcoming and they should do whatever research and pre-production was necessary. Furthermore, Greg would do his best to put wedding photography commissions their way. A wedding was actually scheduled for the coming Saturday. Greg agreed to have a word with the bride and groom.

sixteen

The agenda for the community movie subcommittee was short. It listed apologies—none—minutes of the last meeting—agreed to without discussion—reports—only one, Michael's. He reported that Jack Wilcon was comfortably installed at the Central, thanks to the generosity of Alec and Peggy Grimshaw. He proposed a vote of thanks to them, which was carried by acclamation. The agenda listed only two other items: Any Other Business and Date of the Next Meeting. For a reason that soon become obvious, Michael deferred raising the subject of Jack's associates until Any Other Business. He then began by describing *A Town Like Ours*, referring, as Jack had done, to Dylan Thomas's immortal poem. Fleur, Alec and Trent were enthusiastic.

Fleur, in particular, thought it wonderful that Jack was going to invite Elsie and her friends to write the script. She even wondered if she might have misjudged him. *Perhaps*, she thought, *it's just his manner that is so off-putting, and really he's a very clever and capable man.*

Trent said, 'It'll make Mackay's pageant look a bit ordinary. I'm sure my father will be interested in providing extra finance if it's needed.'

That was Michael's cue to introduce Jack's condition: he needed professional help to manage such a large-scale production and wanted to bring over from LA his associates, Hank Shorn and Studs Collini. Michael added quickly that they would work for nothing; they would need only their airfares and board and lodging.

Howard, Edwin and Greg exchanged glances, knowing that the concept of *A Town Like Ours* was difficult to find fault with, apart from its size. This meant they had to be very careful how they opposed what promised to be a winner with the community. Unfortunately, it would get Michael votes that he otherwise wouldn't have—those of everyone in the movie for a start—and if one added up all the people who'd be involved in the many events, there could be several thousand of them. Edwin felt convinced that, for him, the movie would be a disaster unless he could think of a way of preventing it from going into production.

'There's no doubt, madam chair,' he said, 'that this is a wonderful concept, and I don't want in any way to suggest otherwise. However, it's hugely ambitious, and the more ambitious a project is, the more that can go wrong.'

'So what?' Michael demanded. 'What if one or two of the scenes don't work all that well? We just cut them.'

'The people in them would be very upset,' Trent said, anxious lest a scene he was in ended up on the cutting room floor or—to be more up to date—in the computer's recycling bin.

'Quite,' Michael seized on this statement. 'And that's why it's so important that Jack has the professional help he needs.'

'That's all very well,' Howard argued, 'but we're supposed to be producing a community movie, not a semi-professional one. The whole idea is to use only members of the community. I was opposed to employing even a professional producer, you may remember. It was only because Mackay employed a professional director for their pageant that I withdrew my objection.'

At this point in the discussion, the reverend's mobile phone rang with the first few bars of *Oh God Our Help in Ages Past*. 'Sorry,' he said, standing and moving away from the table. 'I'm afraid being a clergyman is rather like being a doctor in a way— one is always on call.' He took the call, listened gravely, said, 'I'm on my way,' and rang off, then he turned to the meeting. 'I must leave you. One of my parishioners has had a heart attack. She's in the cottage hospital and is asking for me. So sorry.' He hurried out of the room.

Fleur said, 'We'd better postpone further discussion until another time.'

'Nonsense,' Michael snapped. 'We've got a quorum. We can't postpone a major decision just because some old biddy has probably eaten too much and got indigestion. Jack needs a quick decision so he can email his associates and get them here as soon as possible.'

'I'm sure Greg will agree with me that we shouldn't rush into employing more professionals,' Howard said, surprising everyone by his assertiveness. 'He's very in touch with the community. His advice will be invaluable.'

Michael snorted. 'His advice will be irrelevant. He's got a congregation you can get into one of the school buses. Ha! Probably into a taxi. Let's not waste time. I have the support of Trent and Alec. That gives me the numbers, even if there's a tie, because Fleur agrees with me, don't you, Fleur?'

'Well, I don't quite know what to say. I mean, it is a very good idea, but as Howard said, having more professionals will change everything, won't it?'

'I haven't got time to argue,' Michael said. 'I've got a council meeting at seven. It's bloody obvious what we have to do so let's do it. I move that the motion be put.'

'Seconded,' said Alec.

'Oh, very well.' Fleur knew when she was beaten. It was not permissible to have any discussion about whether the motion should be put or not. As soon as someone proposed that the motion be put and it was seconded, it had to be put. Accordingly, there could be no further discussion about Jack's requirements.

'The motion is that the motion be put,' she said. 'Those in favour?'

Up went Michael, Alec and Trent's hands.

'Those against.'

Up went Howard and Edwin's.

Fleur sighed. Unless she exercised her deliberative vote against the motion, it would be carried. If she did exercise it, then there'd be a tie. She would then have to exercise her casting vote. To preserve the status quo, she would have to vote against the motion. This would mean that twice in one evening she'd be defying Michael. It was all so complicated. And it wasn't just the 'Big Thing' that was at stake—her long-wished-for OAM. She owed Michael, as mayor, her position on a number of committees. *Defy people like Michael*, she thought, *and you end up in the wilderness.* She knew that politicians who appointed people to boards and committees could just as easily unappoint them if they rocked their particular boats.

'The motion that the motion be put is carried,' she said. 'We'll now vote for that motion. Oh, there's isn't a motion yet.'

'There is now,' Michael exclaimed. 'The motion is that Jack Wilcon's associates Hank Shorn and Studs Collini be provided with airfares and board and lodging in return for their professional contributions to the community movie.'

'Seconded,' Alec called out firmly.

Fleur took the vote. The result was the same as for the previous motion.

'The motion is carried,' Fleur said. 'Is there any other business?'

There wasn't, so the date of the next meeting was quickly decided.

Michael went into his mayoral chamber well satisfied with the situation so far. Trent and Alec went to The Central Hotel, and Edwin and Howard went to Between the Leaves. Thistle had minded it for Howard until closing time, then she'd stayed on to make herself coffee and hot muffins. She looked up from her book as they walked in.

'Hi! Elsie Woodmarsh came in,' she said, relinquishing Howard's chair. 'She wanted to know if the committee had approved her proposal to Jack Wilcon.'

'Her proposal?' Howard said.

Edwin's eyes opened wide.

'Yeah, apparently she had a meeting with him today. Suggested a collaborative effort called *A Town Like Ours* with her fucking writers' circle. Jesus! Serve the bastard right if he goes along with it.'

'That's very interesting, Thistle,' Howard said. 'Very interesting indeed.'

'What about our project?' Thistle demanded, squeezing out her cigarette and throwing the still-smouldering butt into the waste paper basket. 'Tony's and mine?'

'You've got nothing to worry about. You have my word,' Howard said. 'We just want to work out how we're going to arrange our support.'

'There are one or two things we need to think about,' Edwin explained. 'Don't worry, Thistle. Tony will have the money he needs for new equipment and Sven Ingersson's fares. Just keep our involvement under your hat until we say you can tell people.'

'Fucking fantastic,' Thistle said, smiling broadly. She put her hands behind her head and shook out her mane of red hair.

If only, Edwin thought, *she was less confrontational and coarse, she'd be an extraordinarily attractive young woman.* He wondered, not for the first time, why it was that some people who had so much going for them managed to wreck their lives, and often the lives of people with whom they became involved.

Howard said, 'Edwin and I need to talk, Thistle, so would you mind ...'

She walked to the door. 'I can take a fucking hint. Ciao.'

She'd hardly shut the shop door when it opened and Greg entered.

'How was your parishioner?' Edwin asked.

'At the Coddington St George cottage hospital,' Greg said, his face pale with anger, 'there was no parishioner who'd had a heart attack, no admissions of any kind for two days and none of the patients has given C of E as their religion. Only two have given any religion. Both are Muslims.'

'The bastard!' Howard said. 'That was Milosovic's doing. And Jack Wilcon lied about the movie idea. It wasn't his. It was Elsie Woodmarsh's. And Michael got Greg out of the meeting so he could be sure of the numbers. Yes?'

'He forced the vote, certainly,' Edwin said. 'But how can you know he was responsible for the phone call? Did you recognize the voice, Greg?'

'Not at the time. It was a woman's. Accented.'

'His wife?' Howard suggested.

'Of course it was,' Edwin snapped. 'He controls her. She'd do whatever he told her to do. The man is a total control freak and, to say the very least, seriously ethically challenged. If you want my opinion, we need to get off that committee before the proverbial hits the fan. If we get bad publicity, so be it. But better that than to be associated with what's going on. I now think, in view of developments, that it could be dangerous to leave our resignations until it's too late.'

'What about your electoral chances?' Howard asked.

Edwin shrugged. 'Oh, I'm not all that set on getting onto the shire council. To be honest, the only reason I allowed my name to be put forward as a candidate was to give Milosovic a run for his money.'

'Well,' Howard said, 'we now have evidence that Wilcon is a liar. And what do we know about these associates of his? Nothing. They could be all kinds of trouble.'

'If we do resign,' Greg said quietly, 'we'd need to word our letters of resignation very carefully. We should make our reasons clear without actually mentioning names or situations.' He looked at the ceiling, as if seeking inspiration from on high, and then said, 'How about something like this? "I hereby regretfully tender my resignation from the Coddington St George Cultural Committee and the movie subcommittee with immediate effect. I feel that the composition of the committees is such that my views are of no value."'

'I like it,' Howard said. 'It says it all.'

'I agree,' Edwin said. 'Fleur won't like it, of course.'

'If Fleur wants to stay in Michael's pocket, that's her business,' Howard retorted.

'I suppose so,' Edwin said sadly. 'But she means well, you know. The trouble is, of course, that by withdrawing from the fray, we're giving the forces of darkness a free hand.'

'Oh, I don't know,' Howard observed with a wry smile, 'perhaps we're making it easier for them to sow the seeds of their own destruction. Flat whites, both of you?'

seventeen

While Howard, Edwin and Greg planned their resignation from the movie subcommittee, Jack had an early dinner in the Central Hotel's bistro. He bolted down a half-inch-thick steak covered with mushroom cream sauce, accompanied by a bowl of Peggy's locally famous chips, cooked so they'd absorbed the maximum amount of the cheap oil that she used and re-used until it was as black and thick as drained sump oil. With the meal, he drank three schooners of draught XXXX, a beer that only Queenslanders have the courage to drink, finishing off with a large brandy. He then panted to his room to phone Maybelle in LA.

'Hi, babe. Well, is it all happening or is it all happening? I've got them eating out of my hand, doll.'

'That's great, honey.'

'Whatever Jack wants, Jack gets. Babe, this is the breakthrough. I'm telling you, Maybelle, it's going to be the greatest community movie ever made. Trust me.'

'I'm so glad, honey.'

'Tell Hank and Studs to get their asses over here pronto. They're on the team. You've got money to pay for basic economy, but see if you can find something cheaper. Email me their flight number and ETA, and I'll meet the plane.'

'Right you are, honey. What are they going to be doing?'

'Hank will have to direct. Studs can be his first AD and edit. We've got a DOP.'

'Any money for them, Jack?'

'No, but full board and keep. Here with me at the Central. It's basic but comfortable.'

'They know there's no money, do they, Jack?'

'Yeah, they know.'

'That's good.' A pause. 'Jack?'

'Yeah?'

'You can have your own way, you said.'

'Sure can, babe.'

'Can you find a role for the daughter of a friend of mine?'

'What's she done?' he asked.

'Oh, you know. Just corporate so far. She wants to cross over.'

'That might not be so easy, babe. I mean this is a community movie, right? And there should really be only local actors in it.'

'You owe me, Jack.' He heard steel in Maybelle's voice. 'And she's a real looker. I'll email you a photo.'

Jack decided to do what he could. It occurred to him that Michael wouldn't be averse to having an attractive, young American actress around. And if there was a chance of getting something on Michael that could be used to put pressure on him if problems arose with money, Jack thought the girl might be useful.

'I'll do what I can, babe. But I can't promise anything. It won't be my decision.'

'I understand that, but you'll be doing me a great favour giving this gal a chance. She's a real doll, honey. I mean, I'm telling you, a body to die for. And she can act.'

181

'She'll have to pay her own fare. Work just for her keep.'

'Not a problem.'

'What's her name?'

Maybelle remained silent for a moment or two, thinking hard. 'Roma Sheraton,' she said at last. 'That's right. Roma Sheraton. She's twenty-four. You won't regret giving her a chance.'

'Okay. Tell her to phone me.' He belched. 'Sorry. Ate too much. Ciao.' He put the phone down.

Maybelle felt a little disappointed that he hadn't bothered to ask how she was, but she hadn't really expected it. He couldn't help being what he was. *None of us can,* she thought. She was just very happy, though, that he'd agreed to give her niece, Mary Lou, a chance.

Sue Anne—Maybelle's elder sister—was a lonely, simple-minded woman who, desperate for affection, had found it impossible to say 'No', or to prevent the consequences of saying 'Yes'. She'd had five children by five different men before she turned twenty-four. None of the men had stayed with her much longer than it had taken to get her pregnant. Mary Lou—now to be called Roma Sheraton—was the eldest child, and Sue Anne, realizing how physically appealing the child was, had decided that if she could only get the girl into films or on television, her family's financial future would be secure. She'd made every possible sacrifice to pay for the girl to have dancing and singing lessons, and had entered her for every talent and beauty contest. Although the girl had never won anything important, she had attracted attention, and being the centre of attention became the most important thing in her life. Inevitably, when a porno producer had spotted her in her late teens and offered her a thousand dollars a session, she'd promptly accepted.

The producer wasn't surprised. He found it easy to lure young women into the industry. Porno actresses are very much the centre of attention. They fill the screen, and the camera hardly ever leaves them. No woman, he knew, receives more concentrated attention from so many men than a performing porno actress. It also seemed crazy, many of them thought, not to do for money what they were doing most nights for free. In Mary Lou's case, the offer seemed even more attractive because the man with whom she'd been asked to perform, Rock Hard, was a considerate sort of guy and had unusually promising proportions. The producer told Mary Lou, whose screen name was to be Kandy Kute, that the experience would just be a lot of fun.

Although she'd at first been nervous in front of the camera, Rock's skilful ministrations had soon made her forget where she was and that there were other people in the room. The director had instructed her to look as if she was enjoying it, and this hadn't been difficult to do. She had enjoyed it, and before long she was doing several sessions a week and earning enough money to send some to her mother. Unlike those porno actors who feared being recognized by friends or relations, she had no relations except her mother and siblings, and soon her only friends were all in 'the industry'. She found she'd joined a subculture whose members looked out for one another. Mary Lou felt that she belonged.

The downside to the work, which Mary Lou thought weird and rather sad, was that so much pornography showed men dominating or demeaning women one way or another. For so many people, she thought, sex seemed to be more about power than pleasure. But she assumed that that was the way things were and that she just had to accept it as being a part of life.

A number of the producers were pigs, she thought, for whom the girls were just so much female flesh, and some of the men were appalling, but Mary Lou knew that if she was to stay in the industry and make good, comparatively easy money, she had to take the rough with the smooth. Many of the girls took drugs to keep going, but because Mary Lou was sufficiently in demand to be able to pick and choose who she worked with and what she did, she needed only a little crack from time to time to suppress the worst memories.

She'd also developed enough confidence to plan with her latest boyfriend—also a porno actor—to soon have her own website from which customers would be able to download videos and view her daily sexcam. This was where the real money could be made, she knew. And there should also be opportunities to do some high-priced escorting. One of the girls she'd once worked with charged five hundred dollars an hour. With some of her wealthier business clients she travelled—as their social secretaries or personal assistants—to the world's most exciting and fashionable resorts.

Mary Lou aka Kandy Kute now aka Roma Sheraton was sure that porno and escorting were a much better life than working in a factory, shop, hotel or cafe. And yet, like so many of her colleagues, especially the girls, she still aspired to fame in the mainstream cinema. Very few porno stars ever managed to 'cross over', but a few did, usually with the help of plastic surgery and a name change. When, therefore, she received a call from her aunt telling her about Jack's project in Australia, she was instantly interested.

***

As a result of his huge, fatty meal, Jack had indigestion, which kept him awake for a couple of hours when he went to bed. He wasn't in a good mood, therefore, when at two o'clock in the morning, a phone call from Los Angeles—where it was six o'clock in the evening—awakened him. Roma, whose formal schooling had been fragmentary, was not aware of time zones.

'Yeah?' Jack said.

'Is that Jack Wilcon?'

'Speaking.'

'Hi, Jack. I'm Roma Sheraton.'

Jack vaguely remembered Maybelle telling him about a girl with a name like a hotel. 'Well, hi, Roma. How are you?'

'Fine, Jack. Just fine.'

'Great. I was just thinking about you. So, what's new, Roma?'

'I was told to phone you. That you'd know all about me.'

'Sure, sure. It's great to hear from you. So, Roma, you're ready for your next role?'

'I sure am, Jack.'

'It's a very exciting concept, Roma. This is going to be the big one for all of us. You're going to be famous. Trust me.'

'I do hope so. When will you want me to come?'

'I'm working on the schedule as we speak. Get on the next plane.'

'Sure will, Jack. I know this is my big chance. I've never done anything like this before.'

'I'd better have your latest photo, Roma,' he said. 'Can you email it to me?'   'Sure can, Jack. Should I send you my flight details when I have them?'

'What? Oh, yeah.' This meant she'd have to be met. A job for Trent. 'You do that, doll,' he said. 'Maybelle will organise everything at your end.'

'Thanks, Jack. I'm really grateful for this opportunity. You won't regret it.'

'I'm sure I won't. Well, great to talk to you. And see you soon. Ciao, babe.' He rang off.

185

Jack realized that Roma Sheraton was almost certainly not the girl's real name. She'd chosen it as her screen identity because it was instantly recognizable and easy to remember. Like Paris Hilton. He hoped she was as attractive.

He turned over and went back to sleep.

***

The morning after Roma's phone call, Jack met with the triumvirate in charge of the production—Michael, Alec and Trent—over breakfast.

Jack opened the meeting. 'I've made a decision. I'm determined that nothing will be too good for this movie.'

'That's good to hear, Jack,' Michael mumbled, his mouth full of toast.

'I've engaged an experienced American actress to play the female lead,' Jack announced proudly. 'She's young. She's blonde. She's beautiful, she's long-legged with tits and an ass you can only dream about. And all with the innocent looks of the eternal girl next door.'

Michael and Trent received this news with pleasure: Trent because he'd been promised the role of the male lead in a scene hastily written by Jack just before he came into breakfast—the part of a local farmer's son who falls in love with an American woman who has come to teach in the town under an exchange programme. Perhaps, Trent fantasized, the American might even find him attractive in real life. He imagined the headlines in the celebrity magazines: American Star to Marry Farmer. 'I Want Trent's Child' Says American TV Star.

'What's her name?' he suddenly remembered to ask.

'Roma Sheraton,' Jack said. 'She's got a huge following back home. Daytime soap.'

Trent thought, *Roma and Trent to wed*. Then, *Trent at Birth of Roma's Child*. There would be massive coverage of everything they did and everywhere they went. He grinned with enthusiasm. 'It sounds great to me!'

'What's she going to cost?' Michael demanded. 'Don't think I'm against having a girl like that around, but we do have to watch the expenditure.'

'Her agent has agreed she can work for nothing,' Jack said. 'She wants to get into community movies.'

'Really?' Only Michael saw the absurdity of this explanation. It appeared obvious to him that the girl had to be Jack's mistress or a relation. 'It might not be easy to justify having an American actress in a Coddington St George community movie,' he said. 'I know we have the numbers on the committee, but questions might be asked in the press.'

As always, Jack was ready with an only partly true explanation. 'American cable buyers won't touch anything that hasn't got an American lead in it,' he said. 'It was either get a girl or a guy. In any case, we'll have to dub the movie in American English as well. You Australians are too hard to understand.'

'There might be a problem with the Actors and Media Alliance, Michael,' Trent said. 'They don't like jobs going to foreign actors.'

'To hell with the union,' Michael said. 'This is a not-for-profit venture. We'll give any profits to appropriate charities.'

'Net profits, Mike,' Jack said firmly. 'Make that clear whenever you talk about profits. Net. Not gross.'

Only a Hollywood accountant could explain how a movie that cost fifty million to make and grossed five hundred million at the box office could actually show a net loss.

'When is she coming?' Trent asked.

'I think she's got one more day on her current production,' Jack said, his fantasy circuits humming away. 'It's not the lead, but there's talk about her being up for Best Supporting Actress at The Golden Globes.'

Jack's lies were often so well-crafted that they convinced even experienced sceptics. Sometimes they even convinced himself. At the time of utterance, they were difficult to disprove.

'Well,' Michael said, 'it all sounds very exciting. Roma Sheraton? Have I heard that name?'

'There's been a lot about her in the trades,' Jack said, meaning the magazines about the film and TV industries. 'I think she might even have been on the cover of Vogue.'

Trent sat with his mouth open. *And I'm going to act with this girl*, he thought. *I'm made. My career is made.* 'What's my character, Jack?' he asked.

'We'll give that some thought when she arrives.' Jack visualised Trent milking a cow, while Roma, in hot pants and cleavage to the fore, stood by the cow's panting flanks.

Alec wondered if Roma could be a campaigner for wild-life preservation. He could organise a night shoot. There were ferrets in Australia, perhaps even locally. They could have a night shoot and film them killing and eating something.

Jack's cell phone interrupted their various fantasies.

'Yeah?'

It was Maybelle. Hank and Studs were booked on Air Chechnya Flight AC9 to Vladivostok and from there on Flight AC12 to Port Moresby in Papua New Guinea. From there it would be a short hop by QANTAS to Townsville, arriving Saturday at fourteen twenty-five. Possibly.

'Saturday,' Jack said. 'I'd like to meet them at the airport.'

'I'll lend you a car,' Michael said.

'We're doing the screen tests Saturday,' Alec said, alarmed. He was expecting Jack to help him.

'There's nothing to it, Alec,' Jack said. 'Trust me.'

eiGHTeen

When Alec arrived at the St Jude's Church Hall at nine o'clock on Saturday with his camera, he was surprised to find what appeared to be the entire population of the town in the church yard. A queue had formed at the church-hall door, at the front of which stood or sat people with sleeping bags, folding chairs and a range of camping equipment, including a variety of portable BBQs. A heavy aroma of frying bacon, eggs, sausages, steak and onions filled the usually clean and crisp autumn air.

Many of the other members of the queue had suitcases, carrier bags or other containers that, Alec discovered later, contained costumes they intended to wear for their screen tests. Along with the adults, a large number of children had turned up. They ran around the churchyard screaming, fighting, throwing and kicking balls, being sick, and doing number ones and twos wherever and whenever the need took them, usually behind or even in front of a gravestone. A large mausoleum, a monument to a former alderman of great wealth, was clearly being mistaken, not unreasonably in view of the design, for a public toilet.

The spirit of the crowd was at first festive and good-humoured. Everyone felt excited and full of anticipation. The reason for the size of the turn-up had been not only Michael's column but also a half-page public announcement provided free of charge by *The News Gazette*. The paper had also printed an article based on an interview with Jack in which he'd referred to how famous actors of his acquaintance had been discovered in what the industry referred to as 'cattle calls'. These, the reporter had knowingly explained, were screen tests open to anyone interested in turning up. And, he'd added, Jack Wilcon was confident that at least one potential movie star would be discovered. He would make someone famous. Trust him. He implied that Dustin Hoffman and Julia Roberts both owed their careers to his ability to spot talent. Inevitably the invitation to be screen tested had been widely accepted. A photograph of Jack accompanied the article, taken some thirty years or so previously in which he looked like Stephen Spielberg, but not very much.

Only Alec turned up to conduct the tests. Jack had gone to meet Hank and Studs. Michael had gone to Brisbane for a meeting with a syndicate that was putting together the finance for In Transit Villas, a network of retirement villages and nursing homes. They'd been designed by Michael in one of his exercise books, which, incidentally, he was planning to leave to the nation. In Transit Villas promised to be even more profitable than shopping centres, especially as Milosovic Constructions would be the main contractor.

At Jack's suggestion, strongly endorsed by Michael, Trent had bought some trendy clothes, got himself a more fashionable haircut and arranged appropriate publicity. He intended staying at the Brisbane Marriott until Roma's arrival and perhaps even persuading her to spend a day or two with him there. He thought she'd be suitably impressed.

Howard, Edwin and Greg went to Townsville to a concert. They felt they needed stress release from their involvement in Coddington St George's cultural life.

Fleur arrived just after nine and saw the queue stretching out of the churchyard into and all along the High Street, over the bridge across the River Clare and into the first of the many fields of sugar cane. She went home to bed in shock.

Unaware of how the situation was likely to develop, Alec smiled and waved at the long and, as yet, happy queue. 'We'll soon be underway,' he called.

Then he went into the hall, sat down and began to unpack his equipment. He soon discovered, to his consternation, that the battery in the camera was flat. He'd been filming two possums mating most of the night. They'd taken their time and made some rather strange noises that reminded him of some he'd heard elsewhere. He'd put a replacement battery on charge overnight but had left it at the hotel. He hurried home to fetch it, but then found that although he'd plugged it in, he'd unaccountably omitted to turn on the power. He now possessed two flat batteries.

Panicking, he ran from the hotel to the Coddington St George Pharmacy, which had a small photographic department, hoping they'd have a battery for his model Sony in stock. They did not. The only course of action open to him was to buy a new camera and battery. This he did, but the battery for it was not charged and needed at least twelve hours charge before use. Alec didn't have twelve hours. He bought a spare battery for it, put them both on charge, hoping that he'd get an hour out of each by alternating them until the battery for his Sony had enough charge to be usable.

Just before eleven, he had enough power in the battery of his new camera—which he'd yet to learn how to use—to begin the screen tests. By this time the crowd—which now extended over two kilometres beyond the town—had become restive. Two of the children had been taken to the Coddington St George Cottage Hospital to have minor injuries attended to: one had a bruised eye from an accurately thrown, over-done sausage, and the other had a stab wound in the back of the neck from a deftly inserted ballpoint pen.

When Alec arrived at the hall, his 'gaffer'—the St Jude's verger—awaited him impatiently. He'd explained to the verger—who, being concerned about the possible damage to the hall, had offered his services—that 'gaffer' was the technical term for lighting technician. The verger hadn't been even slightly impressed.

'You're two hours late. I've been here since nine. All those people out there. How can you screen test them all?'

'Just call them in one at a time,' Alec said. 'Ask them to stand where I say, and do their piece.'

'But how will we know who's who?' the verger demanded. Frail and over eighty, he'd been christened Zebediah when such names were permissible.

'They can state their name and phone number before they begin, and I'll record it.' At this point, it occurred to Alec that even if he allowed everyone only five minutes, the screen tests of about a thousand or more men, women and children would take over five thousand minutes or eighty hours. 'We'll never get through them all today,' he said. 'I'd better tell half of them to come back tomorrow.'

'Can't do tomorrow,' the verger said. 'Tomorrow is the Sabbath.'

'I can't send them all home,' Alec said. 'They're all keyed up. I think some of them are in costume.'

He was right. Many of them were. Four Mr Spocks from *Star Trek*, complete with fluorescent plastic ears, had turned up, and among the children and teenagers was an almost-complete cast of *Lord of the Rings*, the Harry Potter movies and the latest *Dr Who*. Darth Vader was well represented, as were Batman and Spiderman. The adult men favoured Hercule Poirot, of whom there were five, and the Incredible Hulk. The female characters from *Sex and the City* and *Desperate Housewives* were over-represented by the town's women, all dressed in the sexiest outfits they could stitch together, or in many cases unstitch. One child, who later achieved fame in a government anti-obesity advertisement, was completely covered in a large, cardboard box that was intended to look like the police phone box from *Dr Who*, but which, being undecorated, was obviously the box in which his parents' giant plasma television had been delivered.

Unwisely, many of the townspeople had chosen characters or stars they remembered from their childhoods. Two infirm old ladies, assisted in their movements by wheeled Zimmer frames, were anxious to mimic Judy Garland as Dorothy in *The Wizard of Oz* or perhaps Julie Andrews in *The Sound of Music;* it was difficult to be sure. Several elderly men, determined to show that they had the bodies of Sylvester Stallone as Rocky, stood around flexing their fat.

The pushiest mother drove into the churchyard in a large Toyota 4WD towing a small caravan. Inside the caravan, her eight-year-old daughter, dressed like a Las Vegas pole dancer, waited to perform. Her mother pushed her way to the front of the queue, pulling the sullen child with her. When told she'd have to wait her turn, she attempted to summon assistance by phoning her husband. He was at the Coddington St George sports field watching his twelve-year-old son by a previous marriage or two play rugby. Every time the boy got near a player on the other side who looked like getting the ball, the man shouted, 'Kick him in the groin!' and similar injunctions. Anticipating a call from his wife, he'd turned off his mobile phone.

Seriously worried by the noise coming from the now less-than-orderly queue, Alec went outside and shouted that he was sorry but there were more people than had been expected. Half of them would have to come back on Monday. The noise changed from a low drone of frustration to a roar of anger. Alec tried to explain that there was no way everyone could be tested, not even if they worked all day and into the night. But no one heard him. The noise became even louder. Fists were shaken. Spittle flew. Several children started to cry. Fights broke out as auditionees attempted to force their way to the front.

Alec ran back into the hall to enlist Zebediah's help, but the old man had worked out how to operate the camera and was busy videoing an almost topless girl posing coyly with a well-worn teddy bear. She'd been practicing what she believed to be a provocative pout since the screen test had been announced.

'Zeb, you've got to come out. They won't listen to me. There's going to be a riot,' Alec cried. 'I'll get the blame. They'll hold me responsible.'

Zebediah ignored him. To the girl he said, moving the camera closer, 'Now let's have you leaning forward, my dear.'

'Don't you want me to say anything?' the girl asked.

Zebediah shook his head. 'Not necessary. I can already tell that the camera loves you.'

Realising that a riot was imminent, and that the verger would be of no help, Alec used his mobile phone to contact Sergeant Bordon, who luckily was not on revenue-creation duty in his patrol car. He agreed to come as soon as he finished booking the four drivers who'd accelerated out of the fifty kilometres per hour limit a few metres too soon.

'What you should have done, Alec,' the sergeant said when he'd restored some kind of order and threatened arrests, and most sensible people had gone home, less than impressed by the poor organisation of the movie, 'was invited people to apply in advance for a screen test. Then you would've known how many you had to deal with. You could then have scheduled it so that people didn't have to wait more than half a morning. Like in a doctor's surgery. I just hope this morning is not a foretaste of what we can expect,' the sergeant concluded, and then returned to the police station where his lunch had just been delivered, compliments of Pete's Perfect Pizzas.

Back at the hall, one by one the remaining hopefuls stood in front of the camera, stated their name and phone number and said their pieces. These ranged from soliloquies from Shakespeare, declaimed with vigorous gesticulation and volume, to favourite jokes rendered pointless by poor timing or inappropriate stress, or both.

Inevitably, complaints of favouritism came when Alec cut short pieces that threatened to occupy what was left of the morning—which was very little. Worse still, the father of the teenage girl in whom Zebediah had shown such interest, on discovering what his daughter had been wearing—or not wearing, depending on one's point of view—threatened Alec with physical violence unless he handed over the memory stick from the camera. This, of course, not only held the screen tests that had been shot so far but was also the stick on which further tests would have to be saved. Alec, who abhorred violence, unless watching various members of the family Mustelidae doing what came naturally, pleaded with the parent to be reasonable and promised to get the shots of his daughter deleted.

The girl's father was adamant, however, and took the memory stick away. Alec now had no means of saving anything he shot. He informed what remained of the crowd that owing to a technical problem further screen tests would have to be postponed.

The bubble of euphoria generated by the possibility of appearing in a community movie had been substantially pricked.

nineteen

Jack had a similarly trying morning at the airport. Air Chechnya Flight 24 had arrived at Port Moresby eight hours late. The passengers remained on the plane, denied access to the airport until overdue landing fees had been paid. Refuelling was also denied, as the pilot's credit card had reached its limit in Vladivostok where he'd bought an entire case of duty-free vodka with which to pacify the passengers during the rest of the flight.

When questioned by Jack, one of the Townsville airport's ground staff informed him that he'd be surprised if the plane ever arrived or was heard of again. A knowledgeable man who'd once worked for Balkan Airlines, he further advised Jack that the Antonov 24s dating from 1959, which the airline had acquired cheaply after every other airline in the Soviet Union and later the Russian Federation had given up on them, were known to have major rivet problems that caused the air frame to rattle and even roll in rough weather.

When, three days late, Studs emerged through the arrival gate, he was without his friend and colleague.

'Where's Hank?' Jack demanded as the two men shook hands.

'He passed out just before we landed,' Studs said. 'He's being stretchered out. I guess they'll keep him in some kind of sick bay till he sobers up and can answer the usual damn-fool immigration questions.'

'We could be here all day,' Jack said.

'Yeah. Where can we eat? There was no food on the plane. The refrigeration system wasn't working.'

'There's a cafeteria here. I guess we can get a hamburger.'

'It was the worst flight, Jack,' Studs said, 'I have ever had, and frankly, if I hadn't had enough dope to keep me going, I'd have freaked out.'

'Jesus!' Jack exploded. 'You haven't got drugs on you?'

'Shit, no. I've used up what I brought with me. I'm not a complete fucking idiot, man. No, I've got to go to Sydney to see about supplies. A man I met in a bar in LA has a contact in a place called King's Cross. Know it?'

Jack didn't know it. 'If Maybelle had known there was free booze on that airline, she'd have put you on a different one. She knows what Hank is like.'

The cafeteria didn't serve hamburgers, so Jack and Studs had to be content with sandwiches. They sat over them and cup after cup of coffee until late afternoon when Hank emerged from immigration. He could hardly walk, so Jack and Studs half carried him to the car and poured him into the back. Jack drove back to Coddington St George with the unconscious Hank. Studs caught a plane to Sydney, promising to be in Coddington in good time for the shoot.

When Jack arrived back at the Central, he discovered a message for him from Elsie Woodmarsh. She required to see him urgently and would be in the Snuggery at seven pm. She trusted that he'd be on time. Jack couldn't think of anyone he wanted to see less, but he had a quick shower and change of clothes, left Hank to sleep off what even for him had been an excessive intake of alcohol, and only a few minutes after seven pm, he approached Elsie in the Snuggery.

'And how are you today, Edwina?' he asked, trying to give the impression he was pleased to see her.

'It's Elsie, and in any case it's Miss Woodmarsh to you. Sit down, Mr Wilcon.'

Jack sat.

'I met Mr Milosovic in the street today. He stopped to inform me that you're employing an American actress for the movie.'

'We have been extremely fortunate, Miss Woodmarsh, in being able to obtain the services of—'

'Nonsense. A community movie such as we're planning does not require the services of professional actors, and certainly not one imported from America. You realize, of course, that having a young woman in some kind of leading role will require my team to undo all the work we've done today, work I may say that is of the highest quality.'

'I'm afraid that's the way of the movie business,' Jack said, forcing a smile. 'Changed circumstances require other changes.'

'You'll be telling me next that a film that begins as *David Copperfield* can end as *Oliver Twist*.'

To this, Jack could think of no useful response, so he just said, 'Miss Woodmarsh, the writer is the servant of the film, not the film the servant of the writer.'

'I've never heard such balderdash,' Elsie said.

'I can assure you that is a fact.'

And Jack indeed could think of many examples of just this kind of situation. It was, he'd once been told, why some novelists refused to allow their works to be turned into movies. Minor roles were often enlarged to meet the requirements of an actor's ego, thereby completely changing the emphasis of the original work: male characters were turned into female characters and vice versa to meet the producer's contractual obligations; locations were frequently changed because of cost factors. Endless reasons existed for making drastic changes to movie scripts throughout a production, from concept to final cut.

'So, you're prepared to further waste my time and that of my team. May I ask how you propose to give this … this American actress a major role in a film that does not have any major roles? The concept, in case you've forgotten it, is that our community movie will consist of a series of linked short stories, each story being set in a different local location.'

'Perhaps,' Jack said, 'Roma … that's the name of the actress, Roma Sheraton … Perhaps Roma could provide the linking narrative.'

'Don't be absurd,' Elsie snapped.

'Then I'm sure you and your team will come up with something.' With both hands on the table, Jack began to push himself to his feet.

'Do sit down, Mr Wilcon,' Elsie said. 'I've not finished yet.'

It occurred to Jack that never, not once, in the history of the movies had a writer ever spoken to a producer in such a way. And she wasn't even a professional! He subsided back onto the chair. 'Well?'

'Fortunately, one of the ladies in my team has produced a possible scenario. I believe that is the word.'

'Scenario will do.'

'A young American woman comes to live in Coddington St George for a year. She is an exchange school teacher. She meets and falls in love with a local boy, a farmer, perhaps, and after a struggle, for he's already engaged to be married, he returns her love. The community is outraged, especially when the jilted local girl finds out something distasteful about the American girl's background. I'm sure you can see the possibilities in such a storyline.'

Jack could hardly believe his ears. She'd stolen his idea! This had never happened to him before, possibly because he'd never had an idea worth stealing. He didn't know whether to dismiss it or enthuse about it.

'I'm sure you will appreciate, Mr Wilcon,' Elsie continued, 'that such a storyline meets our requirement that the film be shot in as many different locations as possible. It would be natural for the hero to take the heroine, if heroine she is, to many different functions and events in the town.'

'Very true.' Jack had had enough of Elsie Woodmarsh for one evening. 'I think it's an excellent suggestion. And now, if you'll excuse me, I have another meeting to go to.' This time he got to his feet uninterrupted. 'Good evening.' And he left the bar to have a lie down in his room.

Jack felt completely exhausted, and his heart pounded away as if he'd just climbed a high mountain, which, in a way, he had. It was widely known in the town that Elsie got her own way by exhausting anyone who opposed her.

TWENTY

While Jack had been on his way to meet Hank and Studs, the Reverend Greg Small had had a meeting at the rectory with Tony and Thistle. He'd explained that Howard and Edwin would help finance a film about Herbie and homelessness in the town, as promised. They'd provide a thousand dollars each towards the purchase of new equipment. He personally, and the church, had no cash to spare, but the church would officially sponsor the film as part of its campaign to address the problem of homelessness. This should help them to get the local co-operation they would need. If Tony needed more money for the film, then, Greg had suggested, he might like to put a card on the church notice board offering a videoing service for weddings, christenings and funerals. In this way, he'd be able to earn at least some, if not all, of what he needed.

'Actually,' he'd said, 'there's a wedding in a couple of days' time. The couple could be interested in hiring you if the price is right. They were thinking of bringing someone from Rocky, but the cost was too great. I think their budget is fifteen hundred dollars for complete coverage of the event, ceremony and reception.'

At first, Tony hadn't been too keen on getting into the wedding video business, but he realised that fifteen hundred dollars would go a long way towards getting Sven to Australia from Sweden on a budget airline of some kind.

Later, to Thistle he said, 'If I shoot and edit your Herbie story, with Sven directing and you writing and speaking the narration, the three of us could create a little masterpiece.'

'Now you're talking, Tone,' Thistle had exclaimed. 'Let's do it. Do you think Sven'll come?'

'I won't lose anything by asking him. What do you think, Howard?'

'Sounds interesting.'

'Can I use your phone to call Sven?'

'Go ahead.'

Tony made the call and explained the situation. 'You can stay with me, so you won't have any expenses. I just can't find a fee for you.'

Sven, who'd not yet begun the day's drinking and was still a long way between productions, had been enthusiastic. He wasn't too concerned about the absence of a fee or even of having to fly by a budget airline. Although none of his films had ever been a box office success, they were nevertheless all available on DVD, and in spite of the pirates, royalties trickled in, providing an adequate income. He'd been hoping to hear from Tony, who'd impressed him with his views on contemporary cinema, and he promised to get on the next plane to Australia. A few minutes later, he phoned to say he'd be arriving by Lap Air the following afternoon, possibly. The airline's schedules were liable to change, depending on reindeer problems on the runway, but like everything Swedish, it had a reputation for reliability. The journey required a bus trip into Lapland from where the aircraft departed, but this was no hardship to Sven.

Howard offered to drive Tony to Townsville where Sven would disembark his Lap Air flight while Thistle minded the shop. She was tempted to say that it wouldn't matter a monkey's if he shut the shop for a day or even a week, since it made so little money, but for once she'd not snapped at the hand that fed her.

***

The next morning, as Howard drove north with Tony, he said, 'Fleur came in to see me yesterday afternoon. Poor woman. I feel sorry for her.'

'Why?' Tony asked.

'She's really worried by what Jack Wilcon's doing, but she's not willing to risk falling out with Michael, who seems to think Wilcon is just what the project needs. The problem is, you see, Fleur lives for her committees. They give her status in the town. She gets invited to things. And they keep her mind busy. She doesn't have time to think how lonely she is.'

'But why is Milosovic so important to her?' Tony asked.

'Well, for a start, she chairs the Cultural Coordinating Committee—the one that disburses the grants. People believe that she's got Michael's ear. In a town this size, all the wheels are linked, you know. Michael gets elected year after year mainly because he's a successful businessman and enough voters think that qualifies him to sit on council. Frankly, if I were God—and I'd need to be to get any changes through—I'd make all estate agents, builders, architects, and developers of all kinds ineligible to stand for any local government office.'

'Who would that leave?'

'Probably school teachers and nurses.' Howard laughed. 'You're right, Tony. It's just as well I'm not God. Things are probably better left as they are.'

'Have we been replaced on the committee?' Tony asked.

204

'Yes. The high school drama teacher's one. Fleur thinks he's been offered chairmanship of the County Drama Advisory Committee if Michael gets elected. And Councillor Winters.'

'Isn't he Deputy Mayor?'

'Yes. And he'll become mayor if Michael is elected to the shire council. The third one … can you guess?'

Tony shook his head.

'Sandra Evans. She's the Social Editor of *The News Gazette*.'

'But she's appalling.'

'She's powerful, Tony. She decides who gets into the social pages and who doesn't. You probably don't realise it because you've got more important things to think about, but there's an A List in this town as there is in every community, and a lot of people want to be on it. Anyway, Michael intends to milk the movie for all the personal publicity he can get. Fleur said he's even thinking about holding a civic reception for the Americans.'

'I still don't understand why he supports Jack Wilcon. The man's a loser. Believe me. He's a nothing in the industry.'

'I think,' Howard said, 'it's because Michael feels comfortable with the man. I don't want to be an intellectual snob—though I am, of course—but Jack Wilcon comes across as a man with little education. Michael is the same. I doubt if he's ever read a book or been to a concert or a play. He never talks about any films he's seen. It's all business and local politics with him. So, Michael doesn't feel intimated by Wilcon, you see. They're two of a kind. From what you've said, Sven's Ingersson's completely different. Michael wouldn't know how to deal with him—and he knows it. He'd be out of his depth and petrified of making a fool of himself. People like Michael have to surround themselves with second and third-raters, Tony.'

'That's very depressing. He has so much influence.'

'Absolutely. Oh, there's one other piece of news from Fleur. Wilcon is providing a young American actress to star in the film. Michael's probably been given the impression that he's in with a chance. He likes young women.'

'An American actress? For the community movie?'

'Yes. Fleur is furious.'

'Who is this actress?'

'Does the name Roma Sheraton mean anything to you?'

Tony shook his head. 'This whole thing stinks, Howard.'

'I agree. And I think it's highly likely that as far as Michael is concerned, it will all end in tears. What we need to do is watch and wait, keep our powder dry, and get on with our own affairs.'

Howard drove in silence for a while. He had a lot to think about. He'd taken on Thistle as a kind of protégé, and now it looked as if he was taking on Tony as well. He liked being a patron of the arts, if only in a small way, and was sufficient of a realist to be aware that his contribution as an actor and director was so small as to be worthless. And yet he loved the arts and wished he had more to offer. He occasionally daydreamed about having his own professional theatre company. He imagined himself as an old-style actor-manager, touring the country with a repertoire of Elizabethan and Jacobean plays, putting them on in country houses and suitable hotels, just like the acting companies had done in Shakespeare's time. It was a lovely daydream, but nothing more; he knew it could never become a reality. He'd never be more than an amateur dabbler in the arts, just enough to have a local reputation.

He'd been pleased when he'd been invited onto the Cultural Coordinating Committee, thinking it a kind of recognition of his place in the artistic life of the town. It hadn't been long, however, before he'd realised that the committee had been established to rubber stamp whatever Michael Milosovic wanted to do.

Edwin had said, 'We only have to oppose Milosovic once, Howard, and we'll find ourselves removed from the committee. Or he'll disband it and form a different one with a different name but the same function with different people. It's how government works. All boards, committees, statutory authorities are stacked with people who will do the chairperson's bidding. Or the chairperson is in the pocket of the politician who appoints all the members. The boards of companies are the same, full of people—the same people—who are known to be 'sound'; in other words, to behave like a rubber stamp and never, ever ask awkward questions.'

'Then why should we waste our time attending meetings?' Howard had demanded.

'Because it's the only way to find out what's going on. With a little luck, sooner or later, that knowledge can be put to good use.' Edwin had laughed. 'What you have to remember, Howard,' he'd pontificated, 'is that there are two kinds of committee: elected and appointed: elected committees usually achieve very little but they do it democratically; appointed committees often achieve a great deal, but do only what the person who appoints them wants them to. We sat on an appointed committee so the important thing, of course, was to resign at the right time and make absolutely sure that our objections have been properly minuted.'

'Well,' Howard had said, 'You, Greg and I resigned because of what Tony said he'd found out about Jack Wilcon. We put our trust in a young man we really know little about.'

'No,' Edwin had objected. 'It was more than that. If we're honest, we'll admit that we've been looking for a reason to oppose Michael. We've resented the way he bulldozed Wilcon's appointment through the committee. There was no proper discussion. The Swede's application wasn't considered."

All this, Howard, thought, was true. He compared the two young people to whom he and Edwin had hitched their wagon. Tony seemed to be very straightforward. It was a pity, though, he thought, that he was not a very impressive young man. He had none of Thistle's fire and dedication. Though Thistle was coarse and confrontational and at times a real pain, she was determined to write what she wanted to write in the way she wanted to write it and to suffer the consequences—poverty and rejection. Tony, on the other hand, was polite and unassertive, anxious to please. And yet … and yet, Howard thought, he'd had the courage, the integrity to stand up to Michael Milosovic. It had been more important to him not to work with a man he despised than to make a movie that could help his own career. In his quiet way, Howard decided, perhaps Tony was as dedicated as Thistle.

If there was one thing, Howard thought, that he knew about the arts, it was that to be really successful one had to be totally dedicated and ruthless. He'd once been to an opening of an exhibition by a nationally famous painter and had overheard a reporter asking the artist—a man as famous for his many failed marriages as for his work—what was important to him. The reply had been brutal. 'The only thing that matters is the work,' he'd said. And he'd meant it.

Thistle, Howard knew, would agree with this. Tony would probably agree but say something like, 'Oh, I suppose, family. Friends. You know.'

Now he turned and glanced at the young man sitting beside him. 'How are you getting on with Thistle?' he asked.

'I really like her. I know she's difficult, but she's so much her own person. And she's very talented.'

'Have you read much of her work?' Howard asked.

'Yeah, quite a bit. She shows me stuff. She writes from the heart. She's not happy, you know.'

Howard drove on in silence for a while, considering this. 'She's a bit extreme, don't you think?' he asked. 'I mean, surely she doesn't have to spend all day writing poetry. What's wrong with having a part-time job? She doesn't need to live in squalor. No, I'm wrong. She does. It's all part of her persona. At some point in the past, she invented herself. She's become what she invented. We all do it in a way.'

'But she's so angry,' Tony said. 'Not like Sven. And he's a true artist, too. But his temperament is so different from Thistle's. She's angry. He's terribly sad. He finds the human condition tragic and intolerable, and his inability to do anything about it has filled him with guilt. The only thing he can do is to make films that bring peoples' attention to how awful it is to be human.'

'Quite,' Howard said, then added, 'as if most of them don't know this already.'

'He has no sense of humour, you know,' Tony, who wasn't himself over-endowed with one, said. 'He's made over fifty films, and not one of them, rather like the Bible, has a single joke in it. When he smiles, which he does rarely, he smiles out of wry sadness, not out of humour.'

'But you like him?'

'Oh, yes. And admire him. And I like Thistle. But I feel sorry for her more than anything. She's going to live on the fringe for the rest of her life.'

'Yes.' After a long pause, Howard added, 'One wants to help, of course, but whatever one does is never quite right somehow.'

They reached the airport in good time for Lap Air's scheduled arrival. Incredibly it was on time to the minute.

Tony waved to Sven as he approached.

'Pleased I am to see you,' he said to Tony as they shook hands.

'This is my friend, Howard Grant,' Tony said. 'He's one of the sponsors of the film.'

'Delighted I am to meet you.' Sven bowed formally.

Howard smiled. He thought he was going to like the Swede. It was a pity, though, that he looked so depressed. The condition could be contagious.

On the journey back to Coddington St George, Tony sat in the back with Sven so they could talk.

'The film will be a documentary,' Tony said, 'about twenty-four hours in the life of a homeless man in a country town. We'll get him to tell us how he feels, how he became homeless, why he doesn't try to change his way of life—all that.'

Sven felt a little disappointed by the project. Tony had told him on the phone only that it was to be a community movie. This had excited him. He'd hoped to make a film in which the actors made up a story as he filmed them sitting around adlibbing dialogue and creating characters totally unrelated to one another.

This kind of film-making was the most recent development in Danish cinema, and Sven believed that an Australian version of it would be awarded at least the Bronze Plaque for Best Ambiguous Foreign Entry at the Sikkim Film Festival. Sven also planned to take this development in cinema a stage further. The actors would not speak. There would be no dialogue. They would sit in a half circle, occasionally moving a facial muscle as their thoughts and emotions dictated. Audiences would have to guess what, if anything, the actors were thinking and what, if any, relationship they had with one another.

But the most exciting development would be that each member of the audience would be provided with a video camera. They would then film the actors. As each of them would be filming from a slightly different position, each film would be different. It was to be the ultimate in audience participation cinema. An extension of video art. An installation, no less, occupying a vast space in a gallery. Sven himself would film the audience filming the actors. There could even possibly be film of someone filming Sven filming everything. The film needed to have many layers and be symbolic of the alienation of people from one another. It would be a record of the pointlessness of any attempt at communication.

When he suggested to Tony that perhaps it would be sufficient just to point the camera at Herbie and let it observe him, and have another camera filming the first camera filming Herbie, Tony said, 'I think Thistle O'Reilly, she's our writer, wants to have a story, Sven. We need to know why he is homeless. How does he feel about it? Does he ever think of his future? All that. She's got a title for it, *Grunts and Groans.*'

'That title, a homeless old man up it sums,' Sven said. 'I like it. Now about this man, everything you know you tell me.'

Tony told Sven what he knew about Herbie—it took him about twenty seconds.

When he'd finished, Sven asked, 'Has he relatives not?'

'No one knows,' Tony replied. 'Apparently he has some kind of birth certificate. It's all greasy and torn, but just legible.'

'How do you know his birth certificate it is?' Sven asked.

'We don't. I suppose it could be anyone's. He could have found or stolen it.'

'Oh, this I like. What is his true identity? Does he have one? How will the film allow us to enter his life?'

On one of Sergeant Bordon's many quiet days, having nothing better to do, and being unable to undertake any revenue collection—the patrol car was being serviced—he'd spent a few hours on the phone and computer trying to find out something about Herbie. He wasn't especially interested in the vagrant, but he thought that he ought to attempt to find out something in case a superior officer wanted to know if he'd done so. One day Herbie might be found dead, and then questions might be asked. The sergeant had found out nothing except that Herbie had a birth certificate that may or may not be his. It indicated that, if it were, he was fifty-three years old and had been born in Charter's Towers, at one time a prosperous gold town but now as depressed as Coddington St George. His father's occupation was given as fisherman, which was interesting as the town was hundreds of kilometres from the sea and was not on a river. Herbie's mother's was listed as a domestic servant. Further inquiries had revealed that both his parents, if they were in fact his parents and not somebody else's, were deceased. No other relatives could be found. He had no criminal record, no bank account, and no credit rating. He had never claimed a pension or made a tax return. He refused to answer any questions about himself, and was within his rights to do so. He was a complete mystery.

Sven was delighted by him. 'He the perfect subject is for our film. The man nothing is.'

'I'm a little worried about the film being a bit boring,' Tony said.

Sven smiled slightly. He never worried about his films being boring. He had made too many films about characters whose lives were completely empty for this to be an issue.

By the time they reached Coddington St George, Tony and Sven had agreed that they would begin filming without delay.

Sven decided to film Herbie in real time for twenty-four hours. He, Tony and Thistle would sleep only when Herbie slept, and they would take it in turns to watch him so that they didn't miss anything. Tony would take a day or so to edit the footage, assisted by Sven, and would record Thistle's narration. They would screen the movie as soon as possible at the St Jude's Church Hall, and invite everyone in the town free of charge to see what moviemaking should really be about.

It was already early evening, but Howard hurried away to make sure his shop had not burned down in his absence or been the location of an outburst of Thistle's anger. Tony took Sven home so that he could shower and change his clothes after his long flight. On the way, he said, 'I wonder, Sven, if you'd like to direct a sort of wedding video we have to make tomorrow. I mean, it would be fantastic to make something different from the usual sort of thing.'

'A wedding? Sad, they are.'

'Sad?'

'Divorce they all end in.'

But he agreed to direct the first of Tony and Thistle's professional engagements.

Mrs Andover had not given a lot of thought to what her guest would look like. The only Swedish men she'd seen had been athletes of one kind or another on the television. She assumed that Sven would be like them, tall and blonde and rather good-looking. She was surprised, therefore, when Tony introduced a long, thin, bald man who looked as if he'd just been told he had terminal cancer.

'I'm very pleased to meet you,' she said.

'And pleased to meet you I am,' he said sadly.

'Tony, show Mr Ingersson to his room,' Mrs Andover said, and retreated to the kitchen where she felt more in charge of the situation.

Tony left Sven to unpack and joined his mother in the kitchen.

'He's not very impressive, is he?' she said. 'I mean, you wouldn't think he was a film director. He reminds me of the man who used to keep the general store on the corner. Before the supermarket put him out of business.'

'What's a film director supposed to look like?' Tony asked wearily.

'Well, you know,' Mrs Andover said. Then, moving on, 'Would he want a cup of tea?'

Tony thought he would. Then they'd go and collect Thistle, find Herbie and introduce him to Sven.

TWENTY-one

Trent wore his new outfit the day he bought it so it wouldn't look too new when he met Roma. He decided that as she'd normally be surrounded by actors wearing the trendiest gear they could afford, he'd offer something different—the prosperous pastoralist look. He'd be comfortable in it, and she might be more impressed by his Australianness than by any attempt to be a male fashion statement. Accordingly, he wore a pair of pale-khaki drill trousers, knee-length, highly polished boots, a cream open-necked shirt and a Harris Tweed jacket. The final touch was the Akubra hat. He'd given the size of this a great deal of thought. It was widely believed that the larger the hat, the smaller the property, but Trent felt sure Roma wouldn't know this. Therefore, if he wore a smallish hat, she might think it reflected the size of his parent's property. He eventually decided on a medium-sized Akubra and hoped for the best. He also decided it would be safer not to shave, so he nurtured some designer stub. Hopefully when Roma saw the Bentley and later the pile that was his home, she would accept him for what he was—the heir to thousands of hectares of prime, well-watered land.

Having no idea how to arrange publicity for Roma's arrival, he consulted the Yellow Pages and under Publicists found 'Instant Celebrity Creations—Complete Service—all media'. He phoned for an appointment and within the hour was in the poster and photograph-lined office of Suzanna Fringe-Markam, the managing director. Aiming at thirty-five, but reaching sixty with ease, she wore loose, brightly coloured, flowing clothes, an immense amount of costume jewellery, which jingled like a horse harness, and a lot of blonde hair. Her shocking smoker's cough came courtesy of the thin, black cheroots she smoked.

The woman petrified Trent, as well she should. Her fee for organising a reporter and photographer at the airport, placing articles and photographs in three celebrity magazines, *Celebrity Today, Hello Tomorrow* and *Who's On Top* would be twenty thousand dollars payable in advance. Of this, most would go to the editors of the magazines to ensure not only publication but also choice positions. If Trent wanted part of the front cover, this would be another five thousand per magazine.

He explained the situation. Suzanna suggested Rent-A-Crowd for a further five thousand, but Trent thought this excessive. Suzanne didn't argue.

'There's always a crowd at the airport anyway,' she said. 'Who's to know they're not there to meet Roma?'

She smiled, toothily—she had a full mouth of them and they were rather large. 'Tell me about Roma,' she said. 'You said she's a soapie star. What shows has she been in?'

'I'm afraid I don't know.'

'Not a problem. We don't get half the American soaps here. Now let's think, she needs to have been in something like *Sex and the City* or *Desperate Housewives*. I know, what about *Suburban Divorcees?*' She made a note.

'Is there such a series?' Trent asked.

'There could be for all I or anybody here knows. If there isn't, there should be. The title says it all, don't you think?'

'Is this quite honest?' Trent asked quietly.

'My dear boy,' Suzanna said, carelessly giving her age away, 'if we had to rely on facts, we'd have no stories. You can have no idea how empty and boring most celebrities' lives are. Now, we need a romantic element, of course. I suggest for the headline for *Celebrity Today* something dramatic such as "Has Tom Lost Roma to Trent?" This gets your name in and hers and links you to an instantly recognizable name.'

'Tom,' Trent said. 'Tom who?'

'In the article we won't actually refer to him. The headline screams Tom Cruise, of course. The important thing is to get your pictures in the magazines, and your names. Whatever we say about you is irrelevant. Even if someone reads it, she'll forget what she reads as soon as she turns the page. Now let's think of some more headlines and captions. How about, "Roma and Trent Hit it Off. Exclusive."'

Trent decided to enter into the spirit of the thing. '"Is Trent Roma's New Man?"'

'Good. But we want to build you up, too. Let's make that one "Is Roma Trent's New Woman?"'

'I like it. I know! "I Want Trent's Baby, Roma Says",' Trent suggested.

'Roma cries, dear. Cries. Says is too mild.'

The conversation continued along these lines for some time, then Suzanna decided it was time for lunch. She knew a delightfully intimate little place. They needn't hurry. She had a completely free afternoon.

On the way to the restaurant, she said, 'You said you're a farmer in real life. Can you get a photo of yourself standing next to a champion Angus bull?'

217

'We don't have one,' Trent said. 'We grow sugar cane.'

'Oh,' Suzanne said. 'A pity. It's not quite the same, is it?'

***

Roma Sheraton arrived at Brisbane two days later. She'd emailed Jack her flight number, date and time of arrival: United Airlines Flight 839 arriving 6.06. Trent was there, dressed in his new outfit, to meet her. He'd decided against the white stretched limo suggested by Suzanne. His countryman's instinct told him that his father's Bentley, which he'd driven down in, was far more likely to impress Roma than the kind of car she was probably used to in LA. He had, however, hired a chauffeur for the drive back to Coddington St George, and the smartly uniformed army veteran was to hold up a placard bearing the legend Coddington St George Welcomes Roma Sheraton on it, neatly printed and correctly spelt. Suzanne had provided a photographer and a reporter.

Roma's flight was on time. It was the first time she'd flown first class, and she'd enjoyed it. The checker had recognised her, leant forward and said with a noticeable leer, 'Love your movies, Kandy. Problem with your reservation, though. I'll have to upgrade you.'

The fawning flight attendants on board had then helped her to feel important, and she'd soon convinced herself that she was now an up-and-coming star in a legitimate movie, and that somehow, she wasn't sure how and it didn't matter anyway, she'd already acquired celebrity status. She was in the movies, and she accepted it as her right.

She would've enjoyed the flight more, though, if the middle-aged man sitting next to her had shown at least some interest in her, but the Japanese accountant, when not asleep, stared only at the graphs and tables on the screen of his laptop. Being completely ignored was a new experience for Roma, but she consoled herself with the thought that now she was on her way to stardom, she could expect better things in the future.

Essentially sentimental, Roma hoped that the male lead in her movie might even be a man to become romantically involved with, if only briefly and for publicity purposes. She knew so little about him, only that he was a wealthy farmer's son called Trent Frobisher. Knowing nothing about Australian agriculture, she assumed he would live on a one-hundred-thousand-acre spread, Texas-style. It hadn't occurred to her that by Australian standards, two thousand hectares of sugar cane was considered great rural wealth, as long as the price of sugar held.

As she walked down the passageway to the arrivals gate, pushing her trolley loaded with fashionable fake Gucci luggage, a fake-gold lady's Rolex on her wrist, fake Mikimoto pearl studs in her ears, and fake Prada sandals on her feet, she managed a fixed smile for whoever would be waiting to meet her. With any luck, she thought, her co-star would be there. They'd be photographed shaking hands. She might even kiss him.

Trent stayed out of sight at first, hovering behind several hundred Chinese waiting patiently for relatives to arrive on another flight. He wondered if some of them lived at the airport. They had the look of people who'd been there a long time, part of the fixtures and fittings. Roma, too, scanning the waiting crowd, was surprised to see so many Chinese. She was now sufficiently lost in her new fantasy world of self-importance to think they were all there to meet her. She waved to them. None of them waved back. She blew a kiss, which garnered an alarmed and sudden burst of angry-sounding Cantonese as the waiting Chinese commented among themselves on the absurd behaviour of this mad woman. They weren't interested in celebrities. They were only concerned with whether Uncle Ho or Auntie Wu had been able to smuggle through customs enough dried tiger's penis and other parts of endangered species to alleviate their arthritis and other ailments.

Trent watched Roma walk towards the chauffer who held up the card with her name on it. He couldn't believe what he saw. She was more gorgeous than he thought it was possible for a real live woman to be. He lost all confidence in his ability to attract her. Seducing giggling, often binge-drunk Coddington St George girls at the local dances was one thing, having a relationship with a glamorous Hollywood television star was another.

The hired photographer's camera flashed, and Roma turned her head this way and that, showing the dentistry for which she'd worked so hard. She felt disappointed that Trent hadn't bothered to meet her. Perhaps, she thought, he couldn't get away from filming.

The reporter approached her and said, 'What have you to say about your new role, Miss Sheraton?'

Roma smiled and mouthed the lines her aunt had practised with her. 'It's so wonderful to be in your wonderful country. I can't wait to get to work on this wonderful movie. It's a wonderful script by a wonderful writer, and I just love my role.'

She followed the chauffeur, who pushed her trolley for her, to the waiting Bentley, elegant and dignified in its pale-green conservative lines. Its size helped her to regain her waning confidence. All was going to be well.

As she got into the rear of the car, Trent, having finally summoned up enough courage to present himself, got into it from the other side. Before she could speak, he said, 'I'm Trent. How do you do, Roma?' And offered her his hand. Then, having learnt a thing or two from an afternoon with Suzanne, he said,

'Forgive me for not being at the gate, but all these reporters get on my nerves. The photographer's flashes hurt my eyes.'

'My goodness!' Roma thought. 'He must be famous. And yet he seems so shy.'

She shook his hand and then leant forward and kissed him on the cheek. Just being beside him gave her confidence. *He's cute*, she thought. *He's not going to be a problem.* 'It's lovely to meet you, honey,' she said. 'I think we're going to have a lot of fun.'

***

Meanwhile back in Coddington St George, Jack looked at his watch. Roma had to be half way from the airport, he thought. He'd considered asking Michael to hire a large, luxury caravan for her to stay in, but the local caravan park, inhabited mainly by wives on the run from husbands, husbands on the run from wives, recently released prisoners, and families evicted from their bank-repossessed homes didn't have a reputation as a happy place to stay. Although called the Coddington St George Tourist Park, it hadn't accommodated a tourist van for several years. It was known locally as Heartbreak Hotel. Jack had agreed, therefore, to Alec's suggestion that Roma would stay in the recently named and redecorated honeymoon suite of the Central Hotel.

In mid-afternoon, Trent and Roma arrived. Trent, carrying her luggage, escorted her to her accommodation. She took one look at the circular bed and the ceiling mirrors and burst into tears. The room was almost a replica of the one in which she'd last performed. She wasn't going to be given a chance to cross over and have a new career. That bastard Jack Wilcon had lied to her aunt.

Confused and worried, Trent said, 'What's the matter, Roma? Don't you like the room?'

'What kind of movie are we making?' she snapped. 'What's your role in it?'

'I haven't seen the script,' Trent said, 'but the concept is that you're a young exchange teacher come to teach for a year in the town. I'm a local farmer—rather like I am in real life. At first, we don't get on, you think I'm snobbish or something, but then something happens—there's a fire or accident or something—and you realise that I'm not as awful as you thought I was. We end up becoming friends, and then the movie ends with a big wedding. And off we go into the sunset.'

'Oh, it's a real love story,' Roma said, sniffing her tears away.

'Sort of. You fall in love with the town, though, not just me. The film shows you getting to know what goes on here.'

'It's not porno, I hope,' she said.

Trent's eyes widened in horror. 'Good God, no! What on earth made you think that?'

'This room.'

'It's the hotel's honeymoon suite, Roma. Sorry, but it's the only accommodation there is. I'm afraid Alec Grimshaw, he's the publican, is a man of little taste.' He attempted a joke. 'He probably thinks it's the kind of room weasels, stoats, ferrets and skunks would be happy in.'

Roma looked at him with her botoxed mouth open. She thought he must have been saying something in a foreign language. 'For a minute,' she said, 'I thought … you know …'

Trent smiled. 'Shall we meet for a drink in the bar later? Say seven? Then dinner?'

'I'd love that, honey.'

***

That evening, after a few drinks, which had made Roma giggly and Trent a little more confident, Jack came in with a couple of pages of script.

'I want to shoot this tomorrow,' he said. 'It's going to be fantastic, Roma. The concept is new. It's original. It'll get an Oscar. Trust me.'

'Trent has told me all about it,' Roma said. 'I love it.'

'She's going to be fantastic, Jack,' Trent said. 'The casting is perfect.'

She wasn't quite perfect, though, because any school teacher who looked like Roma would be in serious danger of harassment from the year ten and upwards boys at Coddington St George High. Many of them would probably recognise her from their nightly searches of the internet. And Roma's appearance almost overcame Trent; he could barely stop himself drooling as he gazed at her. Sure that the movie would have to include a love scene of some kind, he stared at Roma, his eyes wandering over her body as if they had a mind of their own, and he imagined what it would be like to hold her in his arms. To avoid criticism, he thought, the movie would have to get no higher than a PG rating, but this wouldn't preclude kissing and a reasonable amount of foreplay. Even a G rating would permit Roma to wear a bikini, scanty underwear or a baby doll nightie.

For her part, Roma had soon decided quickly that Trent was 'rather cute' and very different from the men she usually went with casually. They always assumed that she was prepared, even willing, to provide sex at the flash of a credit card or, insultingly, for the price of a martini or two. They rarely offered dinner. If she dared to baulk at instant sex, they'd suggest that she had a problem and should go into analysis. Sex, not romance, was the only item on their agenda.

Trent, she thought, was different—a strange mixture of shyness and conceit, probably, she presumed, all part of his being an Australian man of the land. He was obviously proud of his comic-book good looks and physique, but she had no problems with that, and if it would be necessary to have some kind of affair with him, then it would help to pass the time.

It wasn't until after they'd had a meal and Trent suggested that they read together the unactable dialogue that Elsie Woodmarsh's committee of writers had produced that Roma had her second bad moment of the day.

'I'm tired,' she said. 'Let's do it tomorrow.'

'Just five minutes, Roma,' Trent pleaded, not wanting to leave her so soon. 'I'd like to get the feel of the part.'

Trent thought she was trying to avoid any advances he might make, but Roma wasn't thinking of sex, or even of having to avoid it. She was worried about something completely different, afraid that eventually an embarrassing truth would come out.

She bit her lip, took a deep breath and decided she may as well get it over with. 'I can't read, honey,' she whispered.

'You've got problems with your eyes?'

'No, honey. I never learned to read. I was too busy singing and dancing to do real schoolwork.'

For a moment Trent didn't know how to respond to this. Then knowing he had to say something, he asked, 'But how have you been able to act in movies?'

Roma didn't tell him that in every movie she'd been in there hadn't been a written script, and she'd had to say exactly the same few words and make the same sounds.

'I've only had small roles, honey. Just a line here and there,' she explained. Then she leant forward and put her hand on his arm. 'Trent, baby, this is my big chance. You've got to help me.'

'Teach you to read?'

'No, honey. Teach me my lines.'

'Oh, I see! But of course, Roma. I'd love to.'

And Trent meant it. He knew that now they'd have to spend even more time together. And she'd be grateful to him. She gave the impression of being an affectionate, touchy-feely kind of girl. Trent's confidence soared. More headlines popped into his mind: 'I Owe Everything to Trent' Superstar Roma Sheraton declares; 'Roma Sheraton Shock! Trent Reveals All. Exclusive.'

'Does Jack know?' he asked.

'I don't know. I don't think so. My agent doesn't know.'

'We should tell him, Roma,' Trent said. 'The director will have to know, then he'll be able to cover for you.'

'But he might take me off the movie,' Roma cried.

'He's more likely to do that if he finds out that you can't read as soon as we start shooting,' Trent said, feeling quite masterful now. 'If we front up to him now, he'll work something out.'

Roma wasn't happy about this, but she thought Trent might be right. She had no experience of any kind of movie apart from the hundred or so porno videos she'd made. Many of the other girls had also been illiterate, which was one of the reasons they'd entered the so-called adult industry.

'I suppose you're right, honey,' she said. 'But what if Jack does want to replace me?'

Trent's new-found talent for headlines came to his rescue: 'Roma Sheraton Outrage. Illiterate Actress Sacked from Movie.'

'I think the publicity would be so bad,' he said, 'that Jack won't dare.' Then he added, 'There are political reasons for this movie, you know. Everyone has to be very careful not to get any bad publicity. I'm on the steering committee for the project.'

He told Roma everything and impressed her with his knowledge. She knew her future was in his hands, so there was only one thing to do. She'd done it before and would do it many times in the future. It solved almost as many problems as it created.

'Why don't you come back with me for a little while, honey?' she said. 'Let's get to know one another real well.'

TWENTY-TWO

The next morning, Trent went to see Jack. 'I need to talk to you about Roma,' he said.

'Yeah?'

'She's a wonderful girl, Jack. Beautiful. Talented. Delightful personality. A real find. She's going to be great.'

Jack knew from all this that Trent had a problem with her. 'I know how to pick 'em,' he said. 'Trust me. I make them famous.'

'That's right, Jack. There's just one small problem.'

'Yeah?'

'She can't read a script. She's illiterate.'

'Fuck!' Jack exclaimed. Then his creativity came to his rescue. 'So, what's the problem? We make her deaf and dumb. Then she doesn't have to speak.'

'But, Jack—'

'No! It's the fucking answer. The pathos! Think of it. Here's a beautiful girl who can't hear or speak. The young farmer falls in love with her and—'

'Jack, she's supposed to be a primary school teacher.'

Jack's mind went into top gear. 'No problem. She teaches deaf and dumb kids. Fantastic.'

'Jack, it's a great idea, but I'll need to communicate with her. She'll need to communicate with me. We'd both have to learn how to sign.'

'Sign? Sign what?' Jack demanded. His producer's instincts were very strong. 'She's not signing anything before I see it.'

'No, Jack. Signing. Deaf and dumb language. If she's deaf and dumb that's how she'll communicate.'

'Okay,' Jack said, once again his keen creative mind solving a problem. 'So, she's blind, too. Jesus, think of it. One of the most beautiful girls in the world and she's deaf, dumb and blind. She'd get an Oscar. We all would.'

Trent, who very occasionally revealed a sense of humour said, 'Fantastic, Jack. Let's put her in a wheelchair as well.'

Jack seriously considered this. He knew that Oscars were frequently awarded to movies about people who were disabled in some way. But then he had a brief encounter with reality. 'No,' he said. 'Wheelchairs are out. We want to see her fucking legs.'

'I think,' Trent said, hoping to bring the conversation back to at least a degree of sanity, 'she shouldn't be disabled. Let's just make her a girl of few words. She's got beautiful eyes. Let her talk with them.'

By now, Jack's attention had strayed. He needed a drink. 'Sure,' he said. 'Who cares a fuck if she can see or not.'

***

Tony's first assignment as a wedding photographer was at two pm that day at St Jude's. Accompanied by Thistle carrying a large, circular silver reflector, and Sven, who was somewhere in that state of mind between alcoholic exuberance and depression, Tony had arrived at the church in good time to film the arrival of the bride and her father. Now he lay on the ground near where the hire car from Coddington St George Luxury Limousines would stop. Sven wanted the camera positioned so it would record the bride's feet—and her father's—emerging from the car. Tony was then to crawl along the path so that the hand-held camera could follow the feet as they walked into the church. Sven then wanted him to stand up and follow the bride and her father, filming their moving feet continuously, but this time from a different angle, until they reached the altar where the groom and his best man would be waiting for them. Here and only here, Tony's camera was to discover the identity of the owner of the bride's feet by slowly moving up her body, taking in the dress and bouquet and finally her glowing face.

Heavily influenced by the many German films he'd seen, Sven was very aware of the importance of symbolism in film, even though he had to admit to himself that there'd been many times when he'd either not noticed the symbols or, if he had noticed them, had been unable to even guess at what they could possibly mean. Feet, though, needed no explanation. They symbolized arrival and departure. Also, by concentrating on the feet, he thought, he would insert an element of suspense into the film. Whose feet were they? Where were they going? Why? The concept was exciting.

Accordingly, he planned to make much of the symbolism of the bride's feet arriving with her father's feet and then, after the ceremony, departing with her husband's feet instead of her father's. This would symbolize a new and different life for her. He also planned a long, lingering shot of the wedding car disappearing into the distance. He'd have Tony hold onto the empty road for a while, making the point that it was empty and that the bride and groom had left for where. ... for what kind of life? The ambiguity would be beautiful. Then he'd film the wedding guests as they stared with mixed emotions into the vacant distance.

Sven was determined that Tony should give his first client value for money and provide not just an ordinary record of a wedding and reception. He would deliver something that existed in its own right as a work of art.

All went well until the bride, groom, bride's father, and best man stood in position, centre aisle, and the Reverend Greg Small approached with his happy-wedding expression on his face. He stopped in front of the short line-up, smiled understandingly at the nearby bride's mother, who'd started to cry and was working herself up to a good old howl that she hoped the photographer would record for future reference, and then intoned the opening words of the ceremony.

As instructed by Sven, Tony crawled on his knees between the vicar and the bride and groom and attempted to capture the expression on the bride's face from an interesting low angle. Thistle stood nearby, positioning the reflector so that it caught the rays of the sun through the church's stained-glass window and lit up with bright, rainbow hues the bride's rather over-made-up face. As requested by Sven, hoping to capture every nuance of the bride's range of emotions, Tony filmed in extreme close-up. As a result, every flaw in the bride's skin—and there were many, hence the over-liberal application of make-up—was in crisp, multi-coloured focus.

Greg, assuming that this kind of thing was what the bride and groom had ordered, and being used to the extraordinary requests made by many couples, young and old, struggled on. Now and then he had to step over Tony in an attempt not to tread on him. For their part, the bride and groom assumed they were getting the kind of wedding photography that came from an award-winning photographer. Only the bride's father had doubts, but he was too cowed from previous arguments with his daughter and wife about the wedding arrangements to risk further defeat. He said nothing, but slowly shook his head from side to side in silent sorrow.

Disaster didn't strike, however, until the groom placed the ring on the bride's finger. Tony couldn't get the shot Sven had asked for—a clear shot of the ring being forced over the bride's less-than-slender knuckle. Thistle held the reflector over the bride's hand to catch what little light was now available, increasing Tony's difficulty of getting the hand into shot. Sven asked for the action to be performed again, and Tony then ascended the nearby pulpit in order to obtain an artistically high shot of the procedure.

Unfortunately, the pulpit, a recent import from China, was decorated with carvings of, presumably, Old Testament characters, though many of them had so many rolls of fat that Chinese mythology appeared to have intruded. This in itself wouldn't have mattered if the glue with which they'd been stuck onto the main structure of the pulpit had been of adequate adhesion. But it was not. Sitting on the pulpit, legs dangling over the side, Tony grasped one of the carved figures with one hand to steady himself while operating the camera with the other. At the crucial moment, when Tony leaned forward as far as he could, the carved figure—it could have been an artist's impression of Job—suddenly detached itself from the pulpit and Tony fell onto a young acolyte who stood nearby holding a large candle. Bruised but not beaten, Tony got to his feet and continued filming from a standing position.

The service came to an end without further video graphic incident. Sven, Tony and Thistle followed the wedding party out of the church. There, Sven's somewhat unintelligible attempts to persuade the bridal party and guests to organize themselves into unusual groups were met with considerable resistance, partly perhaps because Thistle's shepherding, accompanied by her favourite expletive, offended the more elderly relatives of both bride and groom. Eventually, having suffered more embarrassment than he'd experienced in his fifty years, the father of the bride told the little film crew to clear off and that if they showed their faces anywhere near the wedding reception, he'd sue them for attempting to obtain money by false pretences.

As far as the entire wedding party was concerned, it was a disaster. The bride was so upset that she cried throughout the first night of her honeymoon, giving staff and residents of the hotel where they stayed the impression that perhaps there was something seriously wrong with her groom's sexual practices.

For Tony and Thistle, the afternoon wasn't a success if judged solely as an exercise in wedding photography. It was, however, a success in another way. It showed Tony that even something as mundane as a marriage ceremony could be given meaning that far transcended the usual routine productions, which in so far as creative content was concerned, were indistinguishable from one another. Sven had raised a very ordinary wedding to the level of high art. It had been a seminal event as far as Tony was concerned.

PART FOUR:

THE SHOOT

TWenTY-THRee

Preparations for the first day of the shoot went surprisingly smoothly—the credit due largely to the enthusiasm and widespread co-operation of the populace, most of whom were happy to lend props of one kind or another, provide locations, make small cash donations, and participate as extras. Jack's contributions were to hire equipment from a Brisbane film company and decide that the only dialogue in the movie would be very brief conversations between Trent and Roma. Any other utterances would be ad-libbed by members of the community playing themselves—shopkeepers, teachers, council employees, firemen, policemen and so on. A narrator would provide vital information such as backstory and continuity. He or she would either speak to camera or be a voice-over. The narration would be written when the rest of the movie had been shot. In this way, it could fill in any serious gaps in the story, such as it was. Of these, Jack thought there would be quite a few, though he didn't confide his estimate to Michael.

The Ladies' Literary Society argued its way through the list of possible events and locations at which Trent and Roma would be filmed getting to know one another. In Trent's case, at Jack's insistence, this would involve teaching Roma, in fetching peasant blouse, how to milk a cow. Roma was also to be filmed teaching a class of six-year-olds. At first she was to be filmed teaching a child to read, but after strong representations from Trent on Roma's behalf, this was changed to an art class. Dialogue spoken in the school staffroom was to be limited to inquiries concerning whether Roma had had a good flight, took milk and sugar in her tea or coffee, and similar not-too-difficult utterances known to be well within in the range of even the most challenged celebrities, and which could be invented on the spur of the moment.

As a rule, there would be no recorded dialogue in the various situations. Roma would be filmed having a conversation with a teacher, a child or whoever, while the narrator's voice-over informed the viewer what the conversation was about. The great advantages of this approach to feature-film production was that Roma didn't have to read a script, the Ladies' Literary Society didn't have to write much dialogue—both tasks well beyond the capabilities of all concerned—and there were no minor roles to be cast other than people playing themselves. In particular this avoided what would certainly have been an issue of catastrophic proportions had any one child been given more to say than any of the other 343 children enrolled in Coddington Primary.

Everything was ready, therefore, for the first day's shoot. Studs had arrived, well-stocked with whatever substances he hoped there would a demand for from those more adventurous members of the community who wanted to experience life in the fast track. He operated his pharmacy from the back of a hired Land Rover.

The equipment arrived on time. Alec, as DOP, had assistants from among the town's unemployed youth whom he'd trained how to operate a video camera—not a particularly demanding task. Once the cameras had been positioned and the necessary adjustments made for lighting the required images, the operation involved pressing one button for 'Record' and another for 'Stop Recording'.

All the extras knew where they should be, and the support services—police, fire and ambulance—had agreed to attend morning, afternoon and evening shoots. Jack had scheduled two major action scenes for what promised to be a very long day. He was anxious to get them 'in the can' in case the weather changed and the sun disappeared, which, he was informed, could be for weeks. During such a fine weather hiatus, there would be enough rain to turn the countryside into a lake and isolate Coddington St George.

Strong discussion had occurred between Jack and the Cultural Coordinating Committee concerning whether there should be a caterer providing free refreshments such as sausage and steak sandwiches, tea, coffee and soft drinks. Eventually it had been decided to invite the Coddington St George Lions Club to attend the shoot with their caravan. This would provide, for a nominal charge, donuts, tea, coffee and soft drinks, and all profits from sales would flow back into the community. Michael was especially pleased by this as he thought it would attract votes from the Lions—though not, perhaps, from the Rotarians. The two clubs were highly competitive in their endeavours to be of service.

Unfortunately, the rarity of Hank's periods of sobriety caused a problem. No evidence supported his conviction that the quickest way to sober up was to have a few hairs of the dog.

But Jack felt optimistic, in spite of an extraordinary event early on the morning of the shoot. It involved Muriel Cross, one of Howard's phone sex ladies. She entered the High Street news agency where Jack was buying a morning paper.

As if in response to his rather loud voice, she walked up to him, slapped his face, hard, and shouted at him, 'How dare you insult me, you pathetic little man.' She then left the shop without purchasing whatever it was she'd come in for.

Unfortunately, the assault was witnessed not only by Sergeant Bordon, purchasing cigarettes, but also by Gavin Trim, the star reporter—in his own estimation—on *The News Gazette*. As soon as he recovered from the slap, Jack demanded that Sergeant Bordon arrest that 'mad woman' for assault. The sergeant informed him that he'd do this, subject to Jack visiting the police station to make and sign a statement. Jack promised to do this later in the day.

Muriel, appalled by what she'd done—acting impulsively without thinking—hastened to Between the Leaves to tell Howard what she'd done and why.

'That horrid little man,' she explained, 'used our service again.'

'But why did you hit him?' Howard demanded.

'Because he insulted me.'

'But you're used to obscene calls.'

'This was different. He said my voice reminded him of his grandmother's.'

Howard managed to restrain himself and expressed sympathy. In fact, he felt mildly grateful to Jack. Clearly Muriel should soon become a lady in complete retirement.

'I don't think you need worry,' he said. 'I doubt if Jack will press charges when he realises what your defence will be.'

'But, Howard, if I tell the police this, I'll be telling them about our little business. I don't want to do that.'

'You're right, of course. Although we're not doing anything illegal, the management of Golden Fronds certainly won't permit any business to be conducted from the premises—unless, of course, we offer them a percentage.' As the facility was owned by the Shanghai Double Happiness Aged Care Profit Corporation, he was afraid the percentage demanded would be excessive.

Howard considered various possibilities, then said, 'If Sergeant Bordon asks you why you hit Jack, as he's bound to do, just tell him that it's a personal matter and that if Jack presses charges you'll plead guilty and accept the consequences. I expect that the magistrate will simply bind you over for six months to keep the peace. If he asks for a psychiatrist's report, you can tell the shrink the truth. He'll enjoy the joke and pass you as sane.' And with these words, he kissed the old lady on the cheek and told her not to worry.

Unfortunately, Gavin Trim, the reporter, smelt a story. Jack Wilcon, an important guest in the town, was to be the guest of honour at a civic reception. 'Why?' Gavin asked himself, 'did Muriel Cross, a respectable resident of Golden Fronds Retirement Village, slap his face?' There had to be a reason. He decided to investigate Jack's background and spent the next couple of hours on the internet.

Fortunately, Jack decided that he had nothing to gain from pressing charges against a woman who was clearly demented, and the matter was dropped. Howard and Muriel were both rather relieved.

***

At nine-thirty, several thousand Coddington St George citizens turned up at the recreation ground. There, a small army of assistant directors acted as marshals. Mostly young women in tight T-shirts and jeans, they strutted about, flicking their pony-tailed hair self-importantly as they spoke into megaphones, stopped traffic and ordered pedestrians to be 'quiet on set'.

The impression that the assistant directors gave—that all the members of the crew gave—was that making the film was the only thing that mattered. The town existed entirely for the convenience of the film crew, which behaved as if it were an occupying army in a town that had unsuccessfully resisted a siege. The fact that road closures, demands for silence, and the positioning of extras brought everyday activities to a halt was of no interest to the crew. The Coddington St George community patient transport vehicle, with its quota of elderly residents requiring regular life-saving treatments in the hospital, was held up for three hours while a crane was manoeuvred into exactly the right position in the main street. When the driver of the patient transport vehicle objected, he was informed with a haughty sniff that a movie was being shot, and that everyone in the town had to accept a certain amount of inconvenience, 'Do you mind?'

In occasional sober moments, Hank had listed all the possible locations, taking advice from Alec, who'd offered to organise a sporting event—a football match between Coddington United and North Rockhampton Reserves. This turned out to be a mistake. Ignorant of all local events except those involving wildlife, Alec was unaware that the two teams had a history of physical violence. Sporting officialdom had banned them from playing one another since the Coddington right back had picked up a Rockhampton forward and thrown him headfirst to the ground, breaking his neck in several places. Although the football game was to be just background, members of both teams, assuming that their every movement was being recorded on film, became seriously over-enthusiastic. Two of the players, both of whom, after the first game of the season usually spent the rest of it sitting on the bench because of their propensity to king hit other players who got in their way, lost their tempers within seconds of the director shouting 'Action'.

The Coddington player kicked the Rockhampton player in the groin. He retaliated by striking the Coddington player on the neck with his elbow. Both players fell to the ground. Their team mates raced to protect them from further assaults, finding it necessary to kick, punch and headbutt their opponents. A brawl ensued involving not only all the players but also the referee, who exhausted himself flashing yellow and red cards, and many of the spectators, a significant number of whom had been rounded up from the front bar of the Central Hotel and were in their usual condition of pre-lunch inebriation.

It would've been a wonderful action sequence, if Jack had ascertained that Alec was ready before shouting 'Action'. As it was, the camera hadn't been focused. By the time Alec was able to say 'Camera rolling', the Coddington ambulance had departed with the injured. However, all was recorded on their mobile phones by a number of local home-movie enthusiasts. By the end of the morning, they'd sold enough footage to national television stations to buy the latest-model cameras.

Meanwhile, in the playground of Coddington Primary School, Hank instructed Roma in her role of primary school teacher. Having spent the night with Trent, she was as exhausted as Hank was hung-over.

'What do I have to say?' she asked, fearful that a script might have materialised.

'Not a lot. I just want to shoot you in the school playground with some kids. We need to show the audience what your job is, right?'

'Okay.'

It was, perhaps, a little inappropriate that Roma wore her favourite black, vinyl pants that emphasised every curve of her lower half, and a low-slung halter top that stretched so tightly across her silicon-enhanced breasts that it suggested breathing might be a problem. This, though, didn't seriously worry her as she was used to considerable physical discomfort in the workplace. Aware that the costume had been especially effective in *Sex Sluts from Seattle*, her most recent porn epic in which she'd starred as a nymphomaniacal short-order cook in a truck-stop diner, she felt confident that Jack would be pleased by the effect.

When they'd arrived at the school playground, the kids were already there. Never had they looked so neat and tidy. Their mothers had performed miracles of shoe-shining, pants-pressing, hair-wetting and flattening or, in the case of the girls, curling. And now they waited outside the school fence in excited anticipation of watching a scene between their offspring and the Hollywood actress playing the part of a primary school teacher. Several of the school's actual teachers, all women, mostly under fifty, also attended. Though surprised by Roma's costume, they assumed that the script somehow called for the teachers at the school to all dress as call girls on vacation. Not wishing to miss any possible opportunity for personal exposure on the silver screen, they raced home, rummaged through the most secret parts of their wardrobes and returned equally provocatively attired.

Shortly after filming began, the school principal received a phone call from a concerned parent asking whether she'd given permission for what was occurring. Appalled, she hurried to the school, determined to put a stop to what had all the ingredients of a disaster for her career. If it came to the attention of the director of education, she'd be transferred to a ten-pupil school in the smallest, hottest, driest, coldest and most miserable western Queensland remote community—assuming he allowed her to continue in the profession.

By the time she arrived, however, the scene was in the can. Roma had managed eventually to say the words, 'Line up, children,' though it had required fifteen takes to satisfy Hank who, shooting from every possible revealing angle, had taken some lingering close-ups of her bending over two of the younger children. The other primary school teachers, not wanting to be left out, and confident that their mostly natural endowments were as appealing as Roma's surgically assisted pulchritude, had been equally obliging.

The afternoon schedule called for a scene from the annual picnic race. The men of the town wore an assortment of formal wear hired from Briggs' Menswear—You Can Face the World When You Are Dressed By Briggs. Signs of injuries received during the morning's brawl often ruined their attempts at sporting elegance, however. They looked as if they'd just come from a wedding reception or wake that had got seriously out of control. The older women of the town arrived wearing extravagant, home-made race-day hats and voluminous, multi-collared dresses that covered most of their bodies. The younger women wore a few pieces of diaphanous fabric that covered their bodies hardly at all. Inevitably there were some memorable sights.

In time for the first race, Alec had positioned one camera on a crane and another on a dolly where he thought they'd capture the most dramatic aspects of the race. Unfortunately, they frightened the race horses, which were not used to encountering either a train or a crane—and certainly not both—in the middle of the track as they rounded the first bend. They threw their jockeys and bolted into the distance.

Again, the services of the ambulance, police and fire service were required.

It was as if, Fleur thought, a giant circus had come to town and got out of control. The only thing missing was the big top and the animals.

TWENTY-FOUR

During the days leading up to the *A Town Like Ours* shoot, Tony and Thistle, financially assisted by Howard, were in pre-production for their film, now entitled *Twenty-four Hours in the Life of a Homeless Man*. Thistle, who already had a relationship of trust with Herbie, persuaded him, without much argument, to allow his activities to be filmed. He agreed partly out of vanity at being a centre of interest, but also in return for a guaranteed twenty dollars a day for five days.

Howard, who provided the money, insisted on payment by instalments as he feared that Herbie was quite capable of spending the lot in one evening buying drinks for everyone in the public bar of the Grand where, nursing a donated single half of bitter, he usually spent as much of his time as the landlord permitted.

Herbie demanded the first two payments in advance. Tony was willing to give them to him until Thistle pointed out that Herbie would probably spend them in Fred's Gents Hairdressing having a cut-price haircut and shave. A spruced-up Herbie wasn't the intended character of the film.

Tony and Thistle had a problem, but it wasn't Herbie. Having agreed to be on film for twenty-four hours, he promised to ignore the camera and go about his usual business of trying to stay alive. Their problem was Sven. On reflection, Tony, and to an even greater extent Thistle, felt far from happy with the Swede's direction of the wedding video. In Thistle's words, it had been 'a complete and utter fucking wank'.

'Frankly, Tone, I'm not surprised the bride's father did his nut. I would've done, too. What they all wanted was a properly lit video, in focus, of the blushing bride, looking as gorgeous as a thousand-dollar dress and three-hundred-dollar hair-do made possible; the smirking groom dressed up like a mannequin in a hired suit, and a record of the guests at the wedding, in particular of ninety-five-year-old gran who'd travelled from God-knows-where to be with them all on this great day. And what did they get? Fucking feet. Close-ups of the bride's acne, a lingering shot of the groom's dirty index fingernail as he put the ring on the bride's finger, and a slow pan down grandma's leg as her wee flowed beneath her dress and puddled on the chancel floor. It might be art, but a fucking wedding video it isn't.'

'I only did what Sven asked me to do,' Tony said.

'Of course, you did, Tone. I'm not blaming you. I'm just wondering if we did the right thing by inviting Sven here. If we're not careful, he can really fuck up our little project.'

'We can't not let him direct it,' Tony said. 'I mean, he's come all this way.'

'How's he getting on with your mum?' Thistle asked, not quite changing the subject.

'She's a bit stressed to tell the truth.'

Mrs Andover was not just a bit stressed; she was working herself up into a self-induced nervous breakdown.

Sven was used to the comforts and amenities provided by a nation that had managed to adapt itself to its climate. This meant twenty-four-hour reverse cycle air-conditioning, unlimited hot water for showers, spas and saunas, and plumbing designed to deliver them. The tiny terrace weatherboard cottage in which Tony lived with his mother had none of these, and Sven was forced to make do. The cost of his frequent showers had already exceeded Mrs Andover's old age pension for a week.

And then there was his food. Wanting to be hospitable and make him feel at home, Mrs Andover had asked Sven what he wanted to eat for breakfast. He'd told her. Presumably, she thought, he had no idea what fresh cod and herring cost in Australia, assuming one could get it. Her attempt at a compromise—tinned pilchards in tomato sauce—hadn't seemed to please him. Not wanting to embarrass her—and himself—by leaving the gooey mess visible on his plate, he'd daily covered it up with the extra slices of the toast he'd asked for. After two days of this stratagem, which was clearly failing, Sven had braced himself for possible embarrassment and said, 'Mrs Andover, a muesli man I am.'

Relieved, Mrs Andover had spent her last fifty cents on a bag of cut-price muesli from the supermarket. When she poured it into a bowl, it seemed to consist of sweepings from a barn. Sven poured half a bottle of milk onto it in an attempt to make it edible, but failed—it stuck to the roof of his mouth like soggy flour. For nourishment he had to rely on the pile of cold and limp toast his trembling hostess provided. This she made from the cheapest bread in the supermarket, a brand masquerading under the name of Farmer's Own, and was tasteless, with the consistency of a piece of Styrofoam packing.

Mrs Andover's domestic arrangements had been further disturbed by Sven's habit of passing each evening alone in his room except for the company of a bottle of vodka—the supermarket liquor department didn't stock schnapps—and then sleeping in until midday when he descended the stairs shrouded in a cloud of Scandinavian gloom. Then Mrs Andover had to provide him with breakfast, over which he seemed to choke back tears.

Sven's unfailing politeness made it even more difficult for Mrs Andover to cope with it all.

'This house has never been so sad,' she said to her son, 'not even when after having you I returned home from the hospital to find that your father had gone. Deserted me. And not even left a note.'

Having briefly viewed his newborn son in the maternity ward, Tony's father had decided that life had more to offer him elsewhere. By not giving a reason for his sudden departure, he'd felt that he was being considerate.

**

When Sven arrived at Between the Leaves—the production office for *Twenty-four Hours in the Life of a Homeless Man*— shortly before six in the evening on the day of the *A Town Like Ours* shoot, he brought with him a story board he'd prepared during the previous couple of days. It showed each shot, its location and who and what it should contain, the camera angles and suggested lighting. Sven left little to chance or to the creativity of even his most experienced and qualified crew.

'This everything should cover, I think. Especially as asleep Herbie will be for much of the night, yes?' he said.

'Probably.' Tony took the story board from him. The wedding video still much on his mind, he scanned the drawings quickly to see what Sven wanted. What he saw didn't encourage him. Specific instructions included getting extreme close ups of Herbie's snot-encrusted nostril hairs, the lice in his head, his dirt-blackened bare feet—Herbie had long ago worn out his only pair of socks—and the assorted creatures living in his filthy clothes. Sven also required lingering shots of Herbie masticating something repulsive he'd salvaged from a garbage bin with his few remaining teeth—all blackened or yellow, fang-like and deeply pitted with caries.

Tony handed the storyboard to Thistle.

She, too, scanned it quickly. 'Fucking hell!' was her only response.

For once, Tony thought her coarseness justified. Trying to be tactful, he said, 'There's not much story, Sven.'

'Not correct, Tony. The story is all there. The images, show they will, his life. The truth they are. With this film the Golden Samovar at Vladivostok we shall win.'

'It's not quite what I was thinking of,' Tony spoke tentatively, aware that Sven, having given the concept careful thought, was not likely to change his mind without an argument. Thistle was blunter.

'We don't want to make the audience fucking ill, Sven.'

'And why not? This film full of emotion, it must be.'

'Yeah, but the right kind of emotion.'

As the Swedish guru of the film industry, Sven was not used to his co-workers arguing with him. Young people, especially, sat at his feet to learn his philosophy. They studied books about him in the film schools of the world.

'Tell me, Tony, why films do you want to make? Eh? Your motivation, what is it?'

Tony had never seriously asked himself this question. 'I dunno, really,' he said. 'I like, you know, the medium. And it's something, you know, creative to do.'

Sven snorted. No student had ever given him this reason. He was used to such explanations as, 'I want to explore the human condition using visual images to convey the exploitation of the masses by the power-drugged capitalists (or communist apparatchiks).' The replies tended to depend on the student's current political orientation.

'Thistle, why do you want to be a film-maker?'

'I don't, really.'

'You do not? Then why are you here?'

'Tony is a friend. He needed help.'

'That is not a good reason for making films.'

'I reckon it's a fucking good reason for doing anything,' she snapped.

Sven now began to think he'd made a bad mistake by accepting Tony's invitation. The young man and his appalling girlfriend—he assumed Thistle and Tony were in 'a relationship'—were obviously untalented and improperly motivated. And the board and lodging provided was well below minimum Swedish standards.

'Why then do you a film about this vagrant want to make?'

'I think it's an important story,' Tony replied.

Thistle added, 'There are thousands of homeless people in this country. And not just tramps like Herbie. Young couples with babies. And a lot of people with mental problems.'

'I thought, you know,' Tony explained, 'that it would be a good idea to draw people's attention to the problem.'

'So! A propaganda film you want to make. A message.'

'Yeah, I guess so.'

'Messages are not art.'

'Perhaps not, but film can be a good way of communicating them,' Tony objected.

'So, in art you are not interested. In propaganda you are, yes?'

'Propaganda is a very emotive word, Sven. It has all kinds of political connotations,' Thistle argued. 'All Tony means is that he thinks there are some stories that ought to be told, and Herbie's is one of them.'

'The wrong with that is that the real truth about Herbie Tony does not want to tell. He wants a version sanitized. Refusing to film the reality of Herbie's life, censoring the story, he is. Dishonest, he is.'

'He's no more fucking dishonest than you are,' Thistle's voice was hard and her face set.

Howard, who was in the shop unobtrusively getting on with his paperwork during this meeting, wondered if he ought to intervene. Thistle threw things when really aggravated, and her current location had several thousand books to hand. But, on deciding that intervention might make matters worse, he stayed where he was.

'You have your own agenda, and you want to select those images that suit it,' she hissed at the Swede, her fists and teeth clenched.

'I think,' Tony said quietly, hoping to take some of the anger out of the argument, 'it's really a question of what the purpose of the film is and how can we best serve that purpose.'

'Sven's purpose,' Thistle sneered, 'is to win the fucking Golden-whatever-it-is at Vladivostok! To add to his reputation as an experimental film-maker.'

'We have a duty to our art the envelope to push,' Sven said, retreating slightly, aware that Thistle's accusation had rather too much truth in it and not knowing how to counter it. He was totally unused to being spoken to with so little respect. 'Without experiment, progress there is not, yes?'

'Sure. I take your point,' Tony agreed, 'and, of course, there's a place for experimentation and what you want to do. But this is not it. We have a duty to our sponsors.'

'What!' Sven exploded. 'Sponsors you have?'

'Yes. St Jude's church and the local building society.'

'Religion! Property development!' Sven couldn't believe what he heard. Priests. Developers! He had to sit down. He felt like a man who has discovered too late that he's the driver for a gang of bank robbers. If it became known that he'd associated himself with such a production, he'd never live it down. He'd be accused of betraying everything he'd preached for forty years.

'A television commercial you are making!'

'Well, yes, in a way,' Tony said. 'We want our film to convince people that something must be done for homeless people. We want to make viewers feel compassion for Herbie, not disgust. I know we must show the unpleasant aspects of his life, but they need to be chosen carefully.'

'Selectivity. Censorship!' Sven's eyes grew round with dismay.

'For fuck's sake, Sven,' Thistle exclaimed, 'you know fucking well there's selectivity in everything. When we open our mouths to speak, we choose one word and not another. All art is based on selectivity: what colour to use; what note to play. That's the fun of it. And the challenge. So many options and having the right to choose the most effective.'

Thistle became quieter, more measured. 'What we need is the 'oh, the poor old bugger, I wish I could do something for him' response. There's too much of the yuk factor in your approach, Sven. And don't tell me that commercials are dishonest, because they're not. They're probably the most honest films ever shot. We know exactly what they're for—to sell us something—and we know that the people who make them will use every trick in the book to persuade us to buy. If we get taken in by them, it's our lookout.'

Sven sat silently for a few moments, considering his options. Sodom and Gomorrah he could cope with, he knew, but the land of the Philistines was beyond him. At last, slowly, he stood. 'Television commercials,' he said, 'I do not make. A misunderstanding there has been. Goodbye to you both.' He turned and walked out of the room, and out of their lives.

When the door of the bookshop closed behind Sven, Tony said, 'That was a bit of a bummer.'

Thistle grinned. 'We can manage without him. You know what you're doing, and I can write the kind of narration we need.' She lit a cigarette, began to laugh, coughed mightily, then gasped out, 'You know, Tone, the irony of it is, we'd have done better having that asshole Jack Wilcon helping us. At least he wouldn't have had any difficulty understanding what we want to do and why.' She turned to Howard. 'Don't you agree?'

'Yes and no,' Howard said. 'The problem is that Jack would've had his own agenda and, believe me, you'd have suffered from it sooner or later. Now I think we all need a coffee, don't you?'

'I'll make them,' Tony offered. 'Thistle needs a quiet smoke.' He walked towards the little kitchenette at the back of the shop. As he passed Howard's desk, he said, 'Can I phone my mum and tell her Sven's leaving? She'll be so pleased.'

***

The day's events culminated with a civic reception for the Hollywood guests. A 'who's who' of everyone who thought they were a 'who' in the district had been invited. This included the entire town council and wives, husbands or partners; the town manager and his wife; the chairman of the shire council; presidents of most of the Coddington clubs, societies and associations; the local state MP and his wife; the editor of *The News Gazette* and his star reporter, Gavin Trim; a press photographer; everyone who in cash or kind was contributing to the production, and all present and past members of the Cultural Coordinating Committee.

Howard, Greg, and Edwin declined. Tony and Thistle were not invited.

By five o'clock, all the guests—except for two, Trent and Roma—who'd accepted the invitation had arrived. Michael had decided that he'd make a short introductory speech to which Jack would reply and then the guests of honour would mingle.

'I'll have just the guests of honour on the platform with me,' he told Fleur.

She wasn't pleased by this arrangement. She thought that she, as chair of the Cultural and Community Movie Steering Committees, should also be on the platform, and said so, but Michael was determined not to dilute too much of the glory of being in the limelight.

'This is a Coddington Town Council function,' he said. 'You are neither a councillor nor an employee. I'm sorry, Fleur. But if we have you on the platform, I'll have to have all the members of your committee and God knows who else.'

At first, all proceeded according to plan. Michael stood centre stage, flanked on either side by Jack Wilcon and Hank Shorn, who'd been drinking heavily all day. Jack, in a panic, had recently had a few stiff bourbons to give himself courage. He'd never been a guest of honour before or given any kind of public speech. Though he'd attempted many times during the day to write a speech, he'd got no further than 'Distinguished guests, ladies and gentlemen' before inspiration had died on him like a floundering fish out of water.

But before either Michael or Jack could open their mouths, the arrival—timed to perfection—of Trent and Roma stalled the proceedings. Both radiating the afterglow from yet another successful erotic encounter, they entered the town hall chamber and mounted the platform where they stood next to Hank, who swayed slightly in unison with Jack on the other side of Michael. Marilyn Ferguson, looking up at that moment from her music, was so overcome by Roma's physical munificence that she played a more-noticeable-than-usual wrong note. This put the other members of the ensemble off their stroke. The music stopped.

Roma's gown, made of what seemed to be muslin, had been especially made for her favourite role: the lead in *Daphne, Depraved Queen of the Dwarfs*—a fetish movie for vertically challenged viewers, and the biggest-budget movie of her career. The gown was designed to fall away from her body at the appropriate moment when she pulled on a small tab. Hank, standing next to her, noticed this tab through the alcoholic haze from his breath, and not being in a condition to give its function deep thought, he thought it was probably a loose thread which Roma wouldn't want people to see. Vaguely wanting to be helpful, he gave it a sharp tug. The fabric parted at the seams, as it was supposed to do, and slid to the floor, revealing Roma's underwear-free figure in all its surgery-assisted glory.

Roma stood motionless, as if in shock, and then with surprising aplomb, though with gritted teeth, stepped out of the remains of the gown, and bent down to pick it up. This caused a sharp intake of breath among the female guests and moans from some of the men. Smiling now as if nothing unusual had happened, Roma told Trent to get her a few safety pins from somewhere. Then with statuesque dignity, she carried the small bundle of transparent fabric off the platform to the ladies' toilet.

Michael shouted at the musicians, 'For God's sake, play something.'

Aware of the urgency of the situation, Marilyn decided that the ensemble should play something they knew without having to find the music. Raggedly they began to play 'Advance Australia Fair'. The guests, in either outraged shock or paroxysms of laughter, struggled to attention and gradually quietened down.

Trent almost had a nervous breakdown. He knew his first priority was to get a safety pin to alleviate Roma's problem—a dress that wouldn't stay on—but he'd been brought up to respect the national anthem, and he instinctively stood rigidly to attention. Then as the last notes of the anthem faded away, he hurried to where his father had assisted his grandmother to a chair. An eccentric old lady, her vast handbag was believed to contain a complete set of carpenter, plumber and electrician's tools, as well as sundry gardening implements. Feeling around in it, he soon found what he needed and hurried to the ladies' toilet to assist Roma in the necessary repairs.

As he was attempting—rather clumsily since he wasn't used to handling sheer, almost weightless fabric—to put together the two halves of the dress, three elderly Coddington St George matrons, stalwart supporters of the Coddington St George Presbyterian Church and everything it stood for, entered the toilet. Seeing what Trent was doing, they assumed that fornication was about to take place and ran screaming back into the hall.

By this time, Michael had recovered sufficiently to inform the guests, not without a certain irony, that the formal part of the evening was over. Controlling his fury with a great effort, he then left the hall.

For some time, none of the guests made any attempt to leave, except for the three Presbyterian ladies. Desperately needing to pee but unwilling to risk confronting an even worse event than they'd already witnessed, they hurried out to the nearest public toilet, which was located adjacent to the Town Hall.

Everyone else stayed on, hoping for further incidents. Not until the wait-persons stopped providing food and drink did it seem unlikely that anything of further interest would happen. Only then did most of them depart.

Inevitably, *The News Gazette* photographer obtained excellent photos of Roma's front and rear. Of particular interest to Gavin Trim, who in slack periods spent much time on the internet *not* researching a story, was the stunning tattoo on Roma's back. It showed, in brilliant colour and splendid detail, a matador poised to thrust his sword into the neck of a charging bull, complete with steam spurting from its nostrils.

Roma, a devout follower of astrology and born under the star sign of Taurus the bull, listened to her horoscope on the radio every day. In a rash moment she'd commissioned a tattoo artist at a tattooists' convention in Arizona to give her a bull on her back. The tattooist, internationally famed for the intricacy of his art, had somewhat exceeded his brief. By the time Roma had seen what he'd done, it was too late to undo it without major plastic surgery.

Gavin Trim, star reporter of *The Coddington St George News Gazette* and frequent surfer of the internet, knew on whose back he'd seen the tattoo and what she'd been doing at the time. He realised that he could be onto the biggest story of his career. A stringer at the time for *The Sunday Telegraph,* he wondered to which national daily he could send his story when he'd ascertained all the facts and implications.

The subeditor of *The News Gazette* suggested that the caption to the photograph of Roma leaving the room, clutching her gown to her bosom, should be, 'Movie Star Stuns Coddington with Hollywood Fashion Show'. He had the best few hours of his career captioning the many photographs taken at the reception. The photo of Hank, tripping and losing consciousness while attempting to leave the stage, he captioned, 'Hank Shorn, top Hollywood director, is overcome with emotion at the warm welcome from Mayor Michael Milosovic'. It later won News Photo of the Year in the annual Paparazzi Awards.

Below the photograph of the local MP and his wife doubled up and in pain with hysterical laughter, the caption read, 'Timothy Brush, MP, and his wife Clarissa, share a joke'.

Soon after Michael left the town hall, the editor of *The News Gazette,* Simon West, even as he was scrolling through the photos of the civic reception on his photographer's digital camera, received a phone call from Michael.

'Yes, Michael. What can I do for you?'

'We've had a few embarrassing moments at the reception, Simon.'

'Oh dear! What a pity.'

'I'd be grateful if you didn't publish any of the, er, unfortunate photographs that your man took.'

'Local people will be embarrassed?'

Simon knew that only Michael and perhaps his colleagues on the community movie committee would suffer any criticism.

'Well, not really. Our American friends.'

'Cultural differences of behaviour, I suppose.' Simon looked intently at the photo of a retreating Roma. She was certainly a gorgeous-looking bird, he thought, and the positioning of the charging bull was the work of a true artist. *The News Gazette* couldn't publish any nude photos of her, whatever the subeditor wanted to do, but for the pleasure of it he dragged the conversation out, enjoying himself. He strongly disliked Michael Milosovic and had only agreed to print the 'From the Mayor's Parlour' column because he thought it a good idea for the council to have a regular opportunity to explain its often incredible decisions. He'd not intended to publish a promotional piece for Michael Milosovic, containing the pronoun 'I' in almost every line. And he resented Michael's attempts to influence editorial policy.

'As you know,' Michael went on, playing his only card, 'I—and the council—place a great deal of advertising with your paper.'

'Indeed, you do, Michael. And so, of course, do many businesses in the town. And we appreciate the support of all our advertisers.'

'Yes, but I place more than anyone else.'

'The point is, Michael, that *The News Gazette* is a newspaper, not just an advertising medium.' He didn't add that if Michael took his and the council's advertising away there was nowhere else to place it. *The News Gazette* was the only paper in town.

'Simon, the community movie is my project. It can only benefit the town. At this stage, adverse publicity could badly affect the support we get from the community. Without that wholehearted support, the project is doomed.'

And so, Simon thought, *is the possibility of your being elected to the shire council and becoming chairman of the planning committee. The future of the largest shire in the state is in my hands.*

'Leave it with me, Michael,' he said. 'We don't go to press until tomorrow evening. I might need to raise the matter with our proprietor.'

The proprietor of *The News Gazette* was the Provincial Media Group, which owned a hundred or more small-town newspapers and radio stations throughout the country. The PMG was in turn owned, for a reason no one had been able to fathom, by the Fu Chow People's Media Co-operative, which had sent a non-English-speaking representative to sit on the PMG board. Perhaps, the chairman of the PMG board had surmised, he sat on the board in order to find out how to control a free press.

***

Jack, too, left the chamber as quickly as his short legs and alcoholic gait permitted. He'd not lingered to assist Hank or remonstrate with Trent and Roma. Neither had he hurried after Michael to apologise. He didn't think for a second that what had happened had been his fault. Yet again, it seemed that nothing would go right for him. It was as if, he thought, the Fates were conspiring to ensure that whatever he did would end in failure. It was all so unfair, he told himself, as he tottered along the High Street back to his hotel to lie down. People he trusted and tried to help always let him down. It had been Hank's fault that the dead horse had been left in the cave. And he should've seen that Stud's camera case was in shot. As the director he should have had the set checked in advance. And now the drunken fool had wrecked the civic function.

What the fuck had he thought he was doing? And why had that bitch Roma worn such a dress? It was just asking for trouble, even by Hollywood standards; even still on and in one piece it was far too revealing for a civic function. Surely, she should have known that. And what had Maybelle been thinking of foisting the stupid cow on him? And as for that fool Trent Frobisher! He should have told Roma that the dress was wholly wrong for such an occasion. Jack sighed heavily. He could not be expected, he told himself, to check up on everyone's personal wardrobe.

And then, and then … Jack walked faster as he worked himself up into a therapeutic rage. And then there was that idiot Alec Grimshaw. How the hell had the man imagined for a single minute that he could screen test hundreds of potential extras in a single day? Why hadn't he organised the tests properly over

260

several days? It was beyond belief that the man could have been so stupid. 'And it was no good,' Jack told himself, 'him arguing that I should've warned him what might happen. I can't think of everything. A producer has to delegate.'

And then ... and then there'd been that crazy woman in the newsagents! What had he done to deserve that? Nothing. Absolutely nothing.

The more Jack thought about the events of the past few days, the more convinced he became that he was somehow battling against the forces of evil. He was not a superstitious man, he told himself, but he saw no other explanation. It seemed as if all his life he'd been fighting against his destiny.

He reached the cross roads and stood panting as he looked right and left and then right again, and then he remembered, just in time, to look left and right and left again before starting to cross. But then, even as he tentatively put one foot forward, a road train, its three trailers loaded with cattle, blared its horn at him like a machine driven by the devil. He stepped back and waited, breathing heavily as the enormous prime mover and trailers roared past.

When the road was clear, he started to cross. He wanted to hurry across but was afraid that if he did so he'd trip. He forced himself to walk quickly but steadily.

On the opposite corner, Howard's bookshop, Between the Leaves, seemed to be still open. Jack peered through the glass door and saw Tony, Thistle and Howard sitting at a desk drinking coffee or something. Jack hadn't seen Tony since he'd arrived in the town. According to Michael, the young man had withdrawn from the community movie to work on a project of his own.

This information had hurt Jack's feelings. He thought he'd made a good impression on Tony, but he guessed the guy's behaviour was all par for the course. That was how people behaved to him, he told himself, even when he'd done his damnedest to help them out of the goodness of his heart. As for the bookseller, Howard Something or other, well, according to Michael, he and his priest and banker friends had resigned from the committee for political reasons.

Jesus! Jack told himself. If he'd known he was going to be a fucking pawn in a petty local election, he'd never have accepted the offer to make a community movie in the town. He didn't need this kind of aggro.

It then occurred to him that in view of the situation with Michael Milosovic—who'd cut him dead as he left the stage—it might be a sensible strategy to attempt to mend any broken fences with the opposition—for this was presumably what Howard and his friends were. Jack had no idea what was going on between the factions—if this is what they were—but he thought it could make sense to at least try to find out.

He took a few deep breaths, adjusted his clothes, opened the door of the shop and walked in. Once inside, he threw his arms wide open and exclaimed, 'Tony! It's great to see you again. How are you, my boy?' And he walked forward, both hands outstretched to offer a typical Jack Wilcon handshake.

Tony stood up and shook Jack's hand, trying to evade, but without success, the two-handed Wilcon clasp of sincerity. 'Oh, hello, Jack,' he said. 'How's it, er, all going?' This seemed to be the only possible thing to say.

Assuming that none of them had been to the civic reception, Jack said, 'Fantastic. No problems. We've had a great day. Have we got a community movie or have we got a community movie!'

'I'm glad to hear it,' Howard said, and then not wanting to be inhospitable, and curious to know what Jack and his team were up to, he asked, 'Would you like to join us for a coffee?'

'Thank you. I would. Black. Four sugars.'

Tony fetched Jack a chair—one of many placed about the shop for the benefit of browsers. Howard went to make coffee.

Jack smiled at Thistle, who was still deciding whether to acknowledge his presence. 'I was expecting you to come and see me with a draft of your script. Brilliant concept, Briar.'

'Thistle. Somehow I got the impression you weren't keen on it.'

'How come? I was madly enthusiastic.' One of Jack's many power ploys was to try to put other people in the wrong. He felt that if he could begin a meeting with an apology he'd be ahead. 'Not keen? It was one of the best pitches I've ever had from a writer. I just had a few suggestions to make it more suitable as a community movie.'

'Oh, that's what you were fucking doing.' Thistle let the comment hang in the air as she lit another cigarette. 'I hear the Ladies' Literary Society is providing the script.'

'Oh. It's really going to be very much a director's piece.'

Howard handed him his coffee.

'Thank you. So, what are you three up to? Michael said something about you having your own project, Tony.'

'Nothing much. Just a short documentary.'

'A doco. Now, that is interesting. I've got a few contacts in PBS and the Discovery Channel, Tone. I'll be more than happy to do anything I can to get you a US sale. What's it about?'

Jack wasn't even slightly interested in short, long or even medium-length documentaries, and he knew no one who was, but he liked to make everyone he met think he could do something for them. Usually they never followed up his offers, and when they did, he could always find an excuse for doing nothing.

'I don't think it will be of much interest outside of Australia,' Tony said. 'It's about homeless people here.'

'You'd be surprised,' Jack said. There's money to be made from social problems. And politics. Think Michael Moore.'

Although Michael Moore was probably America's most famous documentary film-maker, Thistle was surprised Jack had heard of him. 'You like Moore's work?' she asked.

'Fantastic. What was that one about a mass murderer? Unforgettable.'

Howard said, 'Where are you filming tomorrow?'

'All over the place. I tell you, this movie is going to be the talk of Hollywood. I'm going to make this town famous. Trust me.'

At this moment, the shop door opened and Trevor Spinks, Howard's IT man, came in. Howard introduced him all round.

'Computer problems?' Jack said.

Trevor shook his head. 'No, no, I've come to install Final Cut Pro on Howard's computer for Tony to use. Microsoft Moviemaker's really only powerful enough for home movies.'

'Final Cut Pro,' Jack said. 'Great program. Use it all the time.' Feeling better, and confident that he had nothing to fear from Tony and his friends, Jack drained his cup and stood. 'Well, it's great to see you guys. I won't hold you up. I'm sure you have work to do. And I must get back to my room and do some more work before tomorrow's early start. You all take care now.'

He turned and walked out of the shop. As soon as he'd gone, Thistle demanded, 'What the fuck was that about?'

'Oh, just sniffing around,' Howard said. 'There's nothing for us to worry about.'

Thistle frowned. 'Perhaps we shouldn't have told him what we're doing.'

'I don't think we need worry,' Tony said. 'There's no money in docos, and that's all Jack's interested in. We'll be lucky to get the ABC or SBS to even look at it. Thousands of people like us are knocking on their doors trying to sell them programs. But I don't care. We'll get it screened by church groups and service clubs.'

'Fair enough.' Thistle put her cigarette out in her cup. 'Herbie'll be waiting for us. We'd better get going. It's going to be a long night.'

She handed Howard a sheet of paper on which she'd listed where she expected them to be filming at different times over the next twenty-four hours. Howard's contribution was to bring food and drink.

Tony and Thistle collected the gear—camera, tripod, single light, bag with fully charged batteries and extra lenses, shotgun mike and boom—and they set off for the Coddington St George War Memorial, where they'd agreed to meet Herbie at six pm.

PART FIVE:

POST PRODUCTION

TWENTY-FIVE

As soon as Michael Milosovic arrived home from the civic reception, he went to his study—a room unsurprisingly free of books and anything of an artistic nature—and poured a large scotch. He then sat at his desk and considered his situation. In the public's mind, as he intended, he was closely associated with the community movie. He'd made it clear in his column and in the various press releases that the project was his idea. This meant, he was aware, that he'd be held responsible for whatever disasters occurred. So far there'd been four: Alec's absurd screen test debacle; the football match and picnic race disasters, and the events that had just occurred at the civic function. Apart from the problem of Roma's dress—and it would've been a problem even if it hadn't fallen off—there was the question of Hank's drunkenness and directorial incompetence.

And he had to consider Alec Grimshaw's cinematography. Alec's work with weasels, stoats, ferrets and skunks had impressed Michael, but he was far from confident that the ability to position a time-lapse camera and then go home for a good night's sleep indicated the necessary skills to shoot a feature.

Unlike Jack, who always blamed everyone else when things went wrong, Michael blamed himself for any errors and omissions. He realised, too late, he thought, that he'd been far too trusting of Jack. He'd failed completely to ensure that everything that ought to have been done, had been done. *Damn it,* he thought. He wasn't even sure that the man Jack had engaged to edit the movie—Studs Collini—was going to turn up. Jack had insisted that Studs Collini would arrive in time to prepare the dailies of the first day's shoot, but Michael had only Jack's word for this, and his word was becoming less and less valuable as the days passed.

Michael knew, in short, that he had to do something. If he didn't, the production would be a catastrophe, and he, Michael, would be blamed. He'd lose a great deal of credibility in the community, and this loss would manifest itself in the election results.

Whereas the movie itself was of little interest to Michael, the votes he'd expected to get resulting from it were of vital importance. He'd done a deal with Trent's father to purchase a hundred acres of his farm if and when it was re-zoned residential. If he were elected to the shire council, he'd have sufficient support from other entrepreneurial county councillors to be elected as chairman of the planning committee, in which position he'd be able to push through the necessary re-zoning for a fifty-villa retirement village. It would then be a simple matter for the In Transit Group PLC to acquire the land from the Frobisher Sugar Cane Trust. Michael had calculated that his net profit from providing architectural and construction services would exceed three million dollars. The incompetence of Jack Wilcon and his cronies was putting this substantial profit at risk.

Michael decided that he couldn't afford to allow the situation to continue unchecked. He had to do something, even if doing it cost him money. Only one thing could be done. Whatever the cost, he had to get rid of Jack, Hank, Studs and Roma and hire an experienced film crew to finish the film. There was no way he could ask the Coddington Council to put more money into the movie. He'd have to find it himself.

In the Brisbane Yellow Pages, he found Queensland TV and Film Production Services Pty Ltd listing an office number and a mobile. He phoned the mobile. Stewart Throsby, the production manager, answered. Michael explained the situation.

'Yeah, we can help,' Stewart said. 'We've got a free day tomorrow. A commercial fell through.'

In actual fact, Queensland TV and Film Production Services, like most businesses and individuals in the film and TV industry, had lots of free days. Most film crew were lucky to get a few days' work once a year, which was why they charged so much for their services when they did get work. The fee for a few days' work a year had to keep them alive for months, in some cases forever.

Stewart Throsby, realising that this was the chance of a lifetime and that the caller was desperate, quickly calculated how many crew he had on his books and how many of them would probably be available. He then worked out a daily rate for each and added twenty percent for himself. He multiplied all this by two to be on the safe side and added ten percent for possible contingences. The total came to two hundred and fifteen thousand dollars, give or take five percent.

To give himself time to think, Michael asked Stewart to repeat the amount and explain how he arrived at it. This Stewart did, adding another ten percent for insurance.

Now came perhaps the most momentous moment of truth of Michael's career. Should he invest almost a quarter of a million dollars in an attempt to avoid a disaster that could cost him three million or more, as well as his reputation? Or should he save his money and hope for the best. He took a deep breath. It was not, he told himself, that he couldn't afford it. He could write a cheque for this amount without really noticing it. And it wasn't that he didn't like to take chances. The construction industry is an enormous gamble from start to finish. His Paradise Plaza shopping centre had been one such gamble, and for a time it had looked as if it would bankrupt him. But gradually the shops had been let, and the more shops became occupied, the easier it was to get occupants for the remaining vacant ones. He'd had to offer a year's rent free to the supermarket, and this had been worth a hundred thou, but as soon as the supermarket was operating, the other retailers had come on board.

An investment in a professional crew, he told himself, would mean that the shoot would be trouble-free. He'd be able to screen the result for the community to see. This would prove to the doubters that the movie was a reality and that he knew what he was doing. The Americans would return to Hollywood before they could do any more damage, and all would be well.

'All right,' he told Stewart Throsby. 'But I want the whole crew up here at six in the morning. We need to plan the day.'

'I'll need fifty percent of the budget up front,' Stewart said. He'd been caught before.

Michael understood this. In his early days as a jobbing builder, he, too, had been caught by customers who for one reason or another had decided not to pay his account.

'No problem. Make your invoice out to INCOMOPRO. Jack Wilcon, the president.' Michael wasn't sure why he'd said this, but it was probably because there might be a possibility of getting out of having to pay the bill himself. Throsby would attempt to get payment from Jack Wilcon, who would be safely home in LA. Stewart would then begin proceedings against Milosovic Holdings Pty Ltd, which could be drawn out for years, well after the day of Throsby's almost certain bankruptcy, by which time Michael would have re-organised his corporate entities in such a way that Milosovic Holdings Pty Ltd had no assets. The art of getting and staying rich, he knew, was to ensure that other people paid for one's mistakes.

Stewart Throsby, not realising what Michael had in mind, guaranteed that he'd be in Coddington St George with a crew and equipment on time the next day.

***

Even as Michael told himself that his troubles were almost over, Gavin Trim, star reporter of *The News Gazette*, was phoning his editor, Simon West.

'Simon, sorry to trouble you so late, but there's been a fantastic development. The story of the year.'

'Oh? Do tell.' Simon's reporters' enthusiasms rarely impressed him.

'The actress, Roma Sheraton.'

'She of the falling dress.'

'That's not all that falls, Simon. She's no more a TV soapie star than I am.'

'And you're certainly not. Go on.'

'She's a porno girl. Kandy Kute. Two "k"s.'

'My goodness.'

Assuming the young man had been trawling the porn sites in his spare time, Simon wanted to ask Gavin how he'd discovered this interesting fact. 'I suppose,' he said, 'a friend of yours who visits porn sites brought this to your attention.'

'Spot on, Simon. He was at the function, saw the bull tattoo on Roma's back, realised he'd seen it before—it's not something you'd forget—and went on the internet to check. Bob's your uncle, as my gran likes to say.'

'And no doubt, Gavin,' Simon said, 'you already have a headline.'

'Two, actually. For *The News Gazette*, it could be 'Porno Girl Stars in Milosovic Flick', and for one of the nationals, 'Porn Comes to Coddington St George'.

'Yes, well, the latter could be worth a couple of pars in *The Courier Mail*, I suppose. Under your by-line as our special correspondent. You'd hit the big time. Even if ever so briefly. They'd need a pic, of course. No doubt you think we could provide one.'

'It's a real scoop, Simon.'

'That's as maybe. However, you'll not write a word, or talk to anyone about your discovery, until and unless I specifically tell you to. Is that understood?'

Gavin was appalled. This wasn't the response he'd expected. 'But, Simon—'

'Is that understood? If it's not, you need not return to work. You'll be fired. Is *that* understood?'

'The public has a right to know what's going on, Simon.'

'The public has a right to know what it needs to know. I'm yet to convince myself that it needs to know what kind of a mess our mayor, unwittingly, I believe, has got himself into. Go to bed, Gavin. Have an early night. Tomorrow is going to be a busy day.'

Simon West put down the phone. 'Shit!' he exclaimed. 'Now what do I do?' He had it in his power to destroy Michael Milosovic's future in the shire. The porno girl story would be enough to lose him at least a hundred or so votes. These would go to Edwin, who would squeak home by a narrow majority. Edwin was a good man, but of very limited ambition and even more limited entrepreneurial ability. He'd sit quietly on the shire council, innovating nothing, and always voting for the conservative, with a small 'c', course of action. This would usually be no action at all.

Without Michael chairing the planning committee, the rumoured re-zoning of the Frobisher land wouldn't happen and the In Transit Retirement Village would not be built. Coddington St George would lose a perfectly worthwhile development to another town. A lot of people in Coddington, and not only potential tenants of the retirement village, would lose financially if the village went elsewhere. Certainly, Michael stood to make a packet if he built the village, but he'd make it reasonably honestly by the standards of local government. A kind of democracy would've been at work.

It seemed to Simon that to drop Michael in it would be to make the town suffer, and this he didn't want to do. He felt fond of the town. He knew hundreds of the residents personally, and he did his best to use his position as editor of the local paper for the benefit of the town. It was hardly worth damaging it for the sake of a cheap headline and a seven-day wonder.

And there was also the Frobisher family to consider. Young Trent, an idiot, but harmless enough, was obviously besotted by the girl, as who wouldn't be, Simon thought. She was attractive enough without the benefit of the sexual skills she must've acquired as part of her profession. But if Trent's parents found out what kind of girl their son was dating and might even be thinking of marrying, they'd be beside themselves with shame and worry. The falling dress, of course, would probably have put the kibosh on anything permanent, or semi-permanent—she'd probably already been married at least three times—though one never knew what stupidity a young man in sexual thrall would perpetrate. So, it was still a possibility.

Simon was afraid that the shame Trent's mother and father would feel might well send either or both of them to an early grave. Reading the story on the front page of *The News Gazette* could generate either a heart attack or a stroke, and Simon didn't want to be responsible for such an event. The Frobishers were good people. As far as he knew, they led decent lives, treated their employees well and donated generously to all kinds of community activities. They were pillars of the Anglican church of St Jude's—an institution with enough troubles of its own without the chairman of the parish council and a churchwarden being linked to pornographic movies. Simon imagined a typical headline—'Churchwarden in Porno Movie Shock'—or something equally misleading. The scandal would almost certainly cause the family to withdraw from public life, and this would be a great loss to the community. The Coddington St George schools and clubs were full of shields and cups paid for by the Frobisher Trust. To pillory the family in the local press would achieve nothing, Simon was sure. It would be an act of unspeakable irresponsibility.

He picked up the phone and dialled Michael's number. 'Michael. Simon.'

'Ah, Simon, you've come to a decision about the photographs.'

'Listen carefully. That girl, Roma Sheraton.'

'Oh, God! Now what's she done?'

'That would be telling indeed. Suffice it to say, Michael, that my ace investigative reporter has discovered that as Kandy Kute our Roma Sheraton performs acts of seriously explicit sex on the internet.'

'Bloody hell.'

'I think it highly likely, Michael, that Mr Wilcon and his associates, being what they are, and incapable of being anything else, will manage almost without trying to destroy your reputation.'

'Are you going to publish this, about the girl?'

'Send the lot of them packing, Michael, before they do you any more harm, and I'll kill the story. Put a spike through it.'

'I'm grateful, Simon. Really grateful. I've actually already decided to get rid of them before something else disastrous occurs.' He told Simon about his hiring a professional crew for the shoot. Then he said, 'Have you said anything to Edwin about this?'

'Absolutely not. It's not the kind of information he'd use anyway. He doesn't want to be elected that badly.' He laughed. 'It's not as if we'd discovered that you'd been acting in a porno movie. You haven't, have you, Mr Mayor? Of course you haven't. 'Night, Michael. Sweet dreams.'

As soon as Simon rang off, Michael dialled the Central and asked to be put through to Jack's room. Jack was asleep, but he gradually returned to consciousness.

'Listen carefully,' Michael said. 'I don't want any arguments. Queensland TV and Film Production Services will finish the movie. You and your cronies are off it. I want you out of this town by eight o'clock tomorrow morning. Do you understand?'

Jack wanted to protest, but he knew it would be pointless. Even he could see the end approaching. He muttered, not very hopefully. 'You owe me the rest of my fee.'

'I owe you nothing, you fucking fraud.' Michael slammed down the phone.

TWENTY-six

At this time, neither Hank nor Roma knew they'd been sacked. Neither were they at all concerned by the evening's events. Studs was probably still up, happily counting his day's takings. Hank would be still unconscious—he'd been returned to his hotel room in this state by the St John's Ambulance team on duty at the reception, and they'd left him to sleep it off. His snores reverberated throughout the room, rattling the cups and saucers on their tray on top of the little bar fridge.

Roma, too, was unconscious, but not from an excess of alcohol. It was one of her habits as soon as the man of the evening left her—and none of them ever stayed the night—to take a couple of sleeping pills that would put her out for at least eight hours. Occasionally she talked and cried in her sleep, but the noises were little more than a quiet whimper.

Jack, though, was wide awake. He grated his dentures so hard that they moved in his mouth, pinching his gum. He took them out. Without his teeth he looked only slightly more repulsive than when he had them in. His cheeks were a little more sunken, that was all.

He was so angry that his whole body trembled. What the fuck did Maybelle think she was doing, dumping the bitch on him? She should've known that the truth would come out. Had she imagined for one moment that there wouldn't be a problem? And as for Hank! The bastard hadn't been sober since he'd arrived. Not that it mattered now. The whole project was fucked. This had been his main chance—his only chance—to get himself a new start, and his so-called friends had blown it. He was back to square one. He'd put all this work into the project—he convinced himself that he'd actually done some work, other than talked up the project and himself—and he was convinced now that he'd have nothing to show for it.

Instead of a community movie, written, directed and produced by Jack Wilcon, executive producer, Jack Wilcon, a Wilcon Community Movie Production, he had nothing—not even a few minutes of screen time. Fuck all!

The only person who would come out of the disaster with anything, he thought, was young Tony. 'And it was meeting me,' Jack told himself, 'that inspired him. And what does the little motherfucker do? He betrays me. Makes a movie on his own without me.'

'All those hours I spent with him in Cannes,' Jack seethed through gritted gums, 'giving him advice, telling him everything I knew about making movies, distribution, financing—I was the boy's mentor, his guru, his inspiration. And what does he do? Ignores me. Makes a movie in competition with me. Turns half the Cultural Coordinating Committee against me.'

A tiny jump from this line of thought brought Jack to the conclusion that Tony was responsible for his sacking. *He wants me out of the way. He wants my movie aborted so that he has the field to himself.*

Jack could hardly contain his rage. He'd been deceived, betrayed, cheated, let down by people he'd trusted and relied on all his years in the movie business, but never so cunningly and calculatedly as by Tony Andover. 'Well,' Jack decided, 'he's not going to get away with it.'

He lay back on his bed and, staring at the ceiling, plotted his revenge. Various wholly impractical ideas passed through his mind, but at last, in the early hours of the morning, he knew what he could do. Studs would know how to do it. Sales of assorted recreational substances had been most satisfactory. Studs owed him one. He picked up the phone.

***

While Jack plotted his revenge, Tony and Thistle filmed *A Day in the Life of a Homeless Man*. Tony, as producer, director, cinema-photographer and editor, had exercised his authority, and after prolonged argument, and not a little abuse, had persuaded Thistle that as Herbie spent most of his time dozing, a complete record of his day, even compressed, might be a little boring, if not unbearably tedious. Accordingly, the film was now called *Homeless: Scenes from the Life of a Homeless Man* and consisted of shots—some prolonged—of Herbie in action.

Inevitably, Thistle had insisted that nothing Herbie did should be censored. The record had to be complete and accurate. This raised considerable problems for Tony, as Herbie had a number of what some viewers might consider offensive ways of passing the time—such as extensive nose picking and other bodily pastimes. A compromise had been reached with Thistle. Tony would film whatever Herbie was up to—or down to—at the time, and a decision on what to include would be made after discussion during the editing.

Other decisions Tony had made concerned camera placement and Thistle's narration. The former presented no problems. Tony suggested using two cameras—one hand-held by himself and one strapped to Herbie's forehead, infantryman style, as shown in TV news from various war zones. This, Tony believed, would make it possible for much of the film to be from Herbie's point of view (POV in film jargon). Herbie had raised no objection.

The unedited scenes consisted, therefore, of Herbie rummaging in rubbish bins for something to eat, finding something repulsive and eating it, throwing it up, sitting alone at a table in the public bar of the Grand nursing a half pint of beer that someone had bought him, until he was turned out, gazing into shop windows until he was told to clear off, visiting the town's public toilet, sleeping on a bench in the park, being disgusting, being moved on by Sergeant Bordon, muttering abuse at passers-by, looking for somewhere to doss down for the night, settling for a doorway out of a draught or a gap in the concrete of the bridge over the river, sleeping restlessly and having the most fearsome dreams and nightmares.

As for the narration, Tony had happily agreed to Thistle's suggestion that this should be in free verse—whatever that was—and would provide the backstory to Herbie's present existence. It would not comment on the action, but would be a kind of counterpoint to it. Thistle was a fast worker, and she'd written and recorded her narration before filming had begun. It was to be the only sound apart from the actual sounds of Herbie's environment. Here again the question of censorship had arisen; Herbie's diet tended to produce flatulence of an amazingly varied kind, ranging in noise from a quiet, barely audible hiss to a full-bottomed roar. Tony had to agree to record whatever sounds Herbie made, but would decide which to include during the editing.

He hoped that Thistle might either be indisposed or suddenly have to visit a seriously ill relative in another town throughout the editing process. He wasn't ungrateful for her input and support, though. In fact, he thought her narration, though perhaps needing a little editing, was very moving and perfect for its purpose. The raw material she'd had to work with hadn't been promising.

They'd discovered that Herbie had been educated up to Year Twelve, and had even passed his HSC and spent a year at Wagga Wagga University studying for a sociology degree. There, his mental weakness had manifested. Overwhelmed by the quantity of jargon to which he'd been exposed, he'd experienced a psychotic episode after attempting to extract meaning from 'Acquisitive individualism was systematically embedded as a psychocultural driver in a global monetarist economic project that was more concerned with finance capital than with productive capital'. He'd thrown the stapled bundle of photocopied pages from a dozen or more textbooks at the lecturer, lain on his back on the floor of the lecture theatre in front of the usual thousand or so students, many from India and China and understanding even less of their course than he did, and allowed a stream of expletives to pour out of his mouth. The lecturer had sent for the police. Herbie had been sectioned and hospitalized in a high-security psychiatric wing, heavily drugged with medications that turned him into a zombie and then later released into the community to fend for himself.

Only partly recovered from his psychotic condition, and lacking the funds necessary to purchase the recommended medication for which he'd lost the prescription, Herbie had begun a new life on the streets. He could think only of one thing: that he was a failure and had let down his mother, who, he'd convinced himself, had made many sacrifices to give him an education. It hadn't occurred to him that if anyone had failed it was the author of the textbook who'd triggered his breakdown. Had the man been capable of expressing himself in plain English—or taken the academic risk of doing so—Herbie would likely have completed his university course and led a reasonably normal life. As it was, believing himself worthless, he'd withdrawn from society, and his mental state had gradually deteriorated.

Thistle managed to communicate this brief biography in a reasonably poetic form. Tony thought the last lines of her narration were especially poignant:

Nobody knows where he comes from.
Nobody cares where he's been.
Nobody cares that nobody cares.
He's got nothing to spend and nothing to lend.
He's got nothing that anyone wants.
He could just as well be dead.
No one would notice.
No, that's not true.
Somebody would say, for something to say,
'Haven't seen Herbie a while.'
And they'd get the reply,
'He's probably dead.'
And that would be that.
No grief. No concern. No guilt.
Just relief that an embarrassment had moved on.

Tony felt pleased with the footage he'd already shot and believed that he could turn it into a moving mini-documentary, something the church could use as part of its campaign to alleviate the suffering of the homeless, many of whom suffered from mental health issues, though certainly not all. Hundreds of homeless young couples, often with children, lived on the streets—though not in Coddington St George. However, theirs was a different problem, and Tony thought it sensible to concentrate on the Herbie kind of homeless man or woman.

Thistle also felt pleased with her narration. She'd even been able to accept that her usual sprinkling of four-letter words was possibly not acceptable in a film sponsored by a religious organisation.

But she'd taken a lot of convincing.

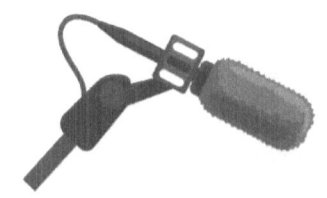

epilogue

Studs took some time to wrench his mind back from where it had wandered to, but eventually he became sufficiently focussed to cope with what Jack was asking of him.

'The situation is this, Studs,' Jack had explained on the phone. 'I've been stitched up by that bastard Tony Andover. Milosovic's in it, too. Unless I do something, I'll leave here without a movie. My plan to make a few bucks in the US as a community movie producer will be fucked. You've got to help me.'

'What the fuck are you talking about?' Studs had demanded.

'I want you to steal the footage of Tony Andover's shoot of *Homeless*,' Jack said, as if asking him not to forget to take home the empty picnic basket. 'Edit it as an INCOMOPRO (International Community Movie Production) with me as executive producer, producer and director. I'll use it to support my cv. No one in the States will know I had nothing to do with it. Right?'

'Yeah, I guess so,' Studs had agreed. 'But what's in it for me, Jack?'

'You'll be part of my team. We'll clean up.'

'How do I get the footage?'

'Unless I'm mistaken, it's on the new iMac computer that was delivered yesterday to the bookshop, Between the Leaves. Howard bought it for his shop, but he's letting that bastard Andover edit his movie on it. All the footage should be in Final Cut Pro.'

'You want me to break into the shop now and unload the footage?' Studs asked.

'Right. We have to be out of town by eight o'clock.'

'Shit. Are the cops—'

'No. Trust me, Studs. When have I ever let you down?'

Studs knew better than to answer this question. It would take too long. 'For you, Jack,' he said and put down the phone.

What Jack suggested wouldn't be very difficult. If the shop wasn't alarmed, and in a town like Coddington St George it almost certainly wouldn't be, he wouldn't be disturbed. Downloading the files onto a blank DVD would be simple.

And it was.

By nine o'clock the next morning, Jack, Hank, Studs, Roma and the DVD containing all Tony's unedited footage were in Michael's spare car and on their way to Brisbane. Confident that the footage could be turned into a new career, Jack spent his last dollars on standby airfares for his team to LA. The Australian venture was over. A new US venture was about to begin.

Knowing that he was going to need Maybelle's assistance in setting up his community movie venture, Jack decided not to make too much fuss about Roma. *After all*, he thought, *what happened to her dress happened to girls like her all the time. It went with the territory.*

'What went wrong, Jack?' Maybelle demanded as soon as he walked into the office. 'I didn't expect you back for weeks.'

'There's been a development, hon.' He collapsed into his chair, exhausted from the flight, during which he'd been crammed between two middle-aged women who seemed to be participants in an obesity contest, one which, he'd thought, they were certain to be tied winners. Now he explained briefly to Maybelle how he'd been set up by Tony Andover, but that he'd got even with the son of a bitch by bringing away with him footage that was going to provide him with a new career in the movie business—consultant producer of community movies. He'd make a fortune. Everything was going to be great. 'Trust me, babe.'

But Maybelle trusted him no longer. She knew he was at the end of his road as a producer. She could provide him with enough lies to get one consultancy, but that would be the only one. He'd stuff it up the way he stuffed everything up. There was only one future for him. He had to become an academic.

'Now you listen to me, Jack,' she said. 'If that footage is any good and Studs does a competent job with it, you can use it to get yourself a teaching job at some fifth-rate college. Faculty of Film Studies or something. There are thousands of them in the country, and most of them are staffed by people who've never made any kind of movie in their lives.'

'For fuck's sake,' Jack exclaimed, 'are you out of your mind? I don't have no qualifications.'

'That we can attend to,' Maybelle said. 'A fake cv, fake testimonials—all from the UK and Europe. You know what suckers academics and film buffs are for foreign movies.'

Jack's creative skills came to his rescue, as they so often did. 'We could call the movie *Belches and Farts*,' he said. 'That's what the Swede Sven Ingersson would call it.' He grinned. 'We could say it won the Golden Pisspot at Minsk.'

And thus it was that three months later, Jack took up his appointment as Adjunct Professor (whatever that meant, he thought) at the University of Southern New Mexico, an institution well-known for its marking system, one that was so generous that no student had ever failed to graduate. This policy it owed to certain of Britain's older universities where students who didn't manage to achieve even a third-class honours degree and did little more than turn up for the final examinations were usually awarded a pass.

Jack coped with his teaching load surprisingly well. Following the example of most of the academic staff, he created his own textbook by photocopying vast sections of little-known books on various aspects of movie production. He delivered his lectures by reading from it in a barely audible monotone. He marked all assignments 'B+ Promising', which was fair as most of them were acquired from various 'Rent an Essay' services on the Internet.

For once true to his word, he arranged for Hank and Studs to be engaged as technicians in the university's communications block. Roma returned to her boyfriend, sexcam and escort duties. Maybelle, having nowhere else to go, moved in with Jack, who did his best to show his gratitude for her help. Entitled, as a professor, even an adjunct one, to secretarial services, he employed her on a part-time basis to do his photocopying and assignment marking.

Meanwhile, back in Coddington St George, life went on very much as before. The Reverend Greg Small didn't find his faith, but his bishop, knowing him to be a decent, caring man, promoted him to the position of rural dean, which he greatly enjoyed.

Life remained unchanged for Edwin, for which he was grateful.

Howard devoted more time to developing his network of phone sex ladies, installing call centres in the new Coddington St George In Transit Retirement Village, Mumbai, Manilla and Kampala. He appointed Tony as manager of Between the Leaves. Tony abandoned film-making as a hobby and gave all his attention to developing the shop as a successful online book store. He employed Thistle as a part-time assistant. They were comfortable with one another and became the best of platonic friends.

Thistle developed her career as a performance poet and reached the world through her web page and Facebook. She became quite famous and spent much of her time blogging and communicating with thousands of virtual 'friends' and 'fans'.

She remained romantically unattached and financially poor.

Almost no one in Coddington St George was surprised that the community movie ran for only fifteen minutes and lacked in story, characterisation and coherence. But several thousand residents had had a great day out, watched a film crew at work— which seemed to consist mainly of standing about chatting and not doing very much—and were well satisfied with the event, especially the assorted disasters. The most enjoyable parts of the production, though, were the twenty minutes of bloopers. Everyone agreed they were hilarious and unforgettable. It was widely believed that it was the bloopers that got Michael elected to the shire council. Anyone who could generate such fun had to be a good chap.

He was soon appointed chairman of the County Planning Committee. The necessary re-zoning of some of the Frobisher fields of sugar cane soon took place, and within the year, construction began on the Coddington St George In Transit Retirement Village. Michael invested his profit from this in In Transit Homes Ltd, in which he became the majority shareholder. He became too important to remain in Coddington St George and moved his home to Sydney's eastern suburbs. He opened offices in Melbourne, Adelaide and Perth. Over the next five years he covered a considerable acreage with his idea of retirement heaven. Inevitably he was later awarded the Order of Australia for services to the community.

Stewart Throsby attempted for several years to obtain payment from INCOMOPRO, but he had absolutely no success. INCOMOPRO had never been registered as a company or anything else. Its Sunset Boulevard address turned out to be vacant. No one knew where Jack Wilcon had gone. Stewart's lawyer advised him not to waste time and money employing a private investigator to track Wilcon down, as even if and when he was found, he'd simply refuse to admit that he owed the money. American lawyers' fees in attempting to obtain the payment would quickly be greater than the amount owed.

Stewart's attempts to get payment from Michael Milosovic and the Coddington Council were similarly unsuccessful because of the way Michael had planned the hire. Any contract, verbal or otherwise, had been between Queensland TV and Film Production Services and either INCOMOPRO or Jack Wilcon. Therefore, neither Michael Milosovic nor the Coddington St George Town Council had any contractual responsibility for the debt.

Fleur continued to chair many meetings in Coddington St George. She did not get her OAM. Michael, having moved on to much greater things, forgot all about her.

a note from the author

Did you enjoy my book?

If so, I would be very grateful if you could write a review for *A Town Like Ours* and publish it at your point of purchase.

Your review, even a brief one, will help other readers to decide whether or not they will enjoy my work.

Do you want to be notified of new releases?

If so, please sign up to the AIA Publishing email list. You'll find the sign-up button on the right-hand side under the photo at www.aiapublishing.com. Of course, your information will never be shared, and the publisher won't inundate you with emails, just let you know of new releases.

www.ingramcontent.com/pod-product-compliance
Lightning Source LLC
Chambersburg PA
CBHW030628110726
47901CB00002B/363